KING
in
WAITING

Also By Griff Hosker

Lord Edward's Archer series:
King in Waiting

The Sword of Cartimandua series
The Anarchy series
Norman Genesis series
Border Knight series
Struggle For a Crown series
Combined Operations series
Aelfraed series
Wolf Brethren series
Dragonheart series
New World series
British Ace series
Carnage at Cannes

KING
in
WAITING

GRIFF HOSKER

LUME BOOKS

LUME BOOKS

First published in 2019 by Lume Books
30 Great Guildford St,
London, SE1 0HS

ISBN 978-1-83901-453-6

www.lumebooks.co.uk

ABOUT THE AUTHOR

Griff Hosker qualified as an English and Drama teacher in 1972 and worked in the north east of England for the next thirty-five years, writing plays, pantos and musicals for his students. He then set up his own consultancy firm and worked as an adviser in schools and colleges. The financial crash of 2010 ended that avenue of work, and he found that he had time on his hands. Griff started researching the Roman invasion of Britain and began to create a novel. The result was *The Sword of Cartimandua*.

King in Waiting is Griff's 130th book and is the sequel to runaway bestseller *Lord Edward's Archer*, which dominated the Kindle charts throughout 2019. Compared to the works of Bernard Cornwell and C.J. Sansom, the *Lord Edward's Archer* series imagines the Second Barons' War through the eyes of an English bowman.

Praise for Lord Edward's Archer:

'Medieval adventure with the pace and power of a war arrow in flight. Griff Hosker has sold over a million books and I can see why!' – Matthew Harffy, bestselling author of the *Bernicia Chronicles*

'From the first page to the last, *Lord Edward's Archer* grabbed me and did not let go. Hosker's depiction of life and struggles in that slice of early English history is real, brutal and utterly captivating.' – Eric Schumacher, award-winning historical fiction author of *Hakon's Saga*

Map of
England
and Wales,
1264

N
W E
S

Badequelle
Namentwihc
Chedle
Ludlow
Biggleswade
Evesham
Gloucester Leueton
Newport Oxford Hertfordshire
Slo London
Bricstow
Winchester Lewes

CHAPTER 1

I am the captain of Lord Edward's archers. One day he will be King of England, and I hope that I will still be serving him when he is crowned. Some men mocked him, calling him either Longshanks or Squinty Eye! They did not do that to his face or within his hearing, for he was a most vengeful man. The London mob had recently insulted his mother, the Queen, and, as we rode south to Rochester Castle, he had let all of us know his feelings towards those who had jeered her. When the siege was relieved, he would turn his attention to them.

I am Gerald War Bow, and I command the handful of archers employed by the future King of England. I know that I am young for the task but my men, most of whom are older than I am, seem happy to serve under me. We get on well together. I was born the son of an archer and to me, they were the best of men and I liked them all.

Neither King Henry nor his son, Edward, were likeable men. I was under no illusions; I was used because I was useful. I had helped to capture the son of Simon de Montfort, but I had been accorded no honours for doing so. It was seen as my job. Now, while the king, his son and their entourage of barons and knights headed south to confront the rebels, we were sent with Captain William and Lord Edward's men at arms to ride into the wild forests north of Nottingham. The slippery Earl of Derby, Robert de Ferrers, had managed to avoid being in Northampton and Tutbury when those two strongholds were captured. Lord Edward had heard the wily and elusive earl had taken refuge in the forests. This was not the work of nobles – and so we had been detached from the army to find him, if we could, and put him with the other prisoners we had taken in the campaign thus far.

I had just ten archers left to me. A third of my archers had died in the campaigns against the Welsh and the rebels. Only Jack of Lincoln remained of the outlaws I had first hired. I think that was why Lord Edward sent us on this errand. I heard him say to Henry Almain, his cousin, as we left, "Set a thief to catch a thief, eh cuz!"

Another reason was that he believed he had the rebels defeated. Simon de Montfort's support lay in the Welsh Marches, London and in the Midlands. We had destroyed the Midlands power base while the Welsh, effectively, threatened the west, and only London remained. When Rochester fell, the royal army could turn its attention to Simon de Montfort and London. The rebellion and threat to the king's power would be over, and Lord Edward's future as King of England would be assured. When the king and his son headed south, in the third week of April, we turned north and headed for the forests which stretched from Nottingham to north of Doncaster.

I liked Captain William, who commanded the men at arms. We had fought together in Poitou and Wales, and we understood each other. They too had lost men, and just eight remained under his command. We worked well together, for my men could use swords as well as the bows of which we were masters.

As we watched the royal army head south, Captain William turned to me. "Well Captain Gerald, this is your sort of land. I know not why the Prince sends us here. You and your archers could easily capture the earl if he hides close to Nottingham. We are only here to ensure that they are held."

I nodded. "He needs us when there is dirty work to do. This de Ferrers is a thorn in the king's side but, from what I can gather, he is a clever man. I cannot see an earl hiding out in a forest. We may find his men, but I think we look further south if we wish to apprehend this elusive lord."

"Further south?"

I nodded again. "He slipped through our fingers at Northampton and Tutbury and I fear he has done so again. While our eye is drawn north, he will head south for London and de Montfort. But," I turned in the saddle and waved forward John of Nottingham and Jack of Lincoln, "Lord Edward is our paymaster and we obey him."

My ex-outlaw and most senior archer joined me. "Captain?"

"You know our task?"

"Aye, Captain, we seek a needle in a field full of haystacks."

My men had an open way with them. I knew that Captain William would not have endured such familiarity, but these were my men. They were older than me and I allowed it, within reason.

"John, you are a Nottingham man. Where would *you* seek the Earl of Derby?"

He gestured with his thumb behind him. "South, Captain, towards London."

I looked at Jack of Lincoln, who nodded his agreement. "He is right, Captain. Robert de Ferrers likes his wine and his comfort. There is precious little of either in the greenwood."

"Let us say I agree with you. His men are not with him. Where would they go?"

Jack of Lincoln grinned. "Ah, Captain, now you ask the right question. To the north-west of Chinemarelie, there is a part of the forest where there is an absent lord. The master of Codnor castle, Sir Robert de Grey, is on a crusade and there is just a castellan. We found the hunting easy there, sir. No gamekeeper. Men would not have to travel far into the forest to have a safe home and food to hunt. It is not far from Derby and it is close to the main road to London."

Captain William frowned. "And why would that be important?"

"You should know, sir, we all like to stay close to our paymaster. Robert of Derby will need his men if he is to continue this rebellion. His men wait to be summoned."

I shook my head. Captain William would not endure the same level of familiarity as I did. "Captain William, my men and I will be the vanguard. I would not ask you to do this, but I have few enough archers as it is. Would you and your men be the rear-guard with the baggage? We can move in the woods and forests a little more easily than you."

The captain could not really argue. Although none of the men were as well armed and armoured as knights, they each had a mail hauberk, coif and mail mittens. Some even had poleyn and cuisse. You could hear a man at arms moving through the trees from a mile away. We would only need them when we had cornered these rebels.

"Aye, so we take the Codnor road?"

I looked at Jack and answered, "Yes, Captain, and it is there we take the road to Chinemarelie."

"Then we will see if the castellan of Codnor can put us up for the night. I daresay it will take you more than half a day to find them."

"That it will."

"Then we will see you at Codnor."

We got on well with the men at arms but all of us, me included, preferred to be on our own. Archers like the company of other archers. We dug our heels in and our horses headed up the road. The men at arms would be slower for they had the horses with the baggage. Most of it was theirs. They had their spears, tents and spare clothes. We just had our spare arrows and food. We would make hovels if we could not find a roof. Archers like to move quickly, for speed and agility are two weapons we know how to use well. I waved Jack of Lincoln forward. "Take the lead. The sooner we find the earl or his men, the sooner we rejoin Lord Edward."

As he rode briefly alongside me, he grinned. "I quite like this freedom, Captain."

"And what about your pay? The longer we are apart from Lord Edward the more likely it is that he can do without us. I do not see a line of lords waiting to hire us."

He shrugged and rode ahead. John of Nottingham took his place. "Then more fool them, Captain. You have proved that we are of more use than men at arms. Would he have captured young de Montfort without us?"

I knew that I had little reason to fear being released, but I knew how lucky I was to be one of the captains of the future King of England. I might not like the man, but I recognised in him a leader and a good warrior. John could see that I was not in the mood to talk and so he rode next to me in silence. I looked at the land through which we travelled. We were still in farmland but the hedges were becoming taller and, in the distance, I saw the dark shadow that was the forest. John of Nottingham had told me that it covered three counties but that, once, it had stretched almost to York. It was hard to believe. It made sense that the men who followed de Ferrers would stay on the southern side of the forest, and we would head there first. Jack of Lincoln knew the forest well, and he would save us much time in fruitless searching.

We were riding the Great North Road, which had been made by the Romans. It went south to London and north to York and beyond. The task, which might have seemed daunting to another, did not worry us. If we chose to hide in the woods then none would find us, but if a lord or a large number of men tried to hide then they would leave clear signs. It was another reason why I had wished to hunt alone. The men at arms would have muddied the water and masked the trail.

We had left the main road and passed Codnor when Jack of Lincoln emerged from the forest. He had strung his bow, and that was always a sign of danger. I did not need to issue orders. My men all took their bows from their leather cases and strung them. I did not. I was the captain.

"I have found a trail, Captain. There are men with mail in these woods, and that means they are not outlaws. I think that these are the men we seek." He grinned. "They are lazy men and have not ventured far."

I reined in. "Are they close to the edge of the woods?"

"I rode a mile or so and I didn't smell them."

I looked at the sky. It would be night soon. As captain I was paid more than the others, and it was up to me to make a decision. I decided it made sense to spend a night in the forest. The rebels would cook, and that would give us smell and a light to follow. I did not know the men we hunted but I knew my own. I turned in my saddle. "Ronan, ride back to Codnor and tell Captain William that we will be spending a night in the forest."

Ronan was the youngest of my men and keen to impress. "Should I return to you, Captain?"

"No, have a night in a bed. Bring the men at arms here on the morrow. We will leave a sign for you to follow."

He looked disappointed but he nodded. "Aye, Captain." He turned his horse around and rode back to the castle.

John of Nottingham nodded his approval. "He is still not over the wound he got when Peter was killed."

"And that is another reason for sending him. I am taking no chances with any of my men. We have perilously few of them as it is. I will not risk a night attack unless I am sure that we can win." I pumped my arm and we headed into the forest.

When first we had followed Lord Edward, we had ridden any old nag and sumpter. Our success meant that we had managed to acquire better horses for ourselves. Most of my men rode palfreys and I had a courser. Only a war horse was better. The squire from whom I had taken that courser had died, as had his master. It was the spoils of war. I did not know her name and so I gave her one. I liked Eleanor as a name, and she soon responded to its use. Captain William thought I should have chosen a shorter name. Perhaps he was right, but I did things my way; I liked the way the word rolled off my tongue, and my horse liked it. That was enough.

At first, the forest was thin. Men had come into the eaves and taken smaller trees for wood. It was a crime, but if there was no lord at Codnor then men would take risks. It meant that the trees at the edge were thicker around the bole and had a mighty spread. Archers notice such things, for a tree with a large canopy gives shelter. As I followed Jack, I saw the trees becoming thinner but more numerous and the trail more tortuous. Jack had dismounted and tied his horse to a branch on a rowan tree. I dismounted and tied mine to another branch. He had stopped for a reason. I went close to him and spoke quietly.

"You have seen something?"

"It could be nothing, Captain, but I smelled dung." He tapped the split nose which marked him as a former outlaw. "Men don't go too far from a camp when they drop their breeks. They like to go downwind of the camp. The wind is blowing in our faces. By the time the lads have dismounted, I should have found it."

How he knew such things I would never know, but he had survived in the woods as an outlaw for some years. My men all chose other trees to tether their horses. We knew which horses got on with others. Mine was the leader, and Jack of Lincoln's would happily let the courser have the best grass. I took my own bow from its case and, removing my cap, took out a string. I strung the bow. I was pleased that it was hard to do; it meant that neither the bow nor the string needed replacing. I took out a war arrow and a bodkin and put them in my belt.

Jack came back and used hand signals. We had all been together long enough to have worked out such signals. Dick, son of Robin, Will Yew Tree and Tom, John's son, dropped to the rear. Matty Straw Hair took the left and Robin of Barnsley the right. My other men followed Jack and myself.

Jackpointed to a barely discernible path, which led up a slight slope, next to the smallest of becks. I nocked a war arrow, as we would be more likely to see a warrior without mail rather than a knight or man at arms. We knew that we were looking for a very distinctive livery. Captain William had told me it was '*vairy or and gules*'. I did not know what it meant but I knew what it looked like; red chalices next to yellow helmets. I had decided that if we came upon outlaws, we would just leave them. Peter of Wakefield and Jack of Lincoln's tales had given me sympathy for the men of the greenwood.

We seemed to walk for a long time, and I saw the sun beginning to set in the west. Jack of Lincoln had told me that we were walking into the wind and, a few steps later, I smelled wood smoke. This was an open outdoor fire and there was food being cooked upon it. Jack was still leading us, for this was his land, but I gave the signals to order my men into position. I waved my hand for Stephen Green Feather to join Matty Straw Hair, while David the Welshman joined Robin of Barnsley. They spread further out. I needed as large a circle of bows to surround however many men we discovered.

This had not been my plan. I had hoped merely to find them and then use Captain William and his men. The fact that we had discovered them within a short time changed my plans.

I heard the noise of laughter and also of argument. Both told me that there was a camp ahead. Jack crouched as he led us closer. When he held up his hand for us to stop, all of us obeyed him. We were one company, and we trusted each other implicitly. He dropped his bow and crawled forward.

He seemed to be away for a long time and, when he returned, he almost ghosted next to me. He held up twenty-two fingers. Then he tapped his sword and held up five. He patted his chest. He held up five fingers and tapped his bow. There were five men at arms, and they wore the livery of de Ferrers. There were five archers and the rest, the other twelve, were just de Ferrers' retainers. I patted him on the back; he had done well. The surprise would be on our side.

With John of Nottingham on one side of me and Jack of Lincoln on the other, I led Matty and Will towards the camp. It soon became obvious where it was, as there was a glow in the dark of the gloomy forest. The men on our flanks were invisible. They would know exactly what to do when we neared the camp. Archers, unlike men at arms, needed to fight together, to nock, draw and release as though they were one person, and to hit the same target at the same time.

I stepped ahead of Jack, for I was captain and I had to lead. It helped that I was the best archer in our company, thus my men had total respect for me. This was our kind of battlefield; all of us could move silently. We looked for the branches and leaves and almost slipped through, without disturbing them too much. We scoured the ground for the tell-tale twigs that would break, alerting an enemy. The camp was a confident one and they had no sentries out; I knew that from Jack's signals. Had there been sentries, then he would have given me the numbers and pointed at his eyes with two fingers from his right hand.

I stopped just thirty paces from the edge of their camp. They had lit a good fire and were roasting what looked like a young deer. Jack had good eyes. I saw that there were four men at arms and they wore de Ferrers' livery, but there was also another man at arms who had no tunic. I knew him to be a man at arms for he was sharpening a sword – and it was a good one. The other five men at arms had mail hauberks beneath their tunics, but the sixth one did not wear his; I saw it lying on the ground.

None of the archers were close to their bows. They had the leggings of liveried archers. The other eleven men were hired men. They were paid less than archers and men at arms. Lord Edward employed none, for he wanted professional soldiers and not the kind of men who might run when a battle turned against them. I saw that some had spears, for they had stacked them together. I spied another man sharpening an axe. These were de Ferrers' men.

I changed my arrow. Five mailed men meant I needed a needle bodkin. I hoped that we would be able to take them without a fight, but I was ready to kill if I had to.

I began to move closer, but all the time I kept my bow aimed at the man at arms who was sharpening his sword. He was the one closest to a weapon. I had not fully drawn the bow; that weakened both the weapon and the archer. I could draw and release in a heartbeat if I had to. I heard fragments of their conversation and as I moved, I listened.

"So, how long do we stay here?"

"Rafe the Grumbler, you are well named. We have been here just a sennight and you have eaten well." It was the man sharpening his sword who spoke, and that marked him as the leader. I had been right to cover him with my bow.

"Aye, and his lordship has abandoned us here, Henry Sharp Sword. That knight might come back from the Holy Land any day now. What then?"

"We find somewhere deeper in the forest! God's blood but the forest is big enough, and the land to the north-west belongs to our master."

"And that is why we cannot go near it. I agree that we have had food, but the ale is almost gone and I need a woman!" Rafe the Grumbler appeared to be well named.

Some of the others laughed. One sneered, "You have not enough money left in your purse to pay for a decent-looking woman. Find a sheep. They complain less." The man had a Welsh accent.

"Owen of Newport you are a Welshman and you put up with anything. Some of your women have better beards than their men."

The Welsh archer stood and his hand went to his dagger. The one called Rafe the Grumbler stood and they faced each other; there would be a fight. He was a man at arms, and he pulled a short dagger. The man at arms who had been sharpening his sword walked between them with his sword drawn. "And I am captain! Stand down or face me: Henry Sharp Sword!"

It was the perfect time to make our presence known. The attention of the whole camp was on the tableau close to the fire, and men would enjoy watching a fight between the two. I slid from the undergrowth and pulled back on the bow. I was less than twenty paces from them.

"Put your weapons down, for I am here on the orders of the king and his son! We seek Robert de Ferrers."

I was watching the leader, for he had his hand on his sword, but it was the one called Rafe the Grumbler who turned and threw his dagger at me. I adjusted my aim and the bodkin-tipped arrow tore through his mail until just the fletch was showing. He fell back into the fire.

I had barely managed to move my head from the flight of the flying dagger. Three more arrows struck the men in the camp. The three had made the mistake of reaching for weapons, and my men would take no chances. In a heartbeat, I had nocked a war arrow.

The one called Henry Sharp Sword dropped his weapon and shouted, "Hold! These are trained archers!" I could barely be seen through the trees, but the direction of my arrow told him where I was. "Who are you, archer?"

"I am Captain Gerald War Bow."

The one called Owen sheathed his weapon and said, "I have heard of him. He is as good as me."

My men had not killed the three men they had hit. They had wounded them, and I saw blood dripping from wounds. "Drop your weapons and move to the fire, then we can tend to your wounds."

"Do as he says!"

Weapons were sheathed or dropped, and the men moved towards the three who were injured. I kicked the body of the man who had fallen in the fire over to the side, where it smouldered. The smell of burning flesh was already in the air. "Keep them covered. Jack of Lincoln, I want an arrow aimed at their captain!"

"Aye, Captain. It is aimed at his heart!" The body of the dead man at arms was a testament to our skill.

I saw the surprise on the faces of the men at arms when my men came from all around them. Our bows were ready to release, and our eyes were on the potential captives. "Captain, you may see to your men but keep your hands from your weapons."

It was only then I realised that I had not seen any horses. It was obvious now – but we had been concentrating so much on the men that the obvious had escaped us.

I was the first to reach the men and, when I was sure that my men had them covered, I took my arrow and placed it in my belt. Slinging my bow over my back, I drew my sword. I saw the eyes of the captain and the men at arms take in the fact that it was a swordsman's weapon.

"Where is your master, the Earl of Derby?"

Their captain looked up at me and I saw the lie forming in his eyes.

"Captain, you and your men talk loudly. We heard what you said. You serve the earl and he has fled. We will take you to Northampton for judgement, but it is your master we seek."

Resignation filled his face and he told me a version of the truth. "He has gone to find Simon de Montfort. We await his orders."

"Better. John of Nottingham, collect the weapons. Matty and Will, fetch the horses."

John of Nottingham began to do as I asked and said, "We leave tonight?"

I nodded but I did not elaborate. I did not relish trying to watch the men who survived, in a wood. Codnor Castle was a better place to guard them, and Captain William and his men could earn their silver, too. The castle was strongly made with a good moat and a drawbridge, which explained why it could be held by so few men.

I watched as two of the men at arms looked at each other while John collected weapons. They were weighing up the odds of taking us. They still wore their mail and must have fancied their chances. My hand slid around my back for my dagger.

The two men must have had a signal, for they suddenly launched themselves at me, pulling short swords which they had hidden beneath their blankets. Stephen Green Feather's arrow threw one of the men from his feet as it punched into his back, but the other was on me so quickly that my men risked hitting me if they released a bodkin. Stephen's arrow had penetrated so much that barely a handspan protruded from the man's back.

The man at arms was confident and thought he had me, for his short sword came directly for my throat. It was a bold strike, intended to end the battle quickly. It was the wrong move, for I was able to block it with my sword while whipping my dagger around and driving it up under the raised arm of the man at arms. He wore a hauberk, but it afforded no protection under his arm. The tip slid directly into flesh and I rammed a little harder; I struck something vital. I saw the light go from his eyes as I gave him a quick death. His body slipped to the ground and I glared at the rest.

"I do not need to take you back! I do so as a service! Does anyone else relish a woodland grave?"

There remained just two men at arms who were wearing mail, the captain and one other. The archers were too far from their weapons and I dismissed the rest. They were not a threat; the two men at arms were the ones to worry about.

The captain said, "All of you, we are captured and we take our medicine. Our time will come. This is not over!" He had finished tending to his wounded man and he stood. "You will have no more trouble Captain Gerald War Bow, but I will remember this night's work. I now have men at arms to replace!"

I nodded towards the three dead men at arms. "Have your men take the mail from your dead men and then bury them. You have no horses and we cannot carry them."

The stripping of their dead and the burial of the corpses kept their hands occupied, and Matty and Will had returned with our horses by the time each man had been given a shallow grave. Animals would come and dig them up, but we had done the best we could. I reflected that the ones who did the burying did not shed tears over the dead. Even the captain did not ask to say words over them.

With Jack leading and John of Nottingham at the rear, we made our way back through the dark woods. Each man we had captured had a halter around his neck. Their captain was tethered next to me. He seemed in a chatty mood and spoke as we walked; the threat made before the burial was now replaced with an attempt to persuade me to change sides. Henry Sharp Sword was a clever man. "I know you serve Lord Edward, archer, but you and your men would be better paid serving de Montfort. I know a good archer when I see one, and you are better than most. An archer who can use a bow as well as you and is also a swordsman is valuable. Where did you learn to handle a sword so well?"

"Fighting the Welsh."

"Ah, then you have fought sneaky men before. John and James were both cunning fighters." He shrugged. "We do not have to like the men we lead."

"I do."

He turned, his face white in the dark. "Your lord did not hire these men?"

Shaking my head, I said, "He gave me the coins but I did the choosing. Why do you think I was so confident about taking you with so few men? Had our positions been reversed then would you have done what I did?"

I saw him glance around and then shake his head. "These are not all my men. My lord asked me to keep them close to his lands."

"You said it is not over, which means you know more than you are saying."

"I just know that your king was lucky at Northampton. Luck is a wilful and precocious mistress. She can desert you at the wrong time."

I noticed that he had said, '*your king*', which meant he believed Simon de Montfort was right. I stored that information.

"You do not seem overly concerned about your capture, Captain."

He shrugged. "We will be fed in Northampton, and my men will have their hurts healed. Our lord has suffered a setback, as has our leader, but we have the Right and together they will prevail. King Henry has abused his position. I am a patient man, Captain Gerald."

The threat was back in his words. I had not been deceived by his apparent change. This man was a professional and he would need to be watched closely.

His words worried me, and I fretted about them all the way to Codnor Castle. Lord Edward and his father thought that the war was over, but this captain did not and he was no fool. What were the rebels planning?

All were abed by the time we reached the castle, and we had to wait for entry. Captain Williams grinned when he saw our captives. "You have saved us both time and men, Captain. Well done. And Robert de Ferrers?"

"From what I can gather he is with de Montfort and heading for Rochester. I do not think there are others in the forest." I was telling him that we need not search any further. We could rejoin Lord Edward.

He nodded. "Aye, we have wasted enough time. We will leave these at Northampton. Mayhap we can catch our lord before the battle is fought."

Both of us were confident about Lord Edward's skill in battle. Although he was young and sometimes reckless, he was also a clever leader who knew how to deploy men on a battlefield. He would relieve the siege and then we would have a reward for our efforts.

We fought for his money. When the war was over, we would be dismissed and we would need to earn a living. A full purse gave us choices.

CHAPTER 2

It took six days to reach Northampton, for we had walking men with us, and by that time we heard that the siege was over. We still headed south, towards Winchelsea and Rochester. The king and his son had recaptured the mighty castle of Rochester; this part of England was back in royal hands. Simon de Montfort had fled to London and the Earl of Derby was with him. We rode directly to the camp of the king and his son, which was close to Winchelsea for, with de Montfort holding London, the king needed men to blockade the River Thames: the Cinque Ports were his only hope. As we rode down the road towards the huge camp outside Winchelsea, I saw heads on spears lining the road.

The king had placed groups of men to guard the road. We reined in at one, and Captain William asked, "Who are these fellows, friend?"

The sergeant at arms pointed at me. "They are like the captain here. They are archers. They have caused the king much trouble of late and hurt our men. They have been punished." The men of the Weald were good archers; they knew the forests well and were to be respected. "They made the mistake of holding us up as we advanced, and then they killed the king's cook. When he captured them, he had three hundred beheaded and their heads left as a warning." The sergeant at arms grinned at me. "The king does not like archers!"

Continuing towards the camp, I wondered if Lord Edward regretted sending us on the wild goose chase to capture de Ferrers. We might have been able to neutralize the archers of the Weald, for we knew how to sniff out an ambush.

When we reached the camp, Captain William and I left our lieutenants to organise our own area while we walked into Winchelsea to speak with the king. The grumbling of the men we passed told us there was little food to be had. Apparently, the Cinque Ports had not welcomed the king as generously as he might have liked.

It was Baron Mortimer who came to us, as we cooled our heels outside the home of the wine merchant that the king was using as his base. Sir Roger was a fierce warrior, with lands in Herefordshire. I liked him as he was loyal to Lord Edward and a good man in a fight. He recognised us. "You succeeded in your mission, Captain William?"

Captain William was senior, and it was he who reported to Sir Roger, "No, my lord. We captured his men, but Sir Robert is in London with de Montfort."

He nodded. "Just so. I will tell Lord Edward of your return. Where are you camped?" We told him. "Then I will send for you when the king decides where we go."

"And food, my lord?"

He grinned. "If you find any, then I pray you share it with us! There is perilously little to be had, but I do not think we will be here long."

As we walked back to the camp Captain William said, "I think we will need you and your men to hunt for us."

"They do not mind hunting. So long as they have full bellies and coins in their purses, they are happy," I said.

We stopped at a tavern. There was little food but more than enough ale and wine. We spoke with other captains who were gathered there and learned much. The king had left twenty banners and four hundred men at Tonbridge, to guard the castle which guarded the river. With Rochester reinforced, the king did not have as many men as he might have liked and, alarmingly, those he had were mainly mounted men. I discovered that we were amongst the only archers in the king's retinue.

As we headed back to our new camp, I voiced my fears to Captain William. "This land through which we travel is perfect for archers. The archers of Weald are good, and if they choose to ambush the king and his knights then all we have gained might be lost."

Captain William believed in mail armour and horsemen. Despite our closeness, he still thought that men at arms were superior to archers. Most men at arms came from the stock of landowners; archers, by and large, came from poorer families or outlaws. "Trust in Lord Edward," he said.

I was not as confident as Captain William, but I obeyed orders and I would do as he suggested. What choice did we have?

I sent my best hunters into the woods to find game. We needed to eat, and Sir Roger had been a little vague in his timetable. Better to have food to hand when we began our march than to wait until we were ordered to leave. When John of Nottingham and the other hunters returned, they brought disquieting news. "Captain, there are signs of many men marching through these woods and heading north."

"Towards London?"

"That would be my guess, Captain."

"Thank you, John, I will speak with Lord Edward when time allows."

We busied ourselves preparing the meat. We would eat fresh, and then we would salt and dry the rest. All the time my men wrestled with the worry that Lord Edward and his father might have miscalculated. In the event, we had but one day to wait to discover what this news heralded.

Simon de Montfort had raised what Lord Edward called '*the rabble of London.*' The Prince of England himself came to our camp to tell us that we would be leaving, and that we would be the van of the royal army which went to fight them. We would have to be ready to ride before dawn.

After he had told us I said, "Lord, my men saw signs of archers and other such warriors heading north from the Weald. Your news confirms that they are headed for your enemies. Archers could hurt our army."

He laughed. "He can bring all the rabble he likes. It is knights who will win this battle, Captain Gerald. We fight not the wild men of Wales this time. We have many more knights than our enemy. This will be the last battle, and our knights shall win it! You and your archers have done good work in the past, but this time you will be spectators and can watch mighty heavy horse sweep the scum of London back to that rat-infested bolt hole. The men of London will pay for their many and varied insults to my family and to my father; de Montfort will be put in his place once and for all. Do not worry, Captain Gerald, this war is over, and soon you and your men will be able to return to your former lives, for my father's realm will be at peace."

As Captain William and I returned to our men, I said, "I thought that we would be Lord Edward's men, well… forever."

Captain William shook his head. "In the grand scheme of things, we are not expensive. We cost less each year than a new warhorse, but the great and the good do not need us, Gerald. They prefer their own around them. I heard the insult. He thinks knights are our only mounted force. My men may not all be noble-born, but I would back them against any of de Montfort's knights."

"Then I suppose I should plan for life after Lord Edward. It seems that there will be perilously little available for us when Lord Edward wins."

"There are many knights who wish to have archers when they go on a crusade."

I shook my head. "I would like to stay in this country." He shrugged. "I suppose we could always hire ourselves out as guards for merchants."

"Could you live such a dismal existence?"

"We need coins in our purses. The alternative is the life Jack of Lincoln lived, and that does not appeal."

As we headed towards Lewes, in the early hours of the morning, I confided in my men. They needed to know that if we won the battle then we might well be out of a job. They were more phlegmatic than I had been, for they all had other avenues they could explore.

"There are always knights who are willing to hire good archers, Captain. Baron Mortimer lives on the Welsh borders, and he would hire you in a heartbeat. You could find a place easily. But I confess that I like this company. You know yourself that there are archers like Guy of Sheffield, and they sour a company. Here we are all one. I shall miss that!"

Guy of Sheffield had been a bad archer who had tried to betray us. I would not employ another such as he.

Jack of Lincoln scratched his split nose. "Do not dismiss us so easily, John of Nottingham. We have not won this battle yet, nor has Lord Edward discharged us. If my time in the forest taught me anything, it was not to predict what might happen in the future. Leave that for the witches and soothsayers."

It seemed good advice; Jack's time as an outlaw had given him a different perspective on life.

The rest of the army moved extremely slowly. As the van and moving without baggage, we made Lewes and the castle quickly – and that gave us the opportunity to scout out the battlefield. What I saw, I did not like. The castle was close to the river but the land rose to the north. Worse, there was not only a wood on the top of the slope, but there were also at least two pieces of dead ground where men could be hidden. I believed that Lord Edward was overconfident, as was his father, and his uncle, Richard of Cornwall. It seemed to be a family trait. Simon de Montfort had been a soldier for his whole life and had fought on crusades. He was not to be underestimated.

I made a thorough examination of the site and then headed back to Lewes. It was as I did so that I saw the banners to the east; it was Simon de Montfort's army. They had arrived sooner than ours, and they would take the higher ground. He might have had fewer knights, but de Montfort had the tactical advantage. I determined to tell Lord Edward of the news and offer my advice. It was in my interests to ensure that he did not fail. Success might mean my dismissal, but defeat would mean the complete end to my freedom.

Richard of Cornwall had his men filling up the houses of Lewes. The king and his son had taken the castle and the priory. I sent off my men to make a camp. We would, at least, have food, for we still had deer meat.

"Find somewhere we can graze our animals. It doesn't matter if it is some way from the castle, so long as they get to eat. Perhaps by the River Ouse?"

John of Nottingham waved a hand. "Leave that to us, Captain. You might ask Lord Edward if he has supplies of arrows. We just have fifty left to each of us."

I waved, to show I had heard. We had arrowheads and we had feathers, for we had recovered many after the battles we had fought, but shafts were something different, and I was not sure that we had a supply. I had not seen any other archers with the army.

When I reached the castle, I was made to wait for some time. Perhaps

Lord Edward was in conference; I did not know. Finally, I was admitted to the great hall, where were gathered the king, Richard of Cornwall – who also happened to be king of Germany – Lord Edward and Sir Roger Mortimer, along with Henry Almain, the son of Richard of Cornwall. They were the only noble-born; the rest were servants and squires clearing away after their masters. I was an archer still covered in the dust from the road, and King Henry looked at me with obvious distaste. He seemed to have an aversion to the common man.

"Why is an archer here, Edward? We have no need of him."

"He was sent to scout, Your Majesty. It might be prudent to know the state of the battlefield."

The king waved a dismissive hand. "We know all that there is to know. We have more knights than they do and God is on our side. We beat them at Northampton, we drove them from Rochester and we shall defeat them here at Lewes."

Richard of Cornwall said, "Speak, Gerald War Bow, for I have heard your name spoken by worthy warriors who know the value of a good archer."

I bowed. "There is a wood on Offham Hill, and it lies half a league northeast of the town and the castle. It could conceal large numbers of men. In addition, there are two areas of dead ground. You cannot see them from the castle or the town, but men could be hidden there. The ground rises to the hill and would sap energy from horses."

King Henry was not in the mood to hear my words. "I care not how many men they match against us. We know what you do not, archer, the bulk of the rebel army is made up of ordinary folk like you! We have nobles, we have knights. Our men are better mounted and we will sweep them from the field."

"But, Your Majesty—"

I got no further. "You would counsel a king? Who is this man, Edward, and why does he hold such a high opinion of himself? I would have him whipped if he were my man!"

Lord Edward reddened. "He is an archer, King Henry, and I will deal with him."

Once outside, I thought he would strike me.

"What got into you, fool, that you question my father? You gave your report and that should have been the end of it. When we fight you will guard the baggage at the priory. I would not have you close to the king, for I can see you make him angry."

I contemplated pointing out that we were the only archers with the army and then thought better of it. "Yes, my lord." Lord Edward was still a young man, and he had been embarrassed by my actions. He knew I was right, I could see it in his eyes, but he was still not yet ready to lead our armies.

I left feeling depressed. We would guard the baggage and would not be able to affect the battle. I headed to the priory first to see where we would be stationed. The baggage was there already, and the carters were making their camp. There was marsh and bog close by. It would not be a pleasant camp.

There were servants and there were squires who heard the argument, and soon the news of the king's displeasure spread around the camp. It had reached our camp before I even arrived. Captain William came over to me.

"I am sorry, Captain Gerald, but we should know our place, and I am disappointed that your bows will not protect us when we go to battle."

I shrugged. "We will still be paid and we will not be in danger."

"That is not what is in your heart."

"Perhaps speaking from the heart is not the thing to do. From now on I shall keep my counsel." I closed with him. "Beware the dead ground and the woods. If I was de Montfort, I would use them."

"And we know he is no fool. Thank you, Captain Gerald."

When I reached my men I said, "We need a new camp."

John of Nottingham shook his head. "We heard what was said, Captain, and it is unfair, you were only doing your duty."

"It is in the past. There is a river, the Winterbourne, and a boggy area, the Brooks. Both are close to the priory. If we camp between them, we shall have grazing and water, and the Brooks will afford some protection, but the air will not be wholesome."

"We should not need the grazing, Captain. Most men believe that we will win, and win easily at that."

I smiled and shook my head. "Let us see. Simon de Montfort is a skilled leader and he will have chosen to fight here for a reason. We will do our duty and guard the baggage."

There were baggage guards but they were just hired drivers. I suspect that they may have been thieves, too, for they resented us and our presence. They saw Lord Edward's livery and thought we were spies, sent to keep an eye on them. I did not disillusion them. We were there to guard the baggage against enemies, not light-fingered opportunists.

The campsite I chose was a better one than I had expected, for the grazing was lush and the water so close that we could tether our horses nearby. The marsh and bog were far enough away that the flying insects did not bother us as much as they might have. The destriers of the knights, on the other hand, suffered. The knights wanted them close and they soon overgrazed the pasture.

That might not have caused a problem, but there were two days of negotiation between the two armies. Such conferences were not unusual.

The talks came to nothing and that outcome surprised no one, for all that they did was entrench the two sides and increase the bitterness. Richard of Cornwall stated that he would 'destroy their goods and their bodies'. Nobles were supposed to speak and behave in a slightly different manner. It showed that there would be no reconciliation – and we would fight.

We were at the southern end of the battlefield and had a clear view of the whole battle. The two armies spent time forming lines. I saw the rebels as they filtered down from Offham Hill; I saw that each of them had a white cross sewn on to their tunics or, in the case of the knights, a white cross on an armband. They were using God as a weapon. To the ordinary Londoners who fought for de Montfort, it would convey the belief that God was on their side. The rebels disappeared in the dead ground and then rose to form a line on the ridge. We had seen them descend and we knew that they looked to be fewer than they actually were. I hoped that Lord Edward knew that too, but as only Richard of Cornwall was on the battlefield, it was highly unlikely. The king and his son would see the enemy line and underestimate the numbers.

I saw that the men of London, the enemies of Lord Edward, were on the enemy left – our right. It took until after the hour of seven for the whole of our army to form its lines. They were mailed men, and it took time. Lord Edward's knights formed his front line. He had with him powerful nobles: de Warenne, de Valence and Mortimer. They were our best men. Behind him were his men at arms, and then the foot soldiers of his knights. Richard of Cornwall was closest to us and the king was in the middle.

As was usual in such battles, both sides allowed the other to form up. To the nobles, it was almost a game. They were rarely killed in such battles and, usually, the worst that could happen was that they would be captured and ransomed. The men at arms, hired archers such as us and the ordinary soldiers had no such luxury. I had learned that they faced death. A knight might spare another knight for ransom, but a commoner was worthless and he would die. It was another reason the king did not like us; worthless as we were, we had bodkin arrows and they were knight-killers. Perhaps that was the real reason we were stuck with the baggage.

I had used the carts which had brought the baggage to make a small fort. My men and I stood on them, and we could use the elevation to send our arrows further, while we had a wooden barrier to protect us from charging horses. The baggage drivers mocked our caution, for they did not believe that we would be in any danger.

One unexpected result of our new task was that we had the entire stock of arrows for the army with the wagons. Most of the archers had been left at Rochester and Tonbridge, and we were lucky that they had not taken more of the arrows. We had plenty, and I had them spread out in all of the wagons. John of Nottingham made a good suggestion: he thought we should tether our horses close to the wagons. I approved his idea, for when I saw the two sides arrayed I knew that the rebels held the advantage.

The preliminaries involved priests and bishops marching up and down the lines. All would be shriven; men fought better knowing that if they died, they had a better chance of going to heaven. Then the attack began.

It was started by King Henry who ordered his line forward. I heard his cry, "Spur on!" and saw the dragon standard as it fluttered. His horse was led by two of his men at arms. It allowed the king to use both arms to fight and gave him some protection. Lord Edward did not bother with such bodyguards. He was fearless and he was reckless.

Lord Edward appeared to be a little tardy; perhaps the huge size of his battle caused him some confusion, and I saw a gap appear between his battle and that of his father. As I looked at the body of men facing him, I saw that it was largely made up of the Londoners. There were some mounted men, but the majority appeared to be on foot. They were not trained. As Simon de Montfort, in the centre, wheeled his men around the track leading from the Downs, the Londoners confirmed Lord Edward's opinion and charged him. I knew Lord Edward well enough to know what his reaction would be. He did not wait for the rest of the army; he ordered his own men to charge the Londoners. From across the battlefield, I heard the crash and clash as the two forces met. The few horses and the disorganized Londoners were no match for the four hundred odd men Lord Edward led. It was as though the Londoners ceased to exist. One moment they were facing Lord Edward, and the next they disappeared back up the slope and into the dead ground.

I turned to John of Nottingham. "If Lord Edward turns to take on de Montfort, then the battle is won!"

Lord Edward and his men disappeared in the dead ground and then, to my horror, I saw them pursuing the Londoners up the slope towards Offham Hill. Now it was time for Simon de Montfort to do that which Lord Edward should have done; he extended his line and turned the flank of King Henry. The men they fell upon were not the knights but the royalist foot soldiers. I knew what was coming.

"String your bows and prepare for battle!"

The drivers looked in horror as the king and his brother found themselves facing more knights than they led. Lord Edward led his knights after merchants and fishmongers; Simon de Montfort's newly-knighted men charged King Henry and his men. It soon became a confused mêlée.

Then my worst fears were realised. De Montfort had a mass of slingers and archers; they rained death on the men who followed Richard of

Cornwall. His knights did not die, but some of their horses did. The ordinary men, however, were slaughtered. I saw Richard of Cornwall isolated from his men and take shelter in a mill, half a mile from us. He was too far away for us to help. I knew that we would soon be engaged, for I saw a mob break through the gap his men had left as they tried to reach their leader. These were not knights; these were the sort of men we had captured in the forest close to Codnor.

"Draw." They outnumbered us, but panic would only make us lose. "Choose your own targets!"

I had a needle bodkin, and I aimed my first arrow at a man who wore a mail vest. He led the men, and he was less than two hundred paces from me but, as there were many men around him, I released. If I missed him then the odds were, I would hit another. My arrow was true and he was hit in the chest. I nocked a second bodkin for, when he fell, I saw a second mailed man behind him. It was just a mail vest and, from the rust marks upon it, an old one. He was closer to me and my arrow drove half its length into his body.

I took a war arrow next. We were sending arrows so quickly that, despite their superior numbers, we were thinning them considerably. I sent ten arrows at them before they broke, and the survivors ran back to the knights who were trying to get to the king. They were an easier target than archers who stood behind wooden walls and killed all who tried to get at them.

If the king or his standard fell, then the battle was over. I saw that his household knights were fighting their way back to the priory. The battle was lost: I could see that, but the king was trying to salvage something, and he was relying on his son to return and save the day.

Then, some of his mounted men saw the Brooks behind us and thought to escape that way. Jack of Lincoln shouted at them to warn them, but they did not heed him. We had left it empty, for it protected us from an outflanking manoeuvre. I saw men and horses become stuck in the mire. The rebel archers raced to try to slaughter them.

They reckoned without my handful of archers. We had height and we were better trained. Using war arrows, we began to thin out the archers. They were forced to turn their attention on us.

"Use the wagons for defence!"

I sprang down, but my order was too late for Ronan and Dick, son of Robin. They were a little slow to descend and both were hit by arrows and stones. They died, but their killers paid the price. We had lost good men and we redoubled our efforts. Even my arm began to burn as we loosed arrow after arrow. The order to stay with the baggage saved us, for we had an almost inexhaustible supply of arrows and the rebel archers did not. They fell back, and there was a hiatus for both sides were regrouping. Meanwhile the king's men were heading into the town, and Richard of Cornwall's men were trying to extract themselves.

"Are they dead?"

John of Nottingham was examining the two dead archers. "Aye, lord."

Then Matty Straw Hair shouted, "It is Lord Edward and his men; they have returned!"

I risked climbing up onto the wagon to afford a better view. He was returning but, as he appeared from the dead ground, I saw half of his force turn and ride to the east. They had seen that the battle was lost and were saving their own skins. Lord Edward led fewer than forty banners and the men of Captain William. My old comrade was loyal. Lord Edward was no coward, and he ploughed his way through rebel foot soldiers. Despite his treatment of us, we were still his men.

"To the wagons! Our lord needs us!"

I loosed arrow after arrow into the rear of the men trying to get to Lord Edward. When my men added their arrows, such was the ferocity of the attack by Lord Edward that the opposition melted away. He reined in. I saw that Captain William had just three men left with him and his tunic was red with blood.

Lord Edward lifted his visor. "Thank you, Captain Gerald. It seems my father was wrong and we *did* need you. Where is he?"

"He headed into the castle. Your uncle is captured."

"Then we have lost. Sir Roger, we will go into the castle. Captain Gerald, protect our backs as long as you can and then save yourselves. We will seek terms, for the castle might be held against a siege and many men have died this day."

I think he was talking to himself and not me at that point. He was a clever man and knew that there were many ways to win a war even when one had lost a battle. He would not give in.

"You have done your duty and I shall not forget this."

I had no time to say more, for de Montfort had seen his enemy and ordered knights to charge us. Lord Edward turned and galloped past the priory towards the castle. We needed to loose as one.

"Draw! Release! Nock! Draw! Release!" We had no time to choose arrows and were forced to use war arrows. We did not slay the knights but some of their horses fell, others were wounded. We slowed them down as they moved away from our arrows and away from Lord Edward. As Lord Edward reached the gates, I saw Captain William turn and wave. We could now leave the field with honour.

The king had lost, but we were still alive.

CHAPTER 3

We had been given permission to leave, and we did so with alacrity. The nobles and the knights might be taken for ransom but, as the archers of the Weald had discovered, for us, capture meant death! We were in the south of England in the heartland of de Montfort and his supporters. To the north of us was a barrier of enemies stretching across the country; we were in the greatest danger that any could imagine.

"Take as many arrows as you can and follow me. We have done our duty and now we save ourselves!"

Robin of Barnsley said, "Easier said than done, Captain!"

"Just get on your horse and don't forget to take Ronan's and Dick's. Times will get harder and we will need horses as well as arrows."

I grabbed four bundles of arrows and headed for my horse. I reached Eleanor and hung my sword from my blanket, then I used the leather thongs hanging from her saddle to secure the four bundles of arrows. They had flights and shafts only; the heads were in a separate bag that also hung from Eleanor's saddle.

As I mounted, I scanned the battlefield. The Brooks and the river barred our escape south and west; the enemy were heading for the town and the castle to the east, and that left just one escape route: north. We had no choice, we would have to take it, even though it meant riding through the enemy. We would be in danger, but I hoped that they would not be expecting us.

I shouted, "We use our swords and we head north. We ride until we can ride no more. John, take the rear!"

I drew my sword; it was sharp and I knew how to use it, even from the back of a horse. I dug my heels in and Eleanor responded – she galloped through the gap in the wagons. I determined not to use my sword until I had to.

Those who were of common birth were busy stripping the dead of their belongings and weapons. They just looked up as we galloped past them. We were gone in a blur, and they did not notice that we did not wear the white cross of the rebels. We reached the high point in front of the dead ground before we were noticed.

I spotted ten men at arms who were mailed, and they served Hugh le Despencer – for I recognised the livery. Our only chance was to ride through them. They were at the bottom of the dead ground and we would have the slope with us; I hoped that they would not even notice us approach. Once we passed them, our fresher and well-grazed horses would outrun theirs. The problem would be getting past them unharmed.

Then they spied us, and I knew that there was no hope of evading them. We had to hurt and discourage them.

"We charge them!"

Perhaps the men at arms thought us easy targets, for most archers could not use a sword well. Hugh le Despencer lived in London. He was master of the Tower and did not know my reputation, so I gambled that his men would be equally ignorant. They made the mistake of forming a line to stop us, which meant that they were static and we were moving. I glanced over Eleanor's rump and saw that Will Yew

Tree, Tom, John's son, and Matty Straw Hair were behind me. They knew how to handle a sword.

The sergeant at arms who led the men was overweight. His master was in command of the Tower, and that was an easy duty. He had a shield – and therein lay an advantage for me. I had no shield, and so I rode to his shield side and trusted that Matty could watch my back. The sergeant's horse laboured up the slight slope while Eleanor had her legs open and was galloping.

The helmet covered the sergeant's face; I had no helmet and a better view. However, he was a soldier and, seeing my intention, tried to turn his horse. He was moving more slowly than I was, giving me an advantage. I stood in my stirrups as he tried to swing his sword at me. My sword came down on his helmet while he was still swinging his own weapon over his horse's head. His helmet dented and he slumped over his saddle.

A second man at arms was just behind him. Perhaps he had expected his sergeant to stop me, for he was not ready with his sword; it was by his side. I hacked at his leg and drew blood. He tumbled from his horse. I galloped up the slope to the ridge. Glancing over my shoulder I saw that another two men at arms were unhorsed, and the rest had stopped. Their leader was dead.

Before I could celebrate, I saw Matty Straw Hair's horse as it galloped towards me. Matty's body lay dead, close to the men we had slain. I had lost another archer.

I grabbed the reins of Matty's horse, which obligingly stopped next to me. If we halted, then the men at arms would regroup and follow us. Although it meant abandoning Matty's body, we had to flee. To stay meant either death or, at best, the loss of three fingers on our right hands. Archers who were captured had a bleak future. I dug my heels into Eleanor.

We thundered through the wood on Offham Hill and soon passed through the battlefield which had seen Lord Edward catch the Londoners. It looked like a charnel house, and body parts littered the top of the Downs. Lord Edward had made a mistake and indulged his personal desire for vengeance on the Londoners. He had shown that he was not yet ready to be a king and leader, although his father had hardly covered himself in glory. The wood had hidden the battle from the prince, and he must have assumed that his father and uncle were victorious. Our horses were tired after the climb and I reflected that the same must have been true for Lord Edward; all the more reason for him to have rested and then returned to the battle. I had to risk reining in.

We were the only living creatures on that piece of high ground. The carrion had flown off; when we departed they would return.

I stroked Eleanor's head. "Good girl. What to do now, eh?"

I heard the hooves of my men's mounts as they laboured up the slope. My horse was the best in our company. I did not turn, for my mind was running through all the choices which remained open to us. We had to escape north as quickly as possible, while the enemy celebrated the victory. London was de Montfort's stronghold and we were Lord Edward's men. Had we been with Lord Edward, then we would have had a brighter future. We were not – and any man who found us could kill us, take our horses, our weapons, coins and be considered justified for we were beaten men.

To get to the north, we had to pass through de Montfort's other stronghold, the Midlands, and that would not be easy. The first thing to do was talk to my men. In theory, I was no longer their captain. Any oath they might have made was nullified by our defeat and Lord Edward's order. I turned my horse. Their faces showed a mixture of disappointment at the defeat and anger at our losses.

John of Nottingham swept a hand around at the dead. "A sorry sight, eh Captain?"

I nodded. "And Matty?"

"Two of them came at him, Captain. He hurt the one on your left, but the other split his skull in twain. It was over in an instant. He knew nothing."

"Yet he is dead." I could not hide the bitterness in my voice. These were my men!

Robin of Barnsley shook his head. "Captain, this was not of your doing. We followed our orders, and all of us can hold our heads high. You got us out of that hole and I confess, I thought that our charge down the hill was doomed – but you had the right of it. What now, Captain?"

"We have no employer and we will be hunted, for men have long memories and there are debts to be paid." I was thinking of de Ferrers and his men. "If any of you choose to leave, then go with my blessing."

John of Nottingham shook his head. "Our best hope for us is to stay together. A single arrow can be broken easily, but a bundle holds firm. We are all of one mind and we follow you;, you are our leader. What are your thoughts, Captain?"

I looked around and saw not a dissenting face. I nodded. "To the north-east lies London, and there are enemies who abound in that cesspit. More than that, I know that Simon de Montfort will head there, and we risk running into his army. To the north-west lies the castle at Windsor, which is still the king's. I do not intend to go into the castle, but if we can reach the wood which lies to the south of it, we can camp and consider our choices."

David the Welshman shook his head. "Captain, that is over fifty miles away. We will not make it in one journey. The Surrey Hills are less than thirty miles from here. If we take it steadily then we can make them."

A wise leader heeded the advice of his men. The king and Lord Edward had disregarded mine at great cost. "Aye, David, you are right, for our horses will need their strength if we are to reach safety."

I wheeled Eleanor and we headed away from the line of bodies that marked the road to London. Noon had passed but this was May, and we had many hours to make the journey.

We passed through an England stripped of men. Some had fought for the king, but more had fought for the rebels. The king might have had more knights, but the rebels had the support of the people. That was down to King Henry's high-handed manner. Simon de Montfort won the people over by promising them a parliament that would hear their voices and not those of the nobles.

We later heard that only four knights had been slain in the battle, but more than five thousand of the ordinary soldiers had died. It was a warning to me that our lives were not valued by the men who led us. Perhaps Captain William was right. It might be that we should consider ourselves. If England did not care for us, why should we care for England? King Henry was our king; I would fight for Lord Edward if he was the king… but his father? I had much to dwell on. I thought of the way my father had been killed for a hunting dog: I should have learned my lesson then. Harry, my old friend in my first company of archers, had come up with the right idea: make money while our arms and backs were strong, and then live well for the rest of our lives.

As soon as we saw the Surrey Hills, we left the main road and took the tracks we found. The farmland turned to scrubland and then thin trees as we climbed the gentle slope. We were seen by farmers, but there was nothing we could do about that. Eventually, someone might question them, but by that time I hoped to be north of the Midlands. John of Nottingham had kept a good watch behind, and when we made our regular stops to water our horses, he could report that we were not followed.

I felt relief when we entered the eaves of the forest; we were always safer in woodland. I knew there might be outlaws sheltering here but we were, despite our losses, still a force that would be avoided, and our livery marked us as archers. The trees and the setting sun soon plunged us into a twilight world. Eleanor began to go a little quicker, despite her exhaustion, and I knew that water lay ahead. A small stream headed south, and there was enough of a clearing for us and our mounts.

"We camp here. Jack, look around and see if we are alone."

The former outlaw dismounted and handed his reins to Robin of Barnsley. He nocked an arrow and disappeared into the darkening gloom. I led Matty's horse and Eleanor to the stream. They were too tired to run, and so I dropped their reins to allow them to drink. As I took Matty's saddle from his mount, I saw the sticky blood. It had not yet dried. Matty had been but a little younger than me – and now he was gone. He was proof that life was too short. After I had taken the saddles from both horses and tethered them where they could graze, I unstrung my bow. I would need a new string the next time I used it, having been forced to leave it strung for too long.

Jack came back and his bow was also unstrung. "No one here and little sign that men use this part of the woods."

"Then we risk a fire. It will cheer us, and food which is hot fills a man's belly better." I looked at their faces for any dissension, but even my outlaw seemed to approve.

Will Yew Tree nodded and added sadly, "Aye, Captain, but hot food and a couple of skins of ale is the nectar of the gods!"

I nodded. "When we can, Will, I will buy some ale. You have all deserved it – and more."

We all had tasks to complete, and the camp became a hive of activity. While we waited for the meat to warm through and the pot of water to heat, I looked at the faces of my men. They were not downcast, and that meant there was hope, for we were undefeated. Our army had lost – but not us.

I took a deep breath. "We have no employer and we will have no income. What do we do?"

John of Nottingham was the natural leader of the men. I was their captain, but John was older with more experience. He looked at the others and must have seen that they wished him to speak. "Captain, we would stay together in your company. You are a good captain; the best that I have served. Your youth does not detract from your ability to lead. We would follow you. What do you think are our choices?"

I felt better after his words and I spoke confidently, for I had run through all the possibilities during the ride from Lewes. "We could return to Sherwood and become outlaws." I saw from their faces they did not like that option. "But I for one would not like that. It seems to me that we would then be left with two options. Serve another lord – and that would mean going abroad or finding someone who needs archers. Or we could protect merchants and their wagons. They are not necessarily the best options, but they are all that I can see."

They nodded agreement. "First, we need to get through the land of de Montfort. I suggest we head for York. It is far from de Montfort and the land he holds. We can take a ship from there if we need to, and we are not known there."

Robin of Barnsley said, "I have a brother who lives close by, Captain, although I have not seen him for many years. I think that is a good choice."

The rest nodded and it was decided. We would head north and see what fate had in mind for us. As we consumed a much-needed meal, for it had been before dawn when we last ate, we discussed our route. It would not be direct. We would have to head north-west towards Windsor to avoid London. Then we would head north-east towards Cambridge and then due north. We would have to parallel the Great North Road. I knew from the discussions I heard amongst the high and the mighty that the first thing de Montfort would do in his victory, would be to stop any royalist supporters heading north – and that meant closing the old Roman road. The land to the east of the road was bare and exposed, which meant we would stand out as warriors heading north, while the land to the west was de Montfort land.

We examined what we had. There were now three spare horses and they would be invaluable. We had over five hundred fletched arrow shafts and we each carried our own arrowheads. We had not managed to retrieve any arrowheads from the battlefield and, until we could get some more, would have to be careful. Of course, a skilled archer could improvise. We could use flint to make hunting arrows, but if we had to fight then we would be at a disadvantage. We had the remains of the deer, and if carefully rationed that would last us four more days. By then we should have reached York; if not, then we would have to risk a town.

I mentioned this, and John of Nottingham pointed out the obvious. "Captain, we will need a town sooner rather than later." He swept a hand down his clothes. "These mark us as Lord Edward's archers. The men who serve lesser knights might escape scrutiny, but not us."

I still had the coins given to me by Lord Edward when we hunted de Ferrers' men. I would not ask my men to open their purses. I had gold buried, but that was in Oxford and out of the way. I would save that chest for an emergency. I closed my eyes as I tried to remember the land twixt Windsor and Lincoln. Lincoln was as far north as de Montfort's influence extended and, if we passed there, I would begin to feel safe.

I spoke my thoughts aloud when I opened my eyes. "Bedford is in the hands of the rebels, and that means we must head further east. We need somewhere with a market so that we may buy clothes and perhaps food. Cambridge is too far to the east as a detour. We need somewhere between the two."

My men were all from the north or the west, and their knowledge of the east was worse than mine. Mine came from meetings with Lord Edward and Captain William. I remembered a market town which lay to the south-east of Bedford. Leueton had a market and, as I recalled, was less than thirty miles away. More importantly, the castle there had been pulled down more than a hundred years before, during the anarchy.

"We head for Leueton. There is a market there. I will go in with David the Welshman. I can still affect a Welsh accent if I need one, and the Earl of Gloucester follows the rebels. We will pretend to be his men."

"And your clothes, Captain?"

I smiled. "Between here and Leueton I hope to find a muddy beck in which I will roll. My cloak is plain, and the dirt will explain why I need clothes."

"For eight men?"

I smiled, for I had thought it through. "David and I will go to four sellers to buy." I shrugged. "It is not a perfect plan, but our parlous position means that we clutch at any straw and think on our feet. We are archers, after all! We leave before dawn, for I would be at the market before noon. Some markets close early and, with rebellion in the land, merchants will like to be home before dark."

It was fortunate that we did leave before dawn, for had we left later we might not have evaded the men who waited on the Great West Road from London, which passed through the village of Slo. We had forded the Thames and were riding towards a small road that headed north when we spied the roadblock. It was not intended to catch us specifically, but any royal supporters trying to get to Windsor.

It was still dark as we approached, and I spied their fire at the crossroads. I knew that our hooves had been heard as I saw their white faces, illuminated by the torches that burned at all four corners, turn towards the sound. If we fled then they would be alerted. They had to be less than three hundred paces from us and I said, as I pulled up the hood of my cloak, "We will try to trick our way through. Keep your hands close to your swords and stay close together."

There was a murmur of understanding, and I dug my heels into Eleanor's flanks. Since I fled the castle where I had slain my first lord, I had grown in confidence. The men would not be expecting danger, for we were heading north and east, towards de Montfort's land. They must have been told to stop men heading west.

I saw there was just a handful of men at the crossroads. They had pole weapons, and one appeared to have a sword and a helmet. I quietly drew my sword and held it behind my right leg.

As we neared them, he held up his hand. "Who are you, and why do you ride in the night?"

I made my voice easy and used a Welsh accent. I had grown up with such accents and although I had rid myself of it, I could recall it any time I chose. "Why, we are the Earl of Gloucester's men come from the victory at Lewes. Were you there?"

I knew that my accent and my words had put them at their ease, for the pole weapons were lowered and the suspicion in the sergeant's voice disappeared. "No, friend, we were not – but we heard it was a great victory and the king, his brother and his evil son, Squinty Eye, were taken. It is a great day." We were almost in the light when I saw a frown crease his face. "You have ridden hard to get here. We heard the news from a despatch rider heading for Hereford!"

Before I could say more his eyes spied my breeks, which were in Lord's Edward's livery. "These are royalist dogs! Stop them!"

I dug my heels into Eleanor as I swung my sword up at the sergeant. He was the leader and the best warrior. His guard had, quite literally, been down, and he was slow to raise his sword. The tip of my sword swept up his chest. His own sword rose, but that merely served to accelerate my blade. I kept an edge sharp enough to shave with, and my strike and his sword drove the sword up to bite into his jaw. He might have been a veteran but the blow was a wicked one, and he fell backwards. I turned. Pole weapons were good when held to keep an enemy at bay. The four men had lowered theirs. My men had swords and they used them. I saw that two of the sentries' heads had been split open and the other two were knocked aside.

Seeing that none of my men were hurt I shouted, "Ride!"

We were through, but eventually word would reach Slo. There would be a lord there, and they would pursue us. We headed into the dark. I doubted that the two men who had been unwounded would be in a position to pursue us, for we had spied no horses.

I intended to get off the road that ran north as soon as I could. The roads off the main road were narrow, and there were many side tracks which led off from them. I would ignore most of them until daylight came and allowed me to see further ahead.

Then, I took the first large sideroad, which headed east. It twisted and turned. Along the side grew hawthorn, elder and alder. We kept a steady pace without punishing the horses. There would be pursuit, but I hoped we would have made our purchases and disappeared north by then. I smiled ruefully. They would send men such as we to catch us;

archers and men of the woods. It would be the reverse of our foray into the woods at Codnor. Were we good enough to evade our enemies?

It was not long before noon when we reached Leueton. We had used the smaller roads to twist and turn towards the large market town, and we stopped when we saw it in the distance. David and I dismounted our horses and approached the small beck that ran close by the road.

There were sheep and cattle in a nearby farm, and they had used the stream to drink. They had muddied and fouled the ground close to it and so, taking off our cloaks, we rolled in their slurry. This was the first opportunity we had encountered to do so, and I feared that the wet, fresh mud might create suspicion – but it was too late to do anything about it. We donned our cloaks and headed towards the town. I was reassured as we closed with it, for there was neither castle nor wall around it, and we stopped just outside at a convenient stand of oaks. The trees looked to have been copsed, and obviously the townsfolk used the timber for their fires in winter. Leaving our bows with the others and John of Nottingham in command, David and I dismounted and walked our horses into the town while our men made a small camp in some undergrowth. There were fields nearby, but they contained growing crops and farmers would have no need to visit them.

It was a bustling market, and that afforded us cover so we were hardly noticed. Our swords attracted a little attention, but in the parlous times in which we lived such weaponry was not a surprise. There were plenty of stalls in the market as well as more permanent establishments. No one commented on our dirty clothes, they were just grateful for our coin and happily sold us all that we desired. A civil war was not good for merchants. We bought bread and cheese as well as a bag of oats for the horses, and then went to an alehouse.

Leaving our horses and supplies with a well-paid old man, we entered the Lion and the Lamb tavern. We chose it carefully, avoiding those inns which suggested an affiliation with either the rebels or the king. I bought an ale for each of us and an ale skin to take back for the others. Then we listened, and my heart sank as we heard the news from Lewes. Lord Edward and his cousin, Henry Almain, had been taken hostage as surety for the good behaviour and co-operation of their fathers, the king and Richard of Cornwall. Richard of Cornwall was incarcerated in Kenilworth Castle, while King Henry was kept close to the Earl of Leicester. Their final fate appeared to be a mystery. The king was to be ruled by a de Montfort-appointed council. He was a puppet and could only make decisions approved by his minders. As we left to return to our men, my spirits were as low as any time since my father died. My employer was a prisoner, I was on the run and there seemed little likelihood of employment in England. I would have to go abroad again.

No one appeared to notice us as we left the market, and we reached our men and horses unmolested. We went into a convenient copse of copper beech to change. We did not throw away our livery as I hoped that, someday, we would be able to wear it again. We had been treated badly by Lord Edward, but he and his father were the rightful rulers of England. Simon de Montfort, the Earl of Leicester, was trying to steal a crown!

Once dressed in the motley array of clothes I had bought, we headed north and east from Leueton. We were just a little too close to the Great North Road for my liking, and I wanted to put as much distance as possible between us and any pursuit. I had spied the signs at the crossroads, and now had a better idea of the route we ought to take.

John of Nottingham and Jack of Lincoln flanked me as we headed for Biggleswade. A small town, its old motte and bailey castle was now just a mound and a ditch. It belonged to the Bishop of Lincoln; there was no lord of the manor and that suited us. We would reach there after dark. John asked, "What if there are men following us?"

"There will be. We killed a sergeant from the Tower of London. We were seen on the Great West Road where we also slew rebels and, most importantly, we serve Lord Edward. We are a danger and a threat, so they will send men to pursue us. I just hope that we can now disappear."

"Then why head to Biggleswade, Lord? Why risk people seeing us?"

I shrugged. "That is simple. We need to put as much distance between us as possible. We will not enter Biggleswade, but I wish to be near it so that we can leave before dawn and skirt it. Once we have passed that manor, we have the River Great Ouse to cross at Huntingdon. There are few people there and the castle was pulled down by King Henry the Second, but we must cross that river. I propose that we do so in small groups spread out over the day. After that, we will reach Peterborough where we pretend that we are visiting Peterborough Cathedral."

Jack asked, "Why, what is there?"

John of Nottingham answered for me. "Probably nothing save for priests who like to make money from the gullible poor, but according to legend they have: two pieces of swaddling clothes which wrapped the baby Jesus; pieces of his manger; a part of the five loaves which fed the 5,000; a piece of the raiment of Mary the mother of Jesus; a piece of Aaron's rod and relics of St Peter, St Paul and St Andrew."

Jack laughed. "Aye, and I am the brother of St John!"

I knew that Jack was right and they were not true relics, but that did not matter, for it gave us an excuse to be in Peterborough – and we needed more food and, most importantly, knowledge. The town was important and the people there would know what had happened in the wider world.

"Whatever the truth of the relics, it gives us an excuse. There is no castle at Peterborough, but it is an important place. We can gauge the mood of the people there. Unless they exhibit rebel tendencies I shall begin to feel more comfortable. Despite our best efforts, people will talk of the two men who went to the market in Leueton. They may try other places first, but once they are on our trail, they will stick to it."

Our new clothes and the story that we were returning home from foreign wars appeared to put the people we met at their ease. The battle had been widely reported, but our presence on the road north seemed to be accepted. There had been rebel archers, but the stories people told were that there were no archers on the king's side. We reached Biggleswade just after dark and found an abandoned farm in which to stay. The roof on the farm had long gone, but the walls remained and our horses were hidden from view.

We had a cold supper and I set sentries. I took the last watch and woke my men when I considered it to be an hour before dawn. By the time dawn broke we were north of Biggleswade, and I hoped that we would reach the bridge across the river by late morning.

There was a low ridge, which overlooked the bridge, and we halted there beneath the leaves of a small wood which had been left between two fields. The settlement was larger than I thought, but it did not look to be garrisoned. I saw travellers using the bridge.

"I will ride down first with Robin of Barnsley and Jack of Lincoln. We must each have a different story. Ours will be that we return home to Lincoln after fighting in Poitou. I know enough about Poitou to convince any who questions us closely. John of Nottingham, Will Yew Tree and Tom, John's son, you will bring up the rear. You served at Rochester Castle and were dismissed. You return to Nottingham to seek work, and the rest of you are pilgrims heading for Durham to visit the tomb of St. Cuthbert. We will wait north of the town. If you find trouble then sound your hunting horn. We all go to the aid of whichever group is attacked. Remember to smile and keep your hands from your swords."

"Aye, Captain."

We rode towards the stone bridge at a steady pace. I saw two men who were obviously locals and were fishing from the middle of the bridge. We nodded and smiled back at the travellers we passed who were heading south. The two fishermen turned at the sound of our horses' hooves. Most of the other travellers were either afoot or had a cart pulled by a donkey. Eleanor stood out as the horse of a soldier.

"A fine horse, my friend." The man who spoke to me had the look of an old soldier, but one who now led a comfortable life. He had a healthy beer belly and the red face of a man who drinks often. He smiled all the time he spoke.

"Aye, she suits me." I had not stopped, even though I spoke politely to the man.

He persisted. "Have you come from the Battle of Lewes?"

I shook my head and reined in Eleanor. If I hurried off it would look suspicious. "We were in Poitou, fighting Frenchmen. Fighting Englishmen is not profitable. We prefer to take coin from foreign masters."

My answer seemed to satisfy the man. "Aye, well, the war in England is over now, so if you want money you will need to go abroad again."

I patted my purse. "Never fear, my friend, our days of fighting are over. I head north to buy an alehouse and find some pretty wenches to serve in it."

It was the right thing to say and he laughed. "Aye, the dream of all old soldiers. Well, good luck to you all."

After we had left him, I said, quietly, "We stop at the first alehouse.

That man was just a little too nosey for my liking. Robin, buy the ale, and I will walk back to the bridge to see the others get safely across."

There was an inn that was so close to the river they could have used the lower rooms to fish from. I gave my reins to Jack of Lincoln and took my bow, still in its case. I jammed three arrows in my belt. I saw my next men approach. In Leueton, David the Welshman had impressed me with his ability to dissemble, and when I saw the suspicious man laugh, I knew that he had convinced them of a story. I wondered if I was being unduly cautious. My men passed me without acknowledgement and carried on through the town.

It was when I saw the suspicious man's companion stride towards the town that my suspicions rose once more. I slipped behind a building and turned my back so that he did not see me as he passed. I took my bow from its case and strung it.

I had seen no castle, but there had to have been a hall, for a few moments after the man had passed me, I heard the strident peal of a bell. It was at that moment that John of Nottingham and my last men began to cross the bridge. The ex-soldier belied his size and ran towards me. From behind me, I heard shouts.

We were undone!

CHAPTER 4

I nocked an arrow. I saw John of Nottingham draw a sword: he recognised the danger. Men ran from behind me but, as my bow was hidden by my body, they ignored me. I guessed the hall lay in the western end of the small town. I cursed myself, for I should have scouted it out – and now we might pay for my carelessness with our lives.

Jack and Robin had heard the noise and emerged from the inn. They stood by the horses with the others who had followed them from within the inn to see what was amiss. The veteran pointed up the road David the Welshman had taken. "They are heading up the road, my lord, and I think there are more coming over the bridge! They are supporters of the king!"

"Tom, take five men and get after them. The rest, come with me!" I said.

We were saved by the fact I was hidden and my two men were shielded by horses. Even so, the other fisherman was now racing down the bridge and following John of Nottingham. I turned, with an arrow nocked, as the lord led six men at arms to apprehend him, Will and Tom. I saw that they all wore the white cross I had seen at Lewes.

I stepped into the middle of the bridge and aimed the arrow at the lord's chest. He was less than twenty paces from me. Jack and Robin had each nocked an arrow and they stood ready too, although they were hidden from the lord and his men. They were facing me and the bridge.

"My lord, we mean no harm. Let us pass, or there will be blood."

I saw that he was a young lord. I did not recognise his livery. He had a sword but no shield, and he wore his mail hauberk even though there was no war close by. His men at arms were similarly armed, but they wore helmets. Behind me, I heard the hooves of John and the others.

"You are an enemy of the people and I arrest you in the name of the barons of England, put up your bow. Take him!"

One of his men, braver than the others, stepped forward. I made a slight adjustment to my bow and pinned his foot to the ground with an arrow. He would be crippled, for it was a war arrow and the broad head would break bones and tear tendons. Even as he screamed in pain and the lord and his men looked on in shock, I had another arrow nocked.

"And this arrow is aimed at you, my lord. If you look to your left you will see two more bows are aimed at you, and I have three more men behind me."

I saw the dilemma on his face. He wished to risk all, but he dared not. Further north I heard the clash of steel and shouts of pain as David the Welshman and Stephen Green Feather dealt with the ex-soldier and the other men.

"Your men are hurting and you can stop the pain. Lower your weapons and we will leave you and your town."

The man I had wounded was an old sergeant. He sat down and removed his helmet. There was blood seeping from his boot. "Do it, Sir Roger, I beg of you. He has crippled me. I need a surgeon, and these men know their business. There will be time to take our vengeance." He glared at me.

Sir Roger sheathed his sword as John of Nottingham appeared behind me. "I have your back, Captain. You may mount!"

I slipped up onto Eleanor's back and we backed up the street. There had been people at the sides of the street, but they had wisely moved off into the alleys and side roads. I whipped Eleanor's head around and we galloped after David and Stephen. I saw two of the men sent after them, and they had both been struck by arrows. One was wounded in the arm and the other in the leg. The ex-soldier raised his fist as we passed.

"Archer scum!"

John of Nottingham smacked him on the back of his head for his pains as he rode next to him. "Keep a civil tongue in your head. We let you live did we not?"

The man clutched his bleeding head, but he moved away from John in case there was another angry blow.

We were now in trouble. We had passed our last major obstacle, but the hounds would be after us now. I knew not the lord, nor his name, but he had struck me as a vengeful knight. He had fought at Lewes – his tunic showed me that – and an archer had humiliated him. I would remember the red tunic with yellow songbirds, for he would seek me out.

We said nothing to each other as we galloped north. The men we had hurt would take time in gathering horses and following us, but follow us they would. We could not head to Peterborough now. It was too large a place.

Even as we rode north, I was calculating what we would do. Peterborough was the largest town in the area, and I had planned on a feigned pilgrimage to lose ourselves in the crowd. Now they would be looking for eight warriors. I worked out that if we headed north-east, we could avoid Stamford, which had a small castle, and then take the road to Lincoln. We had to lose our pursuers. I decided to risk the Great

North Road. We could move faster along it, and I intended to leave the road before the River Nene and lose ourselves in the low lying and swampy land which lay to the north of Stamford and Peterborough. It would be a long ride of twenty-five miles to Stamford, but we had three spare horses.

We rode hard until we were north of Stilton. I reined in and said, "Are we followed?"

John of Nottingham shook his head. "I have seen none yet, but the blood we spilt means that they will come." His voice told me he was worried and, if he was, then the rest, save Jack of Lincoln, would be also.

I nodded. "Fate has intervened and we can do little about it."

Stephen Green Feather said, "It was my fault, Captain. I said something that told that soldier we were Lord Edward's archers. The word slipped out, for the man appeared friendly."

I nodded, for I knew something must have prompted the attack. "That does not matter now, for the carrot is out of the ground. Until we make York, choose each word as though it is an arrowhead!" They all nodded. "We will head for Stamford and ride overnight. Best to be beyond that small castle by dawn. We find a wood and sleep during the day. We will use the three horses to rest ours. Eleanor is the best horse, and I will be the last to change. John of Nottingham, are you happy to be the rear-guard?"

"Aye, for Tom, John's son, does not fart as much as Will Yew Tree."

Will nodded amiably. "I blame the lack of ale, for good beer aids the digestion and makes the body function as it should – but I agree with you there."

The humour showed that the men were in good spirits, and I headed for the Great North Road. Although we were still intact and had suffered no wounds, our position could hardly be worse. There were men who might have followed us from Lewes. The attack at the crossroads near Slo would also have attracted attention, and now the incident at the bridge meant we were leaving clear markers. Eventually, someone would work out our ultimate destination and get ahead of us.

The problem lay on the road we now used. It was the quickest way to the north and everyone used it. Just a couple of miles north of the bridge we had passed two merchants and their servants, heading south. When they reached the bridge, then Sir Roger with the yellow songbirds would know whence we had fled. We stopped only to change horses so that we could keep going at a fast pace. It was getting on for sunset when we reached the River Nene and crossed it.

When we stopped, I saw that Eleanor could not go much further. I saw, just to the east of the road, a track that led to what looked like a deserted farm. The track had a covering of stones. As we remounted, I pointed to it. "We take that track and head for the farm."

Will asked, "Do we camp there, Captain?"

"No, for it is too close to the road. I am using the track as it is covered in stone and will disguise our hoof prints. We are heading across country. We will ride as far as we can and then see if we can find a wood. I would hold up for the day and then risk the road again at night."

I dug my heels into Eleanor. The plan sounded plausible, but it was riddled with potential traps. Riding across country at night was a huge risk, for the last thing we needed was for a horse to fall and hurt the rider. I was taking the greatest risk, as Eleanor was now in the worst condition and therefore the most likely to fall.

We passed the farm and I headed across the fields, now filled with weeds and tares, in a north-easterly direction. The field boundaries had once been dry stone walls, and we were able to pass through them where holes had appeared. We kept going until we came upon a narrow road.

It headed north. A road meant people but, as the sun was setting in the west, it seemed the best route to take. We rode for half a mile and then I held up my hand. "We will walk. Our horses are becoming weary."

We trudged up the road in darkness. We did not pass any village, but I saw many tracks leading off the road and could smell, in the distance, woodsmoke. We crossed many small streams, and I was aware that the road was almost a causeway. In winter this land would be a patchwork of swamps and flooded fields; we were lucky that it was May.

The wood I spied was not a large one, but it was on a tiny island of slightly higher ground. Around it lay shallow pools and swampy land. It would have to do. We crossed the swampy ground and headed for the trees. The mud sucked at our boots. If we had tried to ride our horses they would have struggled. Once we were on the firmer ground of the island, movement became easier, and when we reached the trees, I saw that it was a bigger wood than it had appeared at first. I took us into what I assumed was the centre. There was no area large enough for a single camp, and so we spread ourselves out.

I saw to Eleanor first. I cleaned her as best I could and then used our leather pail to fetch water from one of the pools we had passed. She drank heavily, and I gave her a few handfuls of the oats we had bought. There was enough grazing for all our horses, and they would be able to rest the next day.

All of us cared for our horses before we saw to ourselves. We were spread out under the canopy of the trees and, although weary, we spoke as we ate the bread we had bought in Leueton. That seemed like days ago.

Jack of Lincoln put his hands behind his head. "You know, Captain, I cannot understand those men we saw at the bridge. That lord spoke of the barons as though they ruled England. I thought we had a king."

"We do, and I think Simon de Montfort would be king – but regicide is a grievous sin. This way, the barons rule England, and any blame for the governance can be laid at the door of the king."

John of Nottingham shook his head. "It is no wonder we lost Normandy and Poitou with lords like that. They are all self-serving."

I remained silent but I knew he was right. Baron Henry of Clwyd had just enjoyed the benefits of his manor and had not taken on the responsibility. He had used his archers and men at arms to do the job he should have done. He enjoyed hunting and feasting at the expense of the people who tended the land. The system was not a fair one, and freemen such as my father were the exception. Most men had to work for a lord. We were lucky; we had been paid by Lord Edward and, now that he was a prisoner, we had been given our freedom. At the moment we were hunted but, if we could escape this trap, then we had a chance for a new life. I found myself smiling as I curled up in my blanket.

Robin of Barnsley, who was the closest to me, said, "What makes you smile, Captain?"

I said, "We are still alive and we are our own masters. It may not seem that way now with the dogs of war still snapping at our heels, but while we are together we have a chance, and I would not swap my position with any. Would you?"

He chuckled. "Aye, Captain, you are right. This beaker of ale is half full!"

Will Yew Tree snorted. "Except that we have no ale! I agree with all that you say, Captain, but could we call at an alehouse soon? I have a thirst like you would not believe!"

John of Nottingham laughed. "Will Yew Tree, I have seen you drink cloudy ale, which none other would touch, from the bottom of a barrel. It is not a thirst you have; it is a need for an ale!"

The others laughed, for Will had the lowest standards of any man. I had never seen him refuse to drink any ale, no matter how bad it was.

"Jack of Lincoln, wake me for the next watch."

"Aye, Captain."

I stood my watch with a cloudy sky masking the moon, and I neither smelled nor saw anything. I woke John of Nottingham for his watch and curled up again. I was soon asleep and my dreams were filled with the faces of my dead men. When we reached York – *if* we reached York – then I would pay for a candle for each of them in the minster there.

When I woke, it was daylight. I checked on Eleanor and then made water. I walked to the edge of the wood and, staying in the shelter of the trees, I walked around its edge. The sun had emerged from behind the clouds and I saw farms. Like this wood, they tended to be on islands of land in this fenny country. I saw no towns. Will Yew Tree would have no ale this day!

The road seemed to head north. We would spend most of the day in the wood and leave at sunset. I wished to cross the swamp while there was a vestige of light. I could see there was a track of some sort, we had missed it in the dark.

I returned to my men and told them my plan. We spent the day fitting arrowheads to shafts; we needed to replace the arrows we had used. Each archer chose his own arrowheads. I had five bodkins, ten war arrows and five hunting arrows. The hunting arrows would pierce flesh. We had plenty of blanks, but we were short of arrowheads. That done, we rested or chatted, and the men speculated on the sort of work we might find in York. Most seemed to think we would take ship for the Baltic. They needed men to fight the pagans of Lithuania and the Teutonic knights paid well. I did not relish the thought, but I would go with the view of the majority.

We left an hour before sunset, and I led the men north to the road. We were seen, but there was no avoiding that. The road was slightly elevated, as were the farms in the distance that we passed. We were riding horses and stood out. If any had managed to follow our trail this far, the locals would tell them of our passing. I just hoped that they had lost us and were searching further north.

By the middle of the afternoon, Will's wish was granted, and we found a village with an alehouse. Threekingham was the largest place we had seen and certainly the only one we actually visited. We were less than twenty-five miles from Lincoln, and there was neither hall nor castle. I took the risk. We needed a rest, and we had coins to spend on ale.

As we dismounted, I saw what looked like an old moat and a ruined building. There had been a manor here. The arrival of eight armed men alarmed the folk in the village. I saw men picking up tools to use as weapons.

Will Yew Tree had a beaming smile as he dismounted, and said to the man who leaned over the small stone wall holding a scythe, "Friend, where can a man get a decent ale around here?"

The man smiled and I saw him relax. He pointed to a whitewashed wattle and daub house. "Gammer Gurton brews a good ale. Whence come you fellows? There is no castle around here save for Lincoln."

I dismounted and nodded. "And that is where we are headed. We seek honest employment. What do you think of our chances?"

He shook his head. "Here in Threekingham we keep ourselves to ourselves. The only visitor we see is the bishop's reeve when he comes to collect taxes and, like all reeves, he is a tight-mouthed slippery bastard!"

My men all laughed. Reeves always had that reputation. "Then we shall enjoy an ale or two and continue on our way."

The alehouse was simply the alewife's front room. It doubled as a kitchen, and the house was so small that I guessed she slept in the back. She was almost toothless but her smile was welcoming, especially when

Will slapped two silver pennies on the table upon which stood the barrel. "Gammer, give us ale to the value of two pennies and when that is done, one of my fellows will provide more. I hope you have more ale out of the back, for I have a thirst which would empty this one barrel alone!"

She beamed. "Aye, sir, I have a second and you are welcome – although I must confess, this ale is more than a week old."

Will rubbed his hands. "All the more flavour then! I like you more and more! If I was the marrying kind, Gammer, I would take you as a wife!"

She laughed. "I have buried three husbands already, I need not a fourth! I keep the coin I earn!"

It was Will's humour that put not only the gammer but the rest of the village at their ease. We bought a little food, and Gammer Gurton allowed us to cook it in her kitchen. The price we paid was to cut some firewood for her. It seemed a fair price.

The ale, especially the new barrel, was good, and we spent the night sleeping in the field behind Gammer Gurton's. When we left the next day, we were in a more positive frame of mind. We had full bellies, and we had enjoyed the company of the people of Threekingham. We headed for Lincoln.

Lincoln was the king's castle. It had been so since before the time of King Stephen. With a town wall and a strong castle, it guarded the roads leading to the north. The Earl of Leicester might rule the land to the west of the road, but here we hoped King Henry still held sway.

We walked our horses through the gate. The town watch kept a suspicious eye on us, but they did not try to stop us. I wondered if we could risk wearing the livery of Lord Edward – and then thought better of it.

We found an inn. Pilgrims passed through the town heading both to the north and the south, so it needed somewhere with beds, for travellers with coins. The innkeeper was pleased to have our custom.

The battles of Northampton and Lewes had deterred folk from travelling, and our coins were welcome. I paid, aware that we would need an income soon enough.

The innkeeper was garrulous and happy to talk to us. From him, we learned that Lord Edward and his cousin were incarcerated in Dover Castle, while his father was in the Tower thanks to Simon de Montfort. To all intents and purposes, he too was a prisoner. Simon de Montfort, the Earl of Leicester, now ruled England through his council of barons. He had allowed the king's marcher lords to return to the west. He seemed not to think there was any significance in that, but I saw danger for the rebels and hope for our employment. Roger Mortimer would not allow King Henry to remain a prisoner for long. Soon he would gather men and try to wrest power from de Montfort. I wondered if we should try the west, where we would be amongst allies.

We had eaten a late midday meal when two liveried sergeants came into the alehouse. "Who commands this company of archers?"

I thought about lying and telling them that we were not a company, but there seemed little point. I stood. "I am Captain Gerald, called War Bow."

"The castellan would speak with you."

I nodded, for it was not unexpected. He would be concerned about having armed men in his town, especially those that he did not know. John of Nottingham made to rise and I shook my head. "Stay and enjoy the ale, this will not take long." If I was taken prisoner then John could lead the men and escape.

The constable was Sir Ralph Haie. He was a relative of the famous lady castellan, Nichola de la Haie. He was a greybeard, and his eyes and mind were sharp. He dismissed the officers from around him so that we were alone.

"You are Lord Edward's man!"

He had come directly to the point, and I saw little point in denying it as I had already given my name to his men. "Yes, my lord."

"You were at the battle of Lewes?"

"Yes, lord. It began well and ended badly."

"Aye, I know. The Earl of Leicester has sent a messenger to me telling me to hand over my keys to one of his men." I gave him a questioning look. He smiled. "Messengers take some time to reach here. I sent a vague message back, and I will be safe for some time. You, on the other hand, are hunted."

I started. How did he know? "Whence did you gather this knowledge, my lord?"

"Yesterday an arrogant young rebel, flaunting de Montfort's white cross, arrived. I did not like Sir Roger de la Braie! He spoke to me as though my white hairs and position were worthless. He asked about you and said you had attacked his men." I saw his eyebrows raised in question.

"We did use our weapons, my lord, for they tried to bar our way and take us prisoner. We had done nothing wrong."

"He also said that you had slain men on the Great West Road."

I nodded. "That is true. They also tried to bar our way."

He smiled. "Then I will make certain that we do not bar your way." He poured some wine for us. "I have heard of you, War Bow. I met once with Lord Edward and he told me your tale. He holds you in high regard." That surprised me, for he rarely praised me. "For that reason, I will confide in you. De Montfort thinks he has won, but there are more loyal men who support the king than this rebel who would usurp the crown. It will take time, but we will prevail. For that reason, I ask you to leave tomorrow before dawn. I will give you a pass to leave the city before the gates are opened. Where do you go?"

I hesitated. "Come, Gerald War Bow, if we cannot trust each other, then de Montfort has won already."

"York. We thought to take ship for crusade or find employment there."

"Find employment and stay in England, for Lord Edward will need you. Those of us who support the king and his son will keep in touch. We will send a messenger to York, should we need you." He smiled. "It will be someone you know, for there are many turncoats and traitors."

I nodded. "Thank you, my lord. We will stay in York."

He took a piece of parchment and scribbled on it. He used his seal and handed it to me. "Be careful on the road. You may meet this Sir Roger."

"How many men were with him, my lord?"

"There were four men at arms and another ten who looked like hired swords. They all wear the white cross as though they are blessed by Our Lord! Blasphemy, for they fight against the Lord's anointed king!"

I left in a more positive frame of mind. With men like the castellan there was hope for England and Lord Edward. When I returned to the inn, I paid our bill. "We shall leave before dawn, innkeeper."

I saw the disappointment on his face, for we had spent well. "You will not be able to leave before the gates are open, sir."

"Let me worry about that. Come, men, we shall retire, for I have much to tell you."

We were all accommodated in one cramped little room. Our faces were close when I spoke, as quietly as I dared, of what I had learned. "So, if any of you wish to go on a crusade then leave us at York. For my own part, I will stay there, for I like not this rebellion."

John of Nottingham said, "Then we all stay. We are the company of the War Bow, and I, for one, am happy to continue."

They all nodded and it made me feel inordinately happy.

I smiled. "One piece of good news is that we have now left the Great

71

North Road. That headed north and west. We use smaller roads until we near York. They are still Roman, but there will be fewer travellers. This road we're on is only used by those travelling to either York or Lincoln."

We would be heading due north on the road the Romans had used to march to the city they called Eboracum, and within two days we would be in the relative safety of a northern city – one which lay beyond the influence of Simon de Montfort.

CHAPTER 5

The sentries seemed surprised that we had a pass, but the castellan's seal persuaded them, so they unbarred the gate and allowed us to head north to York. We had over seventy miles to go, and Sir Roger was on the road. We would have to be careful. I should have known that there were men watching for us on our way to Lincoln, and I should have expected the news to reach Sir Roger and his men. My excuse is that, at that time, I was still learning. However, we did at least ride in such a way as to be able to spot any danger. Tom, John's son, was eager to prove himself. With Ronan now dead Tom was the youngest and, as such, was always protected by the others.

As we headed north, he pleaded with me. "Captain, let me be the scout. I have young ears and eyes and my horse, Bess, senses danger even if I do not!"

He did not see the contradiction of his words. I saw John of Nottingham nod. "Very well, but you know what you must do?"

"Aye, Captain, I will ride 200 paces ahead of you. If there is a bend in the road and I am hidden, then I wait until you catch up with me before I move off."

"Good – and if you suspect a trap or ambush?"

"Then I dismount and examine Bess' leg."

"Which leg?"

He grinned. "That depends upon which side I see the ambush."

John laughed. "He will do, Captain, and this is a Roman road with few bends. The places we could be ambushed are known to us."

I waved him off. John had been correct to suggest I allowed the young archer his opportunity. I had learned to scout when I was even younger than Tom. The more you did it, the better you became. I knew that I had taken on the responsibility of scout since Lewes because I felt guilty about losing so many of my men.

We made good time and were able to stop for ale when we passed through Gainsborough. There was no castle there but the lord of the manor, a Mowbray, was part of the rebel alliance. Luckily for us, he was far away in London along with his men. De Montfort was consolidating his hold on that city and advancing his own men. It suited us. We pushed on to Thorne. Thorne had but eight souls living there, and they had neither inn nor tavern. These were not the people of London and were friendly. Many had fought for the king when he and Lord Percy had defeated the Scots. They sold us their ale and food.

I listened to the men as they talked in the barn, which we had been allowed to use by the farmer who sold us the ale. All of my men had dreams and hopes for the future. They each knew that it would take money to realise them. The debate was about how much they might need and how best to spend it. Those like Jack of Lincoln, who had spent some time as an outlaw, wanted nothing more than a farm. Will Yew Tree surprised no one when he asserted that he simply wanted an alehouse and wenches to serve both beer and men!

Stephen Green Feather had the simplest of plans. "I would have a wife and enough bairns to ensure that some survived to become men and women. I do not mind if I have a farm or a tavern, so long as I am my own master and can keep my family. Travelling the land as I have, I envy those who live in peace, but I also know that men like us can take it from them. If I am honest, John of Nottingham, I would live in a home which was close to fellows like you and the rest of the company. I trust all of you."

It was a simple plan, but I envied him. I had no such plan. I knew that I had enough money already to buy a small farm or even a tavern. It was in the chest I had buried in Oxford, but I had yet to dig it up, for there it was as safe as the crown jewels in the castle at Windsor. What was the point in digging it up if I did not know what to do with it? My archers continued to speculate about and plan for what seemed to me uncertain futures. Lord Edward had spoken before the battle of Lewes as though it would be the final act, which would bring peace. He was wrong, and all that I saw, for the foreseeable future, was disharmony and conflict.

I fell asleep with those two cheerful thoughts in my head, but I slept well and rose ready to end the journey and begin our next phase. The castellan's words had given me hope that all was not lost. I thought about Lord Edward; I had believed him grown up, but his action at Lewes had shown me that he was not ready yet to lead. As for being King; that was a different matter, for his father was as poor a king as there could be, and Edward had enough leadership qualities to be better than him. Perhaps that was due to *his* father, King John. I wondered how captivity would affect Lord Edward; perhaps it would mature him and show him how to be a king.

We left the barn after dawn had broken, for to do so earlier would have seemed disrespectful to the people who made us so welcome. We were now fewer than thirty miles from York. We were still vigilant, but

I hoped Sir Roger might have passed us in the night. Thorne was just a little way away from the main road between York and Lincoln – it was after Thorne that the land rose a little and became drier. There were one or two rises and falls. We were riding parallel to the River Don and we used it to water the horses; the last two days of slightly easier travel had seen an improvement in their health. We had to husband our mounts, for we would need them in the future.

As we were all together, I took the opportunity to check up on Tom. He had a great responsibility upon his young shoulders. "Have you seen anything then, Tom?" There was a slight hesitation and I said, "A good scout reports everything; no matter how seemingly insignificant."

"Sorry, Captain. It is just that, for the last mile or so I haven't seen any birds ahead of me. I mean, until the last mile I was the one who spooked them. I had grown used to the pigeons taking flight when I approached." He pointed to the river. "Each time we were close to the river then the ducks and waterfowl made a noise and swam across the river. I haven't seen any for the last mile."

I nodded. "Stephen Green Feather, ride ahead with Tom. The rest of you, string your bows. It may be a waste of time, but Tom here has a bad feeling."

I saw the panic on his face. "But it might be nothing!"

I smiled. "All it costs us is the effort to put a string on a bow. When you spook the next birds let us know, and we will unstring them."

I chose a new string and picked out a war arrow. After mounting Eleanor, I laid the bow across the front of my saddle and tucked the arrow in my belt; I really needed an arrow bag, but did not seem to have time to make one.

We watched as Tom and Stephen rode ahead. I let them ride 170 paces before I pumped my arm and we followed them. I peered ahead and looked for possible ambush sites. So long as the river lay to our left then any attack had to come from our right.

We were passing open fields of beans, for this was fertile country. On the higher ground, in the distance, I saw animals grazing. A drainage ditch lay next to the road. The beans were just coming into flower and they would give an attacker cover. The road rose and, as we neared the top, I saw Tom dismount and go to the right of his horse. I dug my heels into Eleanor and, holding my bow in my right hand, I nocked an arrow in my left. I could transfer them quickly if I needed to. My men were so well trained they needed no words from me. I saw Stephen Green Feather lean down, ostensibly to speak with Tom, but in reality he was nocking an arrow.

We reached them just a few heartbeats too late. The crossbow bolt slammed into Stephen's shoulder. Even so, he tried to turn, to raise his bow and send an arrow back towards his attacker. The second bolt hit him in the chest. He tumbled backwards: it was a mortal wound. We all hated crossbows with a vengeance, and now we had even more reason. Tom had raised his bow and, using his horse for cover, sent an arrow to our right. I heard a cry. By then we had reached the rise and I saw, galloping towards us, Sir Roger and four men at arms. Four other men rode behind him. That meant there were six men hidden, and at least two of them were crossbowmen.

I shouted, "John of Nottingham, take Robin and David, deal with the men in the bean field. They have crossbows."

"Aye, Captain!" He and the other two archers wheeled right while Will and Jack reined in with me next to Tom. As I dismounted, two bolts slammed into my saddle and Eleanor reared. One of them must have pricked her.

"I hit one of the crossbows, Captain, but I think that two remain."

"Don't worry about them; John will deal with them. We have mounted men to deal with. Bodkins!"

The horsemen were eighty paces from us – they must have waited beyond sight. I now cursed my own choice of arrow. I aimed my war arrow at the advancing horsemen; I would not be able to make a damaging hit, but I could worry them. The arrow hit the horse of the man at arms next to Sir Roger. The animal jerked to the right, and horse and rider were so close to the water that they fell into the river. It was a lucky hit, but I would take it.

I nocked a bodkin. Jack and Robin had bodkins ready, and their arrows slammed into two of the men at arms. They were now thirty paces from us, and each arrow went through the mail as though it were a piece of cloth. The men were thrown over the backs of their saddles.

Tom had vengeance on his mind. He was a skilled archer, and his arrow went into the open mouth of another man at arms. He fell, too. I aimed my bodkin at the knight. The other four horsemen had already closed enough for us to strike, when Will and Robin sent their war arrows at them, and one horse, along with a man at arms, was hit. The injured horse and rider turned and galloped into the bean field. I heard cries from my right as John and the others dealt with the crossbowmen and the last of the ambushers. I concentrated on the knight. He had plate armour, a couched lance and a shield. I knew that he expected to win. It was almost impossible to penetrate plate, even with a bodkin.

He was forty paces from me when I released. I had a full draw, and I sent the arrow not at his chest but at his neck. There, he just had his mail coif. The arrow struck him cleanly and almost passed through, only the fletch stopped it.

"Stand aside!" I shouted, as his horse was still galloping without its rider and would not stop. We let the animal pass between us as the lance fell to the ground. "Will, see to Stephen." It was a forlorn hope, for I knew he was dead, but I had to ask.

His voice was sad as he answered, "He is dead, Captain. Damned crossbows! They are the devil's machine!"

I moved the horses aside as I hurried to the bean field. John and Robin were leading two horses. "David the Welshmen is hunting the last of them. Those horsemen you hit joined them. In total, five escaped, Captain. Should we go after them?"

I shook my head. "They are hired brigands. They will run as far from us as they can, and they have a wounded man and a horse. Jack, go and fetch back the war horse and the knight's body."

"Aye, Captain. That was one of the bravest arrows I have ever seen."

I nodded absentmindedly. "Search the bodies, take all of value and then hurl them in the Don."

I looked to my left and saw the horse which had been hit and fallen into the water. Its body was floating. The arrow had not killed but had weakened it, and then it had drowned. Of the man at arms, there was no sign. An archer might have survived the fall, but not a man in hauberk and helmet with a sword at his waist.

David the Welshman returned. "The others have fled. They were heading east as fast as their horses would take them."

It took some time to collect the mail and weapons. We let the bodies slip into the Don and loaded the mail, plate and swords onto the backs of our horses. "Disguise the plate with a piece of sacking. That would be hard to explain when we reach York."

Then we buried Stephen Green Feather. He would never have a wife, nor see his children grow up. His dream had been ended with two crossbow bolts. We made sure that his bow was buried with him and that he was well covered. The river would flood and his body would sink deeper. He would not be disturbed.

We mounted our horses. Jack of Lincoln pointed at the knight's horse, a destrier, and said, "And how do we explain the war horse, Captain?"

"Simple, John, you ride the warhorse. He looks similar to Eleanor, and no one questions my right to ride such a horse. Get rid of the knight's livery."

As we rode towards York, John of Nottingham said, "Men knew he was hunting us. Those who escaped may talk."

"Then let them talk. Aye, they know my name and they know my trade, but you are all unknown. I would argue, if it came to court, that we were attacked."

"He was a knight!"

"And an enemy of Lord Edward. Our fates, it seems, are entwined. I must help Lord Edward and his father regain the throne, or I risk losing my life!" I laughed. "Life is never simple, is it?"

I made it sound frivolous but it was not. I could kill a knight in battle, but at any other time it would be considered murder. Had I fought him with a sword, that would have been different. Life was not fair, but a man made the best of it or he was not a man.

York was the most important city in the north. It was from here that the Scots had been repulsed during the anarchy. The politics of the south were largely irrelevant, for the city was ruled by a sherriff and an archbishop. I hoped that we could find employment, but our first problem was gaining access to the city.

"What is your business?" The sentry's tone was aggressive, and I heard the murmurings from my men. They were not happy.

I smiled. "We are here to trade and then to seek work."

"Have you any coins? The Sherriff will not allow vagabonds to enter."

Thanks to Sir Roger and his men I had a full purse, and I reluctantly opened it for him. His attitude changed immediately and he smiled. "Then welcome, sir. I would recommend The Angel, by the river. It is a good inn and they have a fine stable."

I smiled a false smile such as the one he had given me. "Thank you!"

I had no intention of staying in an inn recommended by him. I had heard that The Saddle was an honest inn and we repaired there. We had been given directions by other warriors who had frequented it. Will Yew Tree's eyes widened when he saw the size of the head on the ale, which was being carried by a buxom wench. "I have died and gone to heaven!" Will had not had enough ale on our journey north.

The inn proved a good choice. There were no bed bugs, the price was reasonable, the ale good and the food edible. We had endured worse. We did nothing that first night, save enjoy the fact that we had food, ale and would have beds. We did not fear a knife in the night, and the enemies who had pursued us were dead. Life was getting better.

The next morning, after checking on our horses, we split up to explore the city. We needed employment, but we also needed other things. We had to have more arrowheads, and we needed a blacksmith. I went with Jack of Lincoln and we headed for the market. John of Nottingham would seek a weaponsmith, while the rest would do as we did and seek a merchant who needed good men to guard their belongings.

The first four we tried did not seem interested. They sought men at arms and, despite our swords, we did not appear robust enough. Having spent all morning on our fruitless quest, we were approaching noon and decided to find an alehouse. Hunting employers was thirsty work.

We found an inn, which was crowded. That was a good sign. As we made our way to the barrels to get served, I bumped into a merchant.

"Sorry, my lord!" I had learned that civility brought its own reward. When the merchant turned, I recognised him. "Dickon of Doncaster!"

The merchant laughed. "I never thought to see you again! What did you say your name was, War Bow?"

"Aye, sir, and I am the captain of a company of archers now!"

His face split into a smile and he said, "Then we are well met. I can see that you and your companion have a thirst. Buy your ale and I will find you and speak with you, for this is a most fortuitous meeting, and I think that Fate has sent you to me."

Jack and I shouldered our way through the crowd to order our ale. We were helped by the fact that we were broad-shouldered archers, and we barrelled our way through. I held up two fingers and the serving wench nodded.

"Who was that, Captain?"

"A merchant, Dickon of Doncaster, whom I served in Poitou. My friend and I helped him to take some wagons through bandit country. With luck, he may wish to employ us."

"In Poitou, Captain? I thought we needed to stay in England."

"We do, but let us hear what he has to say first, eh? He obviously wished to speak with me. Let us find a corner where we can talk."

With our ale in our hands, we looked around for a place to sit. There were no seats, but there was a space where we could stand, so we made our way there. The ale was passable. We had drunk better in the homes of the alewives heading north, but it would do. Jack said, when we were halfway through the ale, "Here is your friend, Captain."

I looked to where he nodded and saw Dickon and what looked like a younger version of himself. He reached us and said, "This is a popular inn! Captain, this is my son, Geoffrey of York, and this is the archer I told you of, Geoffrey, Gerald War Bow."

I bobbed my head. "Sir."

Geoffrey of York grinned. "As we are of an age, archer, I do not think that I yet merit the title sir." He raised his beaker of ale. "Well met, fellows!" We all toasted.

Dickon leaned in to speak to us. Where we stood was quieter than the rest of the alehouse, for the men around us were serious drinkers, but he obviously wanted us to hear his words. "So, Gerald, are you on your way to war? Or," he raised an eyebrow, "are you fleeing a war?"

I had the same uncomfortable feeling when I spoke to Dickon now, that I had experienced when I met him close by the abbey on the Humber. He seemed able to look into my mind and know what secrets I was hiding. But I had changed in the years since I had first met him. I now knew how to keep a straight face.

"We seek employment, sir."

Seemingly satisfied, he beamed. "Capital! That is what we wanted to hear eh, Geoffrey?"

"You may be the answer to my prayers, archer. When my father fetched me here, he told me what you and your friend did in Poitou. Is this the same fellow?"

Dickon shook his head. "It is not. I do not know him. Although the split nose suggests an interesting past!"

"No, this is not he, Roger died in Poitou saving the life of an English lord." I decided, for the moment, to keep Lord Edward's identity to myself. "This is one of my archers, Jack of Lincoln."

"I am sorry to hear of Roger's death. He was a good man and I liked him. You say archers, how many men are in your company?"

"There are now seven of us, sir."

The father and son exchanged a look. Dickon said, "Do you have horses?"

The last time, Dickon had to furnish us with mounts. "We do, sir, and we each have a spare."

"Better and better. Geoffrey, go get more ale, and I will make Gerald a proposal." His son seemed happy to leave us to speak. "My son runs this end of my business, the English end. I work in France, Poitou and Flanders. He is young but he is learning. This unrest in the south has caused him problems. We have had some of our wagons taken by bandits and also by lords who do not obey the law."

"Here, close to York, sir?"

He shook his head. "Despite the Scots, the north is safe. The northern barons keep order. It is once we try to cross to Cheshire or through the Midlands that we have difficulties. You and your men can handle swords?"

"We are all proficient."

His son returned. "I have explained the problem, Geoffrey."

Geoffrey of York handed us our ale. "We have a good business, Captain of Archers. We began by trading sheepskins but we have expanded. My father now imports items from Germany, Flanders and even France. The port fees here in York are a fraction of those in London. We were doing well until we expanded further south, and then we found difficulties."

I was going to ask why they bothered to expand if they were doing so well when he added, "The Marcher Lords in the west also seek that which we trade. The Welsh are belligerent, and men like Richard de Clare and the Sherriff of Gloucester are keen for weapons from Saxony. There, they make good swords and armour. We lost our first consignment north of Derbyshire. Two of my men were slain."

"Bandits?"

"Bandits who were in the employ of a lord, for one of the men who attacked us wore spurs. The work may be dangerous. Are you and your men interested?"

I did not have to look at Jack to know the answer. We had come seeking employment and this sounded perfect for us. "Aye, Master Geoffrey."

He beamed and his father clapped him on the back. "Good! You have your own horses and that means we will not have to lay out money for those." Dickon glanced at Jack. "We just need to settle the fee."

"You can speak in front of Jack. My company has no secrets."

"You have not changed, then. You were ever a loyal man. What say you to twenty shillings for each trip? And we will pay for food and lodgings."

"And you pay for damage and losses to our horses?"

Dickon nodded. "That seems fair."

"And when will you need us?"

Dickon became conspiratorial. "The Battle of Lewes has altered the situation. The first wagon train will need to leave York by August. The journey west will take a month."

I nodded. "And until then?" We would be spending our hard-earned coin, and York was expensive.

Geoffrey understood the problem. I soon learned that he was a clever young man and had inherited all of his father's intuition. "I have a hall at Easingwold. You could stay there. In fact, that might be judicious for you, and your men could act as my guards."

Dickon looked at my face and seemed to read my thoughts. "And of course, you will be paid as such. Five shillings a week?"

I saw the grin on Jack's face. Five shillings a week and food and lodgings were better than we might have hoped. "That is agreeable. We need a couple of days to finish our business in York, first."

With a knowing look Dickon said, "I thought you might. My son's hall is in the middle of Easingwold. He will expect you." He held out his hand. "I am right glad I came to this alehouse."

"As am I." It was fate, for if one of my other men had entered then Dickon would not have approached them.

The others had depressed expressions when we met, but soon brightened when they heard my news. "So, we have a couple of days and we should use them well. We need to sell the warhorse. It will fetch money we can use. Then, we need to find a smith. We need arrowheads, and hopefully we can sell the mail and plate we found." They had taken the swords and daggers from the dead and they would use them. My sword was still satisfactory and I would not change it.

John of Nottingham said, "I found a weaponsmith. His name is Matthew. He has good mail and seems to be an honest man" He told me where to find him.

The next day he went with Robin of Barnsley to sell the horse, while I went with Jack of Lincoln to find the smith. Matthew had a smithy just outside the Roman walls; John had found him through the landlord of The Saddle. A recommendation always helped. I saw him making a sword as we approached, and that was good. He was a true weaponsmith and not a smith who mainly shod horses and dabbled with weapons. On the horses we had brought we had the mail and the plate. I was anxious to be rid of them.

I had bought some better clothes with the coins I had taken from Sir Roger, and now looked a little more like a person who deserved respect.

"Good morning, good sirs, how may I be of service?"

"I lead a company of archers and need to know if you can make arrowheads."

"Aye, sir: hunting, war or bodkin?"

"War and bodkin."

"That will be expensive." I saw him calculating in his head. "How many would you need?"

It was my turn to calculate; we had some already, and we were not going to war. "A hundred war and sixty bodkins."

"That would be ten shillings for the war arrows and twenty shillings for the bodkins."

I heard the sharp intake of breath from Jack. "Acceptable – and we have something to sell to you. Jack, unpack the horses."

I could see that he was intrigued. "Metal? I have scrap metal aplenty."

Jack emptied the mail first. "No, smith, this is good mail. You may need to repair the odd link or two, but this could be resold by you."

The smith rubbed his beard as he worked out a profit margin. I took the sack of plate and took it out piece by piece. "And this, smith, is good plate. We also have half a dozen helmets."

His eyes widened. "How did you come by this?"

"It was not stolen, if that is your question. We are good archers and we took these in battle." I saw the worry on his face. "None will come to seek it!"

"Five pounds for all of it."

He was robbing us, but it was a buyer's market. "Seven – and you make our arrows for nothing."

I saw him calculating. He held out his mighty fist. "Then it is a deal! How soon will you need the arrowheads?"

It was June and we would be leaving in August. "July?"

He nodded. Jack said, "And when can we have the balance of our money?"

"I do not have it here. Let us say… the end of the week?"

I nodded and we left.

"He robbed us, Captain."

"He made a profit. No matter what he paid us, Jack, we are in profit, and we do not have to worry about selling the plate now. When the horse is sold too, then we can begin to think about spending some of this coin!"

I had no plans to spend my share. When I had time, I would return to Oxford for my chest. My funds were growing.

CHAPTER 6

We collected and shared the profits from the plate, the mail and the horse. It allowed us all to buy from the merchants of York, whose prices were much lower than they would have been further south. Each of us had different needs and our bags bulged when we left.

Then we headed to Easingwold. It was a small village, and Geoffrey of York's hall was the largest building in the small gathering of houses. His wife, Margaret, was with child, and she had two other children. Although busy, she was always pleasant to us. His steward, who had been expecting us, accommodated us in the barn. That suited us and, as our new master was away on business with his father, we set to making arrows and performing all the other tasks we needed. The time we were allowed was a luxury, for our food was cooked for us. We had straw beds and the weather was pleasant. Even better was the fact that there was a good alehouse in the village. It was called, appropriately, The Feathers, and we all spent some time there. Will Yew Tree was there each night; his coins diminished faster than ours.

We also took the opportunity of washing and repairing our livery. We would need it again, and now was the time to attend to it. I had bought some leather in York, and I used the time we waited for Geoffrey of York to make myself a bracer for my arm and a pair of boots. When I finished that, I made a canvas bag with spacers for my arrows. I now had the time to make a good one. In battle it was more convenient to have a bundle of arrows stuck in the ground, but if we were riding to protect a wagon train then we needed arrows close to hand.

We had been in the hall for half a month when, not long after having left for the alehouse, Will Yew Tree returned. That was unheard of – and he was with a man and a boy of perhaps eight years of age. This was unusual. Jack of Lincoln rubbed his eyes. "Surely you have not drunk the alehouse dry? That would be a prodigious feat, even for you!"

Will snorted. "Nay, Jack of Lincoln. I come to speak to the captain and introduce Peter, son of Rafe. This is Rafe, his father." The boy bobbed while the father stood straight – I saw that the man had a withered arm, but his body looked to have been that of a warrior. "Can I leave them with you, Captain? There is a game of nine men's morris, and the other players are as much use as a one-legged man in an arse-kicking contest!"

"Of course." I turned to address the newcomers. "Come, it is a pleasant evening, let us go and sit by the duck pond." Once we were seated, I asked, "How can I help you?"

"I was an archer, Captain. I served under the sherriff in the wars against the Scots. I suffered a wound which means this," he tapped his withered left arm with his right hand, "is useless. Better that I had lost the arm altogether."

"I am sorry. How do you make a living now?"

"I was a good archer. I had money put aside, but the sherriff gave me a smallholding. We get by, Captain, and I do not need charity." He was proud. Most archers were. "I have been training the boy here to be an archer. I have done all I can to make his arm strong and to tell him how to draw. Now, he needs a working archer to show him. I have heard

90

of you, Captain, and Will Yew Tree speaks well of you. He might be a blowhard, but I can tell that he knows his business. I would have you take my son as an apprentice and make him an archer."

I looked at the boy. I could see that he was slightly broader than most boys his age. "What do you say, Peter?"

"I would learn to be an archer, Captain, and Will Yew Tree says that you are a good teacher." I knew not why he thought that. "I am a hard worker and I am willing to learn."

"And can you ride a horse?"

He was not expecting the question and looked at his father as I continued. "We are mounted archers, Peter, and we ride to war. If we took you on, then you would need to ride to war and look after the horses as well as fetch us arrows when we fought."

I saw him consider my words. "I like horses, but I will speak the truth, I have never ridden one." I saw his father's face fall.

"You are honest and that counts for much. I will tell you what, spend the next four days with us. We will try to teach you to ride. That way, you can see if you like us and still wish to serve with us."

Rafe looked happy. "That is an honest answer, Captain, and better than Peter and I could have expected." He turned to his son. "I will see you in four days. Do not let the family down, Peter!"

"I will not father, and I will make you proud of me."

His father hugged him. "I already am!"

He turned and headed back to the alehouse and I turned back to the child. "Well Peter, let me introduce you to the others. They are good men, but you may find them a little rough."

In fact, my men were charmed by the keenness of the boy. He had an endearing way with him, and in all the time I knew him, he never told an untruth. He was hard working and, over the next days, he spent as many hours in the saddle as he could. He fell off the horse many times, and his buttocks were red raw, but he persevered and after three days was a rider. More, he got on well with the horses, and even Eleanor took to him. When he was not riding then Jack of Lincoln and John of Nottingham showed him how to fletch and to fit arrowheads to arrows. That was self-interest. He would be able to repair arrows for us.

Half a day was spent with me. We had an old bow that was easy to draw and shorter than the others. I had not known why we kept it, I suspect that if we had not had spare horses to carry our bows, we would have discarded it. The bow was still hard for Peter to draw, but that helped to build his strength. His fingers bled and, each night, I heard him cry himself to sleep – for muscles ached which he did not know he had.

When his father returned, all of my company stood to hear the boy's decision. I said to his father, "We would have him as an apprentice, but I know not if he still wishes to join us."

We all looked at Peter. He smiled and put his bloody hands behind him. "I confess, father, that is has been hard; harder than I thought it would be. It has not deterred me. I am still resolved to be an archer. This is a good company of men, and they are both kind and honest. None has raised a hand to me when I made a mistake. If they will have me, then I will come with you, say farewell to my mother and my sisters, and return here to join the company of the War Bow."

Rafe held out his good arm. "Thank you, Captain."

"Thank *you*. When he is an archer I will return him to you, and he can then make his own decision about his future. For now, we serve Geoffrey of York, but one day we will return to our former master. I will not say who that is, save to say that he is a nobleman. We will look after your son as though he was our own. We will be as foster fathers to him. We will keep him as safe as it is possible, but war…"

He looked ruefully at his left arm. "Aye, Captain, I know better than most."

August was soon upon us, and the carters and their wagons arrived at the hall. There were eight of them and they were laden. Geoffrey of York had arrived back six days before the wagons. He showed me honour by telling me about our destination and cargo.

"We have eight wagons, and they are bound for the Earl of Gloucester. We have to travel over the saltway in Longdendale. It is also called the Pass of Woodhead. As this is north of the lands of de Ferrers in Derbyshire, your services may not be needed."

I kept a straight face. The Earl of Gloucester had fought Lord Edward and de Ferrers was my enemy – however, he was right. That remote route passed through the lands of Chester, and the earldom of Chester belonged to Lord Edward. However, it also passed close to Clwyd, and Baron Henry might remember me.

"We have a cargo of weapons. There are crossbows, swords, pikes and helmets as well as hauberks and German plate. That will need to be guarded carefully, Captain, for each suit of plate is worth more than thirty pounds. We have three of them."

It seemed I had been robbed as I had suspected, and Sir Roger must have been a rich man if he could afford plate armour.

"Would bandits risk the robbing of a wagon for plate and mail? I could understand the swords, but where would they find a market for plate armour?"

He smiled. "It may surprise you to know that I managed to buy a suit of plate armour as well as three hauberks here in York. The weaponsmith was a little evasive about their origins, which led me to believe that they were taken by bandits! As you will learn, bandits and brigands steal first and worry later where to sell it. We pass through Holmfirth, and after that there is nothing save wild country. This is not a journey I would undertake in winter. We get there as soon as we can and then pick up a cargo of salt and cheese from Namentwihc before reversing our journey. That cargo may be more valuable to the bandits of the high country. I hope that you and your men are a waste of money. This is the easier of the trips we will make, our next one will be harder, for we will travel to Oxford with spearheads, swords and jet from Whitby. There we are forced to pass through de Ferrers' lands, and he is a terror to honest merchants. He charges a tax to all who use his road, and if we use the byways, he has his men take the cargo anyway. We will use the byways, and you and your men might be the surprise they do not expect."

As we were leaving the next day I confided in my men. I did not tell them of Baron Henry, but all else they needed to know.

Jack of Lincoln found it amusing that we were transporting the armour we had sold to the weaponsmith, young Peter just took it all in. We had kitted him out, too. He had returned with serviceable clothes, but he needed a cloak. We had the cloaks from our dead comrades. They were good cloaks, which were well oiled and would keep a man dry in all but the worst of storms. We cut one down for him. We also cut down a hood and a cap. If he was training to be an archer then he needed to look like one.

He had his bow and he had arrows; we just gave him hunting arrows. It was unlikely that he would use them in battle, anyway. When we fought, he would be busy carrying arrows for us. We also gave him a pair of daggers. One was long enough for him to use as a sword if he needed to. We had trained him to use a bow and, on the journey across the high land, we would show him how to use his other weapons. We gave him our smallest horse, Daisy – she was a docile mount but still seemed too big for him. We had impressed upon him that he had to keep up with us; he was our apprentice, but we could not be his nurse-maids. We had a job to do.

We headed south, towards Loidis. Here, we were still under the protection of the sheriff. Even so, we started as we meant to go on. Tom rode at the fore as our scout. Stephen's death still hung heavily upon him, but he was rigorous and knew how to spot danger. I rode with Geoffrey of York. He wore a leather byrnie beneath his tunic and a helmet. He had a sword and had told me that he knew how to use it. His father had handled himself well in Poitou. A man named Simon, who had worked for Geoffrey and his father for years, was the lead carter. My men spread out along the side with John of Nottingham, Jack of Lincoln and young Peter at the rear. We had not brought our spare horses as they had been left at Easingwold. Geoffrey of York might be just a merchant, but we had hired on to guard him – and guard him we would. I was no less vigilant than I had been when I watched the heir to the English crown.

We made less than fifteen miles a day, and our progress was tortuous. One benefit was that Peter became a better rider, and he was able to learn how to care for the horses. The carters took to him and gave him tips.

I could see why Geoffrey of York had not chosen this journey in winter. After we crossed the tiny bridge and corn mill that was Holmfirth, our journey became even tougher. We had spent the night in the tiny hamlet; we had to camp but were able to buy fresh bread, and we knew that would be in short supply until we reached the villages of Marple and Marple Bridge. As we ascended the twisting road that led to the Woodhead Pass, the carters had to walk next to their horses, in order to ease their burden. I looked up at the rocks and rough ground ahead. This was perfect bandit country. I made a decision. "Archers, dismount and string your bows. Peter, stay with the pack horse in case we need arrows."

Peter's tiny voice came back, "Aye, Captain."

My men did not need to answer, they just dismounted. Geoffrey of York did not dismount but looked down at me quizzically. "Do you see danger, Captain?"

"No sir, for when you *see* danger then it is too late. This way I have a strung bow and a nocked arrow. If I was a bandit then this is where I would hit us. We climb a slope and we are going so slowly that if we make seven miles this day, I will be surprised. The rocks make perfect places to hide. We will walk."

He stayed in the saddle. I knew it was a mistake, for he made a good target.

I kept watching Tom ahead of us. He was a good scout and he sniffed the air. Bandits would smell differently from us. We had bathed two days before we left Easingwold – bandits would stink. The steep slope might help potential bandits, but as the wind came from the west then it would bring their smell to us.

We came to a flatter part of the pass and the road twisted to the right. It was the sort of place most men would relax, but I did not. I had a war arrow nocked and I was ready. I saw Tom turn and drop to one knee. He was improvising, and I knew that there was danger. His bow pointed to the slope on the right.

"Ware, right!"

We kept moving, but Tom's warning had been enough for the carters to move to the left of their horses, as did my archers. I led Eleanor with my left hand and held my bow and arrow in my right.

The arrows, when they came, were sent from too far away. The bandits had height, but they had hunting bows and arrows – that saved the life of Geoffrey of York. Two arrows plunged down and struck him; they penetrated his tunic but not his leather byrnie. He dropped to the ground and drew his sword.

I had dropped Eleanor's reins and I scanned the rocks. I saw a patch of white, some hundred and twenty paces from me. In one motion I drew and released. The arrow smacked into the head of the bandit. My arrow precipitated the response of my men. Tom, isolated ahead, ran back to us. The poor quality of both the archers and their weapons was shown when an arrow thudded into Tom's saddle; it failed to stick and fell to the ground.

The bandits ran at us. There were more than thirty of them, although accurate numbers were hard to ascertain. I drew and released at the nearest man. The carters drew their swords. The horses pulling the wagons would not move for there was a slope once more, and they were grateful for the rest.

I struck a bandit in the shoulder – my war arrow was barbed. As he fell, writhing, he tried to pull the arrow from the wound but simply tore a large hole. I saw him slump to the ground. My men did not panic. Nock, draw, release! It was something they could do in their sleep. Each archer chose the nearest target. As the bandits were less than one hundred paces from us, we could not miss. Their arrows also fell on us, but the only hurt they caused was when they managed to hit a horse.

Half their number were hit, but still they came – and now they were so close that their clubs, axes and short swords could hurt both horses and the carters. We were the trained warriors. I dropped my bow and ran towards them, drawing my sword. I could have drawn my dagger, but I was a good swordsman and I had skill. I used it.

Simon the Carter was being attacked by two men. Geoffrey of York had been too concerned with watching the battle and failed to react. Simon blocked one blow from a short sword, but I saw the wood axe swinging at his unprotected side. The bandit was a big man and he took a mighty swing; that gave me the chance to cover the ground and, even as his axe was coming around, to deal a mortal blow. I brought my sword from on high and hacked through his arm. My sword was a good one. I took both his arms and then, as his companion looked on in horror, I swung my sword at his neck and hacked through to the bone. The handless man ran! I did not think he would survive. Perhaps he had been the leader, for the rest of the bandits fled, and my men sent arrows after them. We had been a juicy target but they would not repeat their mistake. Fewer than eleven escaped.

"Dispatch the wounded and take their weapons. If the other bandits hereabouts have no weapons then they cannot prey on others. Is anyone hurt?"

"Simon the Carter has an arrow in his leg."

"See to him. Are you alright, sir?"

Geoffrey of York was visibly shaken. "I was too slow. You have earned your money this day – and then some."

Simon came over to me and held out his hand. "And you, Captain, have saved my life. I am in your debt, whatever you need."

"Just doing my job… and we all help each other, do we not?"

The wound to the carter was not serious and we soon pushed on. I thought that we had seen the last of bandits, certainly on this side of the high land, but we remained vigilant.

We camped as the sun was setting on the western side of the pass. It was not an ideal place, but there was water and we were sheltered. I set sentries and then checked the animals. Peter was giving them water and a handful of oats each.

"Captain, how did you manage to kill two men so quickly? Your hands moved so fast that I could barely see the blows."

"I only killed one, although the second was hurt so badly that I doubt he will trouble any traveller again." I stroked Eleanor. I had an old apple I had found in the apple store at Easingwold and I gave it to her. "If you are ever in a situation like that, Peter, then do not panic. Choose a target and a blow. Worry about the second man after the first is hurt."

"How did you learn to fight?"

"By avoiding being killed. I was lucky in my first battles and I know it." I ruffled the boy's hair. "Do not worry, you will be much older when you have to fight – and I think the rest of the journey will be easier!"

I was proved right, although the journey was no quicker, for late summer rains hit us when we reached the Cheshire plain, and we were all grateful that we had good cloaks. Geoffrey of York fretted about the mail and plate for he feared it would rust. It was almost September by the time we rolled into Gloucester.

I had feared that the Earl of Gloucester might recognise us as Lord Edward's archers, but he did not even bother to inspect his cargo; his steward did that. Geoffrey of York was paid, and we spent the night in a town where we slept in beds. While we were in the tavern we heard news about the rebel alliance. The Earl of Gloucester was at home because he had fallen out with de Montfort. Having led one of the battles, he felt he had deserved more from the Earl of Leicester and, when he had not received it, the unpredictable earl had left London. We also heard that Lord Edward and his cousin, Henry Almain, were now in Wallingford Castle. That was not far from Oxford. In the safety of a Gloucester inn, I drank too much and contemplated riding to Wallingford to make contact with Lord Edward. When I rose, the next morning, I realised how foolish that would have been.

We left and headed for Namentwihc, where we filled the wagons with cheese and salt. We had a wet and unpleasant journey back to Easingwold. When we reached the scene of the ambush there was no sign of the bodies. There must have been honour amongst the bandits, that they had taken the time to recover their dead. October was almost upon us when we finally reached Easingwold.

The journey had taken longer than Geoffrey of York had planned, and his wife's time was almost come. "The sheepskins can wait until the new year, Captain. I would have you send a message to the merchant in Oxford to explain the delay and to take him the jet, for that is not a large cargo. You need to take just one sumpter to carry the small chests."

"Me?"

He smiled. "I trust you and know that you will be able to make the journey safely while my steward, good man though he is, may fall foul of some enemy. You shall be paid."

It struck me that this might be an opportunity to recover my chest from the inn. I agreed to go and went with Tom and David the Welshman. The ones I did not take were all disappointed, save Will Yew Tree, who could now spend each night in The Feathers!

CHAPTER 7

This time, we were able to ride the main roads for we wore better clothes and were not a company of archers. The three of us left our bows at home. I felt almost naked as we rode south, but I did not think we would need to use a bow, and the weapon marked our trade; this time we were riding in secret. We rode first to York and thence to Lincoln.

While the others saw to our horses and beds for the night, I sought an audience with the castellan. As I headed through the city, I saw that there were many armed men. The unrest in the country was manifesting itself as swords sought masters. I kept my hood up and hoped I would not be recognised. When I reached the castle I was kept waiting a little while, and when Sir Ralph arrived I saw why. He had been dining.

"I am sorry, my lord, I have but one night in Lincoln, and I thought to ask if there was word of Lord Edward."

He smiled. "I mind not my dinner being disturbed for a loyal Englishman. The news is mixed, Captain. The rebels have allowed the barons from the west to return to their lands, and therein lies hope, for they can build up our forces. The Queen is in France and Sir John de Warenne in Poitou, but it will take time to gather enough men to challenge de Montfort." I nodded, and his face became serious. "The de Braie family sent men to ask me what I knew of Sir Roger. I could honestly say that I had not seen him after he had left for the north. I will not ask you what happened, except to ask that it was done with honour."

"A man died to prove that honour." It was a simple and truthful statement. We had been ambushed and Stephen Green Feather died.

"Good. You say you go to Oxford?" I nodded. "Then take the back roads. The rebels seek Lord Edward's archer."

"There are just three of us, and we did not bring our bows. None would know us for archers. We work for a York merchant, and we have work until the new year. After that…"

"Say no more. Plans are afoot. Watch yourself, these are dangerous times. We will contact you again if we can. There are many spies and traitors!"

I left Lincoln with more hope than I had arrived with, but also apprehension. The de Braie family controlled the land around Huntingdon, de Montfort controlled Leicester and de Ferrers ruled Derbyshire. We would have to sneak through their lands, knowing that they were looking for us. I confided my fears to my men, and it was David the Welshman who came up with the solution. "Captain, we have to bring the wagons down when the lady is delivered of her child. Let us use this as an opportunity to scout out an easier passage south. Our master does not wish to pay the tolls that the men of de Montfort charge, so let us find a way which takes us south without touching their strongholds."

It was a good plan, which I adopted. I quickly realised that our journey to Lincoln, useful though it was, had added thirty-five miles to the journey. If we had used the route further west then, although the road would not have been as flat, it would have been shorter.

We headed south and west to pick up the road through Nottingham. It was when we reached Nottingham, in the late afternoon, that I realised there was a line between the lands of de Montfort and de Ferrers that we could exploit. Nottingham was a royal city and controlled by a sherriff. The present incumbent was a political creature, and Phillip Marc appeared to tread a fine line between not offending the rebels and ensuring that when King Henry was returned as king he would not lose his position. More importantly, Nottingham had many archers, for the nearby forests seemed to produce good ones. Even if we had brought our bows we could have blended in. I now regretted not bringing John of Nottingham, who would have had contacts in the town.

If I had been recruiting archers then I could have had my choice. We spoke with many in the inn, which was close to the castle. Even without a bow, an archer would recognise the three of us by our broad shoulders and oak-knotted arms. We pretended to be ex-archers who were seeking other employment. If we had wished it, we would have had many opportunities for work.

We left the next morning and I decided to push on hard, for my visit to Lincoln had delayed us too long. "We will do this next part of the journey in two days. We have good animals, which are well rested, and we have managed, more by good luck than good management, to evade our enemies."

I was tempting fate but, as events proved, that was the right course of action. We were travelling faster than other travellers, and it was Tom who spotted that we were being followed. He urged Bess next to Eleanor. "Captain, there are four men who follow us."

I did not turn. "You are sure?"

"I was not, but now I am. I had a feeling that there was a man watching us in the inn last night, but it was crowded and I could not be certain. When we left the stable, I saw other horses there and, as we began to gallop, I heard hooves behind us. The others on the road walk. We are the only ones who gallop – and now there are horsemen following us."

"Well done. We will watch for somewhere we can ambush them. They will not close with us for they could have done so before had they wished. They mean to take us. They will watch where we sleep and come in the night."

David the Welshman said, "We should have brought our bows."

I nodded. "Hindsight is always perfect, David, let us use the skills that God has given us. We can all use swords and we know the woods. More, we know that they follow us and that gives us an edge."

This was not a Roman road and it had twists and turns while the ground rose and fell. In places, there were open fields next to the road while at other spots the trees and hedgerow were so close as to form walls. I knew what I was looking for. I needed a place where the road crossed a stream or a small river, where there were trees.

At noon we stopped in a village and used the water trough. We fed our horses oats and we ate our stale bread while they consumed them. Then, we quickly remounted and rode off.

It was the middle of the afternoon when I spied the place we would use. We had just passed Bretford, and the road began to drop and follow a bend of the Avon. There were willows that hung over the road, above the height of a wagon, and beneath them were scrubby blackberry bushes. Some still had fruit on them. As we turned the bend I said, "Dismount. Hide the horses and then secrete yourselves. Have your weapons ready."

"There are four of them, Captain."

"I know – and that is why I will put myself where they can see me, and I will distract them."

As they led Eleanor away I took my dagger and hacked a willow branch, which was longer than me. I sharpened the end as I listened for the horses. I heard them galloping hard as they realised we were out of sight and that they had lost us. The four of them rode around the bend and, seeing me, reined in. I was leaning on the willow as though it was a staff. I took in the fact that their horses were lathered, which told me they were not as good as mounts as ours. The men were not archers, but one had the livery of de Ferrers. It was hidden by a cloak but, as he pulled back his horse to stop it, I had caught a flash of red and yellow. The other three looked like the sort of men we had captured close to Codnor: mercenaries.

"Friend, you have followed us from Nottingham. I do not like having a stiff neck. What is it you wish?" The four of them were fewer than five paces from me. They rode sumpters, so my head was level with their chests.

None wore helmets but the one with the tunic had a metal coif, which hung around his neck. He had the best sword of the four, and I saw his hand go to it. He smiled as he rested his hand upon his sword. "Where are your companions, Gerald War Bow?"

If he thought to surprise me with his words then he was mistaken, for I knew that we had been recognised as soon as I saw the red and yellow tunic. "You answer my question and I will answer yours."

"You are in no position to bargain, archer, for I see you have no bow, and I can take any archer who bears just a sword. However, I will tell you why we seek you. Captain Henry Sharp Sword has offered a bounty for you. It is fortunate that it is dependent upon your being alive. If he would have had your body, then you and your companions would now be dead. We would have slit your throats last night."

I knew then that we had been seen in Lincoln. Henry Sharp Sword had been our prisoner, but the battle of Lewes had reversed our positions. He was on the winning side. I nodded. "Then you may be disappointed, friend, for I will not go quietly. If you want this body then you must kill me."

"Where are your friends?"

I had been buying time for the two of them to move around the rear of the four, and now I saw them. "Oh, they left me, for my horse was hurt. I have this staff to help me walk." I turned as though to point with the staff down the road but in reality, it was to change my grip.

I turned and hurled the staff at the man at arms. It was only a willow, but the point was sharp and I was lucky: it struck the man in the eye. I drew my sword and ran at the other three. Tom and David also had their swords drawn. Tom leapt onto the back of one horse and drew his sword across the throat of the man who had been struggling to draw his own weapon. I swung my sword at the leg of the closest man and hacked through to the saddle; the horse reared and threw him. The last unwounded man looked from me to Tom and did not see David the Welshman. David's sword came up under his ribs.

The man at arms drew his sword and slashed at my head. I sensed rather than saw the strike. Instinctively, my hand came up to block the blow. I saw blood pouring from the damaged orb: my lucky strike had cost him his eye. He slashed again at me and I easily blocked it. I grabbed his boot with my left hand as he raised his sword for another blow and I lifted his foot, stirrup and all. He raised his arm for balance and tumbled from his horse. The animal dragged him a few steps and I ran after him. He was conscious, but only just. I took his foot from the stirrup and removed his sword.

"The others?" I asked.

David spat. "They are dead, but do not waste tears on them, Captain, for they were killers all." He held up a stiletto. It was the classic weapon of an assassin.

"Put their bodies in the ditch and collect their horses." I gathered the horse of the man at arms.

He raised his head as I approached. "And now do you slit my throat?"

I shook my head. "I am no murderer like you. What is your name?"

"William of Glossop."

"Well, William of Glossop, return to Henry Sharp Sword and tell him that I know of his bounty. I will now hunt him – and I am an archer. He should fear me. Take your horse and go."

"My sword?"

"Do you think me a fool? You have your life and that should be enough. Now go!"

He mounted and rode north. I had made another enemy. We waited until he was out of sight and then continued to Oxford.

We reached Oxford at sunset the next day and stayed in the inn where I had buried my chest. We were welcomed, for when we had stayed there before we behaved ourselves and paid well. We said we did not need the ostler to see to our horses and, while Tom watched, I dug up the chest. David the Welshman chuckled. "Clever, Captain!"

"I did not need it then, but I think Easingwold might be a safer place, as this is a little close to de Montfort for my liking."

We ate in the inn and discovered that Lord Edward and his cousin were closely guarded at Wallingford Castle. My plan had been to attempt to speak with him, but I saw now that was impossible. We heard more about the laws that de Montfort was passing. He was not the king, but he was using the mob of London to make him so in all but name – he was trying to make a parliament of commoners. It was a clever plan, for it would undermine the great lords and the king. We would have a monarch but he would not be anointed. He would be the man who controlled the commons.

However, I also saw the fatal flaw in such a plan. Men like the Earl of Gloucester would not be happy to lose power to commoners. Even allies such as the de Ferrers family might take their support from de Montfort. I spied a chink of light in a dark night.

The next day we sought out the merchant whom we had been sent to find, Ralph Widdecombe. Tom and David carried the two large chests and I took the smaller one. Ralph Widdecombe had a large hall, which was attached to his warehouse. He was a portly man with a grey beard, which showed him to be an older man who enjoyed life. He had, however, sharp eyes. He was not a fool.

"I see that you have not brought wagons, which suggests to me that there is something amiss."

I nodded. "My master's lady has gone into labour. I have brought the jet, but the weapons will be brought later. My master sends his apologies, but he does not know when they can be fetched."

He did not seem unhappy and smiled. "If you have the chests placed on the floor then I will have the payment readied." He turned and spoke to one of his servants.

"I hope I am not causing offence when I speak, but you do not seem unhappy about the lack of weapons."

He nodded. "You are clever, and I can see that Geoffrey of York has chosen well. The fact of the matter is that I intended to sell on the weapons to a Marcher Lord, Baron Mortimer. Since the Earl of Leicester has sent Lord Edward to Wallingford, the roads into the marches are well guarded. I need your master to deliver the weapons directly to Wigmore Castle in Hertfordshire."

I was no businessman, but I knew that this would cost Geoffrey of York money; more than the cost of transporting the weapons to Oxford. "And the payment for the weapons? Does that come from you or Baron Mortimer, sir?"

"The baron and your master will not lose out financially. If any has lost out it is I, and I do not mind, for the risks were too high in any case."

The small chest with the payment for the jet arrived. I opened it and checked the amount. I could see that the merchant was unhappy with my action. "When do you return north?"

I was not about to divulge that sort of information. "We have some business here in Oxford, and when that is done we will return to York."

"I hope you have a safe journey and apologise to your master for the changed arrangements. Blame the Earl of Leicester."

As we left for our inn, I knew there were politics involved. This merchant lived too close to the great lords to risk the enmity of either, and so he was playing both sides off against each other. It was Geoffrey of York who would be aiding the enemies of Simon de Montfort and not the prosperous merchant.

We did not wait one moment before I paid our bill, we fetched our horses and we left Oxford, before either the merchant or a rebel spy could report that one of Lord Edward's archers was close enough to pluck. I decided not to go back the way we had come, but to head for Northampton. I knew the land there from the battle, and we could head up towards Lincoln. We now had spare horses and so we pushed hard. We rode the captured sumpters first; if they were broken I would lose no sleep. I intended to make fifty miles in a day and would outrun any who sought us.

We stayed that first night in the market town of Haverberg. There was method in my plan, for Haverberg was a royal manor. We would be safer there than further east in de Montfort land. The talk in the town was of the king. This was a royal manor and their livelihood depended upon him, and de Montfort's attempts to undermine that power did not sit well with them. The mob of London might back the rebels, but the majority of Englishmen did not.

When we left the next day, I was in a more hopeful frame of mind. The conspiracies and plots of the southern merchants and barons were an irritation, nothing more: Lord Edward and his father would prevail. I knew that my lord would be planning an escape, it was not in his nature to sit back and accept captivity.

Our second night was spent in Newark upon Trent. This manor belonged to the Bishop of Lincoln, and he supported the king. Once more, we heard nothing but support for King Henry.

We almost killed our horses completing the last part of our journey: sixty-three miles in one day. When we wearily walked our horses through the York city gates I was as weary as I ever had been, but we had managed to evade our pursuers.

Even though Easingwold was just a few miles north of York, none of us could ride another mile, and so we stayed in The Saddle. With no reason to rush, we ate well, drank well and slept late. Perhaps there was a reason for that. As we had a late breakfast, some disgruntled riders came in from the south. They spoke of bands of de Montfort and de Ferrers' men on the Great North Road, who were seeking three archers and had been less than polite in their questioning. The three of us had neither bow nor arrow about our person and we played dumb, sympathising with the travellers who had been delayed by the search of their carts. My choice of route had been justified, as had my suspicions of Ralph Widdecombe.

When we reached Easingwold, I had much to tell Geoffrey of York. His wife had still to deliver her child, and I saw the worry on his face. I felt guilty about the news I would impart, for it would only add to his worries, but he had to know the potential danger which lay in Oxford.

In the end I had no choice, for he was desperate to know what Ralph Widdecombe had said. I told him and then revealed my suspicions.

"Then what should I do about Baron Mortimer?" The worry about his wife must have made him less confident, which explained why he sought business advice from an archer.

I viewed the problem as a military one. "Sir, Baron Mortimer is an ally and supporter of the king. If you do not deliver the weapons to him, that may be viewed as an act of treason. I believe the king and his son will prevail. You have nothing to lose."

"Except for my life." He waved a hand. "It is September now. I cannot leave my wife until the bairn is born, and I will have to stay a while to ensure that she is well. That means we would not be leaving until October or even November. The Woodhead Pass is impassable to wagons after harvest time. We would have to go further south – and that means risking Simon de Montfort."

I had no answer except for the obvious one. "Then you stay here with your family, and I will deliver the weapons."

He smiled and shook his head. "My father is right, you have more honour than many gentlemen, but I cannot allow you to take on this responsibility. We will leave when we are able. It is in God's hands now!"

Tom and David had told the others of our encounter and the fact there was a price upon my head. Jack of Lincoln seemed almost amused by the fact. "I thought I was the only one to have had that honour!"

John of Nottingham snorted. "An *honour*?"

"Aye, John, how many men do you know who know the value of their lives? Anyway, it is no matter. The captain is too good to be caught by his enemies, and he has us around him!"

The attack seemed to make my company even closer. I noticed that they rarely let me move anywhere, even the village, without one of them accompanying me. I was not afraid, but I was touched by their concern.

Geoffrey of York's wife gave birth to a son. He was healthy and had all his parts. I knew why our master wished to stay, for many babes, more than a quarter, did not live beyond the first month. Half might not survive two years. We did not waste our time but prepared for the journey. We knew that we would be far closer to our foes and we needed to be ready. We made the six wagons we would be using both stronger and faster. We ensured that the wheels were well greased and that we had spares. I suggested to Simon the Carter that we might use a couple of extra horses to pull the wagons. Not all of them would have the same load, and it made sense to me to have more horses pulling the bigger wagons. Simon felt indebted to me and complied. I also suggested that the carters might wear protection. Even a leather jacket might stop a hunting arrow.

It was the middle of October when we eventually left, and autumn had arrived with a vengeance. The rains delayed us by a further day as our master sought oiled canvas to cover the weapons. It would not do, to deliver rusty weapons.

It was a miserable wet day when we set off. We would not be heading for York but for Sheffield. Having to go so close to the de Ferrers' land, Geoffrey of York decided to profit from the danger we would be in. He intended to buy some of the knives they produced there. They were highly prized, and our master knew how to make money.

The road was slow, and it was wet. We made our purchases and had a night in a good inn, for Sheffield was a prosperous town. We had to change a wheel when we left Sheffield and headed towards the hills that lay to the south and west. It meant that we did not stay that night in the inn at Badequelle as we intended, but we camped at the tiny hamlet of Owler Bar, which was some miles short of the larger town. Our spirits were low. We were constantly keeping an eye open for danger, and yet each day dragged like the slow wagons, which seemed reluctant to move. Once we reached Badequelle then the hard part of the journey would be over, but we would have the more dangerous section to come. For although the ground would be easier, we would be in the land of de Ferrers. His captain had put a price on my head, and that money must have come from de Ferrers. If I was caught then, unlike Lord Edward, I would not enjoy a comfortable captivity. I would be killed. My archers knew that already, but the carters only learned of it when my men's apprehension raised questions. I saw, too, the worry on the face of Geoffrey of York. I suspect he was regretting his decision to hire us.

The good news was that it stopped raining as we left our miserable camp at Owler Bar. We hurried to Badequelle, less than six miles away. It was a growing market town, and the bridge over the Wye meant it drew visitors from all around this part of Derbyshire. We closed with the town shortly before noon, but we had changed our plans. A wagon was damaged; changing the broken wheel meant we would push on to Chedle rather than stay in the comfortable inn in the town. It would mean a longer day, but we were all anxious to deliver our goods and get back to Easingwold. My company now regarded the small village as home.

We were spied as we approached Badequelle, for we saw people staring at the six wagons which lumbered down the road. We did not ride with our bows on our saddles, they were in the wagons, but we all wore the hood and cap of an archer. As we stopped in the main square to water our horses, I heard hooves galloping away – I knew it meant trouble but I did not worry the master. Instead, I went around my archers and warned each of them. We all took our bows from the carts and strung them, filled our arrow sacks and took a few spare arrows for our belts.

Tom would continue to be the scout who rode ahead, but I told John and Jack to hang back at least 200 paces from the last wagon. I had Peter close to the leading wagon. If we were to be ambushed, I wanted us spread out as much as possible. If we had been men at arms then the opposite was true, but we were archers, and my arrangement meant we could slow down any who attacked us. Geoffrey of York stopped only long enough to buy fresh bread and some of the local cheese.

We were a mile out of Badequelle when he noticed my new arrangement. "Is there a problem, Gerald?"

I would not lie to him. "There may be. I heard the hooves of a horse leaving as we entered the town. It might well be a coincidence in which case we have lost nothing, but if, as I fear, it means that word has been sent to de Ferrers at Derby, then we may find hunters seeking us. You asked us to guard your wagons because this road is dangerous. The weather has helped us, but we may find an enemy comes to stop us. We will watch ahead, behind and to the side. This land helps us for it is more open and less wooded than an ambusher might like."

The clearer skies aided our ability to see, and as we approached Chedle we saw not an ambush but a column of men, heading from the east. My eyes were sharp and I recognised the de Ferrers' livery. Chedle lay less than a mile ahead. "Master, whip your horses and get to Chedle. There you will be safe."

"What will you do?"

"Why, fight them of course! They are my enemies and the enemies of the king. Archers! To me!"

I dismounted as the carters whipped their horses and raced for the safety of the town. The enemy horsemen began to gallop. I was gambling that they would not only want to capture me but the wagons and whatever they were carrying, too. "This time we do not wait to be attacked. Aim for their horses when they are in range. Peter, hold the horses."

His voice showed his fear. "Aye, Captain." But he grabbed our reins and bravely stood close behind us.

I counted twenty men in the column. The thin sunlight shone from helmets and spears, but we would not know if they were mailed or not until they were much closer. The road they travelled joined our road less than half a mile to the south of us. I saw the wagons nearing the town, and that decided the horsemen. They left the road and galloped across a field of winter barley; they wanted the archers more than the wagons. That would help us, for it would slow them, and they would not be able to strike us as a line.

I nocked a war arrow, as I intended to hit a horse. A horse was a bigger target and had no protection. If a horse was hit then the rider was, effectively, out of the combat; a fall might even disable him. I drew. This was my most powerful bow, and few men could draw it as well as I did. I released then nocked a second war arrow. Even as the first one hit a horse, my second was in the air.

The others began to rain arrows down, and that spurred on de Ferrers' men. They began to spread out, and I nocked a long needle bodkin. I had spied that the leaders and the four warriors at the fore all wore mail. They were now less than a hundred paces from us. They outnumbered us, but we did not panic. We had hit ten of them or their horses, and we had yet to suffer a wound.

I saw six horseless men, and a couple of those had been hurt by their falls. There were still ten mounted. My needle bodkin struck the leading rider. He tumbled from his saddle. A second mailed warrior also fell. I saw that the riders without mail slowed up. When Jack of Lincoln hit a third mailed warrior, they decided that was enough and they fled. Two horses were hit as they did so.

I ran towards the nearest men at arms. One was still alive; Jack of Lincoln's arrow had hit him in the gut. It was a mortal wound – stomach wounds always were. I took his helmet from him. Blood was trickling from his mouth.

He shook his head. "Bastard archers! You cannot fight like men!"

"And why cannot Henry Sharp Sword fight his own battles? Does he always have to send men after me? Let him come, and we can end this blood feud."

The man laughed and it was a mistake, for it hurt him. "It is not just the captain. The earl wishes you dead. It is his bounty! Fear not, archer, he is close… he…"

His eyes glazed over and he died, but his words made me stand and stare east. These men had been sent to slow us. The ones who had fled would return to the captain, and the next time he would be more circumspect. We put the wounded horses out of their misery and took the mail, weapons and coins.

As we headed to Chedle I said, "Sleep with one eye open this night, men, for this is not over!"

CHAPTER 8

The carters and Geoffrey of York waited anxiously for us in the market square. "Well?"

"They are gone and we lost not a man, but they will return."

Geoffrey of York nodded. "How much further do we have to travel to be safe from them?"

"It is forty miles until we are beyond their reach."

I saw his shoulders slump. "Then that is two days of travelling and, even if we make it, we still have the journey home."

"If we make Wigmore Castle then we can take the Woodhead Pass home. Empty wagons might be able to make it."

He nodded. "I have rooms at an inn, but we will need to have men watching the wagons."

"My men and I will sleep in the wagons."

"My carters can—"

"Your carters are not warriors. We are. You pay us for this, and we will earn our money." I did not tell him that the wagons would be easier to defend than the inn, nor that I wished him and his carters safe. If there was to be a knife in the night then it would be my company who would bear the danger. "Take Peter into the inn with you."

Geoffrey nodded. "You are a good man, and there are precious few like you. Come, Peter."

"I would rather stay here with the rest of the company."

Will Yew Tree said, "Now then. What is this? Dissension? An archer obeys his captain. This is another lesson for you."

Peter nodded. "I will obey, but I am not afraid!"

I smiled. "No one thought that for an instant!"

Geoffrey had food and ale sent to us. I drank sparingly and allowed Will to have my share. While the others ate, I spoke with John and Jack.

"I think we are in danger here. We take it in turns to watch."

John nodded at Will who was smiling, drunkenly, at all around him. If we had to fight then he would be fierce but, as a sentry, he would not be alert enough to keep watch. "All of us?"

"No, just we three. We have the most experience."

Jack of Lincoln had lived the hardest life of any of us, and he knew how to kill. He patted his knife. "Aye, Captain. I hope that bastard comes tonight. I would like to stick him with my steel and end this! I hate looking over my shoulder."

As did we all! The wagons were in the yard of the inn. It was a tight fit, but with the horses in the stable and the gates closed, they were as secure as they could be. We had one man in each wagon, and I took the middle watch. The rains might have stopped, but it was still October and it was cold. I wrapped my cloak about me but did not bother with the hood; I kept my head warm with my archer's cap.

When Jack of Lincoln woke me, he took my place in the wagon. I sat in the middle of the wagons with my back against a wheel and placed my sword and dagger on the ground next to me. I had deliberately chosen the middle watch, even though it was the most unpopular. The couple of hours' sleep had refreshed me, and I was still alert. For me, John of Nottingham had a harder watch as he would rise from a deep sleep.

I sat on one of the carter's straw-filled cushions. It stopped the cold from seeping up through my body. I leaned back into the wheel and watched the sky – it was a clear sky and a cold one. My breath formed before my face. I knew how to keep watch; I moved my head slowly to scan the skyline and I listened. The horses in the stable would alert me to any intruder as, I hoped, would the inn's dog. It had growled at us when we arrived. Robin of Barnsley had a way with animals, and he had got it on our side. It slept next to the gate.

I was not sure if I saw the movement on the roof; I wondered if my imagination was playing tricks but, when the dog growled, I knew that there were enemies, and they were not coming through the gate but over the roof. I hissed, "Jack, they come. Wake the others." I knew that he would not yet have fallen into a deep sleep.

I picked up my sword and dagger and stood, by sliding my back up the side of the wagon. I spied a shadow on the roof of the inn. He was sliding down the thatched roof. Having seen one, I then saw another three. It was a clear night, and bright for the time of year. I saw no faces and knew that they were facing the roof to slow their descent. They had ropes. I guessed they were secured, to allow them to lower themselves down the roof and into the yard. I made my way to the gate.

Robin of Barnsley appeared next to me with a knife in his left hand and a small hatchet in his right. I nodded with my head at the roof so that he knew where our enemies were. Our breath would give us away, for it was still like fog before our faces when we breathed. As soon as they turned, they would see us. The dog still growled. Robin reached down to pat it and the dog stopped growling, knowing that Robin was a friend.

When I reached the gate, I put my ear to it: I could hear men on the other side. The three who were sliding down the roof were there to open the gate and let the rest in. I now understood why they would only send three men into an inn filled with armed men: the three were skilled killers.

The rest of my men had risen, and I saw their faces as they stood by the wagons. John of Nottingham had taken charge. He saw just three men and would regard this as an opportunity to take them on two sides. He did not know about the ones beyond the gate.

Above me, I heard a hissed conversation and, although I could not make out the words, it told me the men were above my head. The gate was recessed on both sides, and Robin and I, along with the dog, were hidden. Then I managed to make them out. "I have not heard the dog for a while."

"It has gone back to sleep. Silence, for they may be sleeping in the wagons."

Then events happened rapidly. The three men must have used the wall to walk down, for I saw their legs appear as they slid down the rope. The dog saw enemies, and his teeth fastened onto the leg of one. The dog was a big beast, and the bite must have been fierce, for the man cried out. Then, the other two landed in the yard before us. The dog's bite had alerted them, and they had weapons ready. One slashed at the dog with his short sword, but Robin partially blocked it with his dagger and then chopped at the man with his hatchet. The other killer lunged at me with his sword, and I parried it with mine. John and my archers ran to the man who was being savaged by the dog, and I could hear the noise of people in the inn shouting as they heard the clash of iron. My opponent knew his business. A bodkin dagger in his left hand, he lunged at my eye. His hand was quick and, although I moved my head to the side, he still scored a long cut along my cheek. I instinctively rammed my dagger upwards and felt it cut through material, then flesh, and finally, as blood dripped down my hand, it grated off his ribs. He grunted, but he was a tough man. He tried to headbutt me, but I lowered my head so that his forehead hit the top of my skull and then drove my knee up between his legs. Hands grabbed him from behind as he reeled.

Robin of Barnsley's opponent lay dying in a pool of blood. The one savaged by the dog was the least wounded, and the man I had stabbed did not have long for this world. Geoffrey of York and the innkeeper appeared, along with the carters. All were armed.

I pointed my sword at the gate. "There are more men outside. I will open the gate and we can confront them." I was not sure if it was foolish or calculated but, even as I lifted the bar, I heard the sound of hooves. We opened the gate and ran out to the market square. I saw ten riders galloping east. There was neither wall nor town watch in Chedle, and the men had escaped. This had not ended as I hoped.

Torches had been brought. The man I had stabbed had expired, silently going to his death unshriven, but the other was talking. The innkeeper was questioning him and doing so none too gently. His guard dog had a cut along its side, and men had tried to enter his property. "What were you trying to do?"

I knew that the man was a hired killer. The one I had slain knew his business. The single survivor's eyes flicked from me to the innkeeper, and I saw the lie in them as he spoke. "We saw the wagons arrive and thought they might contain something worth stealing."

The innkeeper nodded, seemingly satisfied, but I asked, "And what about those on horses who waited outside?"

He shook his head. "I know nothing about that. We three came alone. Let me have my leg seen to, for your dog has wickedly sharp teeth."

The innkeeper shook his head. "My dog will have attention before

121

you! Tad, Rafe, bind him and put him in the ale cellar. We will take him to Totmonslow for judgement at the next session."

"You have slain my friends, let me go, for I have learned my lesson!"

"Take him away!" The innkeeper apologised to Geoffrey of York. "I am sorry about this, sir. Since the war, there have been many attacks on innocent people. It is time the king did something."

Geoffrey of York nodded. "Aye, it is safer in the north than here in this land."

"Innkeeper, I would keep a close watch on that one. He is slippery."

"Do not worry, we will watch him." He pointed to two of his other men. "Dispose of the bodies." I held up my hand and knelt to examine the purses of the two men. "You would rob the dead?"

I shook my head as I poured the contents of the purses into the palm of my hand. "Put these coins into the church alms box. These were not poor men, there are fresh-minted coins here. The man was lying." I gave the purses to the innkeeper.

"Then on the morrow, we will question him more rigorously before we take him to Totmonslow."

Left with my men, the carters and Geoffrey of York, I said, "These were sent by de Ferrers. The sooner we leave and get to Cheshire, the better."

"Aye." Geoffrey looked at me and my bleeding face. "You need that wound seeing to."

"My men can do that. We are all awake and it is a clear night, what say we head out before dawn? We could make many miles. If we stop two or three times, we might reach Telford by dark and then Wigmore Castle would be just one day away."

He looked at Simon, who shrugged. "I would rather be on the road, sir, where we can see our enemies, rather than risk an assassin in the dark."

"Then prepare the horses and I will settle our account."

John of Nottingham saw to my wound. "This could have cost you an eye, Captain. Then your days as an archer would be over." He cleaned the wound with vinegar – it stung. "This needs stitches but the light is too poor."

"Just put honey on the wound and cover it with a bandage."

"It will be hard to talk. Better have a drink now while you can." He handed me the ale skin from one of the wagons.

I nodded as I drank. "Then I will listen and let you do the talking. If we can reach Wigmore then we will be safe."

"Until we try to get home."

"Aye, that's the problem, until we have to cross back to the east. This time they will be waiting." With the honey applied and a bandage around the lower half of my face, I would find it hard to either eat or drink, and talking would be almost impossible.

Simon was a good carter, and soon one wagon had its horses hitched and was driven into the market square. It made it easier to move the other wagons We saddled our horses and took them out too. By the time the third wagon had been moved, Geoffrey of York had concluded his business. "The innkeeper felt guilty about the incident. He did not charge us for the stabling, just for our food."

John of Nottingham shook his head. "The purses we took will never see an alms house."

I knew that John was right. The innkeeper had not been concerned that I might take the purses, just that he wanted them for himself. We were about to leave when he rushed out. "The prisoner has escaped and Tad is dead! The man had a dagger in his boot!"

John of Nottingham said, "The captain warned you!" Pointing east, he added, "If you wish to catch the murderer then look towards the lands to the east." He turned back. "We are ready, master."

Geoffrey of York pointed south. "Let us ride!"

We reached Wigmore Castle as a barely visible sun set on a gloomy and fog-filled day. The clear night of the attack seemed a lifetime ago. I had barely eaten, but the itch in the wound, which began as we neared Wigmore, told me that the healing had begun. John had sniffed the wound each time we had stopped and could smell no badness. While Geoffrey of York sought an audience with Baron Mortimer, John took me to see the lord's doctor.

When the bandage was removed, the doctor's eyes narrowed. "How did you come by this wound?"

"The captain was attacked." I still found it hard to speak, and John answered for me.

"Then he is lucky, for another finger higher and he would have lost his eye. I will have to stitch the wound." His hand opened. It would cost. He might heal those in the castle as part of his duties, but I was a stranger and I would pay.

I counted out three silver pennies. He beamed, as it was more than he expected from an archer. "They will be small stitches!"

He gave me a drink of aqua vitae and then, after cleaning the wound, began to sew. It hurt, but I bore it. I would now be able to both eat and drink. I would also be able to speak.

Geoffrey of York returned some time later and looked pleased. "His lordship is happy and we are well paid; we have more than the merchant was going to pay us. Baron Mortimer has many men to arm! It seems he knows you, Gerald, and would speak with you on the morrow. We are to stay here in the castle. We should be safe from assassins here."

Baron Mortimer and his wife, Lady Maud, saw me alone the next morning. Lady Maud was a force to be reckoned with. She was from the

Braose family; a powerful Marcher dynasty, and she knew about political struggles. Had she been a man, she would have led armies. As it was, she guided her husband. Roger Mortimer was a brave knight and a fierce fighter, but it was his wife who had a mind as sharp as any general's.

I had seen Roger Mortimer many times and he knew me. "The youngest captain of archers, welcome Gerald War Bow. It is good to meet another loyal servant of the king. I too almost lost my life at Lewes! I will have vengeance on de Montfort." He leaned forward. "How did you come to be serving this merchant?"

I told him of our flight, our enemies and the threat which remained to us, but not the meeting with the castellan of Lincoln. I believed that the baron was loyal, but I knew how to keep my mouth closed.

"The merchant was a little vague about your attackers, but you know who they were."

"Aye, lord, it was de Ferrers' men." I described our capture of them.

"Then this is personal?"

"It is, but I am seen as Lord Edward's archer too."

Lady Maud smiled and gave her husband a knowing look. "Do not worry, Captain. There are plans in place to free Lord Edward, and you have been sent to us for a reason."

"Aye, you shall stay here with us, and we can plan the rescue of Lord Edward."

I shook my head. "First, I am honour-bound to take my master home. I took his coin, and I will not abandon him."

They both looked surprised, then the baron nodded. "A delay of a month will not hurt us as winter is upon us and…" He realised that he was about to say too much and waved his hand. "Take your master home and then return, for Lord Edward and his father, not to mention England, have great need of you, Gerald War Bow."

Lady Maud asked, "Are there many such as you, archer?"

"Like me, lady?"

"Loyal and with all the attributes of a noble who gives his word to a merchant and keeps it."

I did not give the answer that was in my head, for it would offend a high-born lady. I had seen much ignoble behaviour from apparent nobles and far better behaviour from some commoners like my friend, Roger of Talacre. "In my experience, my lady, such behaviour comes from the way that you were raised, and just reflects my father's hand."

"Then he was a good man."

I remembered a cold man who had brought me up alone. "He was a hard man, but he was a good father and a fine teacher. I owe him much."

The baron said, "We will pay you a salary while you are with us, but I have no doubt that you will wish to return to the service of Lord Edward once he is free."

"Aye, lord, for we swore an oath to Lord Edward, and we would honour those words."

I went to dine with the archers and the men at arms, as well as Geoffrey of York. I told Geoffrey of our conversation, and he seemed relieved that he was not going to be abandoned here, on the other side of the land from his home. John of Nottingham had kept his ears open, and he told me what he had heard. "Lord Edward may be released sooner rather than later. The Earl of Gloucester has returned home because he is unhappy with the way that titles have been awarded, and there are many who feel as he does. It is rumoured that de Montfort is keen to free Lord Edward once he has put in place certain strictures on the power of the king."

"Strictures?"

"He would lose most of his lands and be accountable to a council of commoners and lords."

I thought that was a falsehood and that Lord Edward would not agree – then I thought back to the man I had come to know over the past couple of years. He would agree, if he thought he would soon have his freedom and then he might fight to get them back. He would give a little to gain all. A throne and a crown were at stake, and Lord Edward wanted both. Now I understood the baron's veiled words.

The next morning, we were eager to be off and headed north, towards Chester. This time we would not collect salt, but we would hurry north and east and attempt the Woodhead Pass. The snows had not yet come, even though it was cold enough and there was plenty of rain. My wound itched, but the doctor had been good. He had told me to seek a doctor once I reached York and have the stitches removed in a month. If we could not find a doctor then we would do it ourselves. We had all tended each other's wounds before, and we were not without skill.

The men all knew that we would be leaving Easingwold and, whilst they were in the main sad, they knew that it would bring them closer to our lord, Prince Edward. The exceptions were Peter and Will. Peter rode with me and John of Nottingham, and I think it was for reassurance. He had seen us attacked and knew that the best of our warriors were John and me.

"Captain, have I progressed enough yet for you to think I might be an archer?" His voice was uncertain. He had grown stronger since he had been with us, but he still lacked confidence.

"You are strong enough and you are diligent enough but, as John will tell you, we cannot know until you are a man grown. Do you not like the life?"

He nodded. "I think it is the best of lives, but…"

John finished his sentence for him: "But you now know that you will be far from your family and you are fearful."

"Aye, I am."

I considered my words before I spoke them. "Both of us left our families when we were your age; I was a little older. You would leave home one day in any case. Your father wishes you to be an archer, and so do you. You have another few days to make your decision, for when we reach Easingwold then we will pack our bags, turn around and make this same journey."

"I think I will stay with the company, but I will use the days you have given me to make a sound judgement. I will speak with my father and my mother."

John laughed. "Already you have grown!"

When we reached the pass, the first flurries of snow fell. They did not stick upon the road, but soon they would, and then the pass would be closed. The wagons were empty and we had spare horses. We used our own horses to help pull the empty wagons up the slick slopes made slippery by melting snow and sleet. My men cut down branches from nearby bushes and used them to place under the wheels of the wagons. It was hard work but we were strong, and we negotiated the pass in one day.

We camped at Holmfirth and woke to a white sea of snow. The pass was traversable only by horsemen, and soon it would be closed to those, too. We had barely made it, and it left me with the problem of how to return to Baron Mortimer in the depths of winter.

We were approaching Loidis when Will Yew Tree joined me at the front. He had been largely silent on our journey north and, for the last few miles, I had seen him speaking with Robin of Barnsley who was his closest friend amongst the company. Something troubled him, and I thought I knew what it was. Jack of Lincoln had confided in me that

Will had found a widow who worked in The Feathers. Despite his red nose and cheeks, and the belly which hung over his belt, Will had only seen thirty-two summers. The widow was of an age with him, and I guessed that he was ready to settle down. I was prepared when he spoke.

He was a blunt man, and he came out with his words directly. "Captain, when we reach Easingwold I would stay there." I nodded. "You are not surprised?"

"You have spoken before about your wish to have an alehouse. We have been successful; we profited from the mail, the plate and the warhorse. The men we slew on this journey have added to your funds, so it is no surprise, and I have told all of you that you may leave whenever you chose. Have you enough coins?"

He smiled. "Not yet, but I have a plan. I would speak with our master, for I think he still wishes guards for his wagons. I could seek out archers. I would not be a captain such as you, but I could lead a handful of men."

"Good!"

"You do not mind?"

"I told you after Lewes that any man who chose could leave. You go with my blessing. I shall miss you, for you are a good archer. Who knows, we may come north again when Lord Edward regains what he has lost – his freedom!"

We reached home without any further incident, but we did not leave the next morning as I had initially planned. I realised that would have been unfair on Will and the rest of my men, not to mention Peter. We needed goodbyes. We celebrated as rain and snow lashed down outside. I sat with Geoffrey as men became drunk and laughter and song abounded.

"Will Yew Tree is a good man, sir. He will be able to find other archers, for he has a good eye. If Lord Edward does regain his power then the land will be safer anyway." I was not convinced of my words, for England was filled with greedy men.

Geoffrey nodded. "I shall not need to travel again until after Candlemas anyway. You have earned your pay and more, Captain. I have not lost a single item and, thanks to Baron Mortimer, I received far more for the weapons than I had expected. I am richer for your presence."

"And we are richer for having had home, albeit briefly."

CHAPTER 9

We left the day after the celebration, and it showed as we rode, for my men had thick heads and queasy guts. We now had more than fourteen horses and our war gear, not to mention our spare clothes and treasures were carried upon the horses. We had no route decided upon but, once on the road, John and I decided to go to Nottingham. Jack of Lincoln was convinced that there would be more outlaws willing to leave the forest and join us. The losses we had suffered and Will's departure, allied to the fact that there was now hope that Lord Edward would be freed, meant we needed more men for the company. The forests of Sherwood seemed the best place to find them. "Snow always does that, Captain. The greenwood is bearable in summer, but come winter and snow…" Jack shook his head.

There was little choice for us, in any case. The snows meant that the high passes were ruled out, and that meant passing through Derbyshire or Leicestershire. I just hoped that winter would keep those hunting for us in their castles or occupied in the politics of gaining control of England. However, we were taking a risk; only a fool would willingly go so close to their enemies. We were six such fools and a boy who knew not what he was letting himself in for.

We did not call in at Lincoln. I was convinced that we had been seen there and that had led to the first attack. They might have spies watching for archers. Nor did we visit Nottingham castle and the town. We kept to the smaller towns, which had no castles, and all the time our story remained consistent. We had been hired as guards for wagons, and now that the trading season had ended, we were heading for London to enjoy the pleasures of that city. We had no intention of venturing anywhere near the city, but we had to keep our enemies guessing. They might not be patrolling for us, but we had bloodied their noses too many times for them to forget us.

We used Hucknall Torkard, which lay close to the forest, as our base for the four days we spent seeking archers. We chose it because there was no castle, and the family who dominated the area, the Torkards, were farmers, and so long as men did not cause trouble they were left alone. The outlaws had little to raid close to the town, and the landowners allowed them to take rabbits and the occasional deer. The outlaws did not abuse the privilege.

We found an inn on the road south of the town. When it was not winter, there were many travellers who used it, for Nottingham was expensive as a resting place. We were welcomed. If the landlord wondered why we stayed for three nights, the silver we gave him invited him to keep his suspicions to himself. Jack and John disappeared for two days. They did not take their horses and, when they returned, it was with four men. All were less than twenty summers, and each of them was emaciated. Winter had barely begun, it was just November, and yet already food was scarce.

Jack introduced them one by one. He had not known them before, but he had known where to find them, and his name was known by them and the others who lived in the greenwood. These four had come willingly. Jack later told me that there were others, but they were a little older and had families.

"These, Captain, are the only ones who chose to come with us. I think the rest feared that if they were seen outside the forest then they might risk capture and punishment. This is Geoffrey, son of Martin. I knew Geoffrey's father, for he was also an outlaw. He left our band and was killed last year. Lewis Left Alone is an orphan, taken in by the men of the woods when he had seen just five summers. He would like to see life beyond the trees, for that is all that he has known. William of Matlac had a farm close to his namesake. De Ferrers' men killed his father and took the farm. That was three years since. The rest of William's family perished, but William has the fire of vengeance burning in his heart!"

I nodded, for I could see an angry young man; perhaps he was a little like me with blood to avenge. He would need his anger curbing. I looked over to John, who nodded.

"Finally, this is Mark the Bowyer. His father was also a bowyer, but he was hanged in Leicester by the earl's brother, Henry de Montfort."

I looked at the bow maker. "Why was he hanged?"

"The earl's brother said my father made bows for the outlaws. He did not, but Henry de Montfort had him hanged anyway." He smiled. "So I went and made the best bows that I could for the outlaws. When I heard that you and your archers had fought de Montfort, I knew that I was destined to join you."

I nodded. "I am captain of this company and, if you join us, then you obey me. If you cannot take orders then we will give you food, ale and five silver pennies and you can go on your way. Do any of you wish to take me up on that offer?" They all shook their heads. "We are Lord Edward's archers. We have livery for two of you and, when we can get it, we will have livery made for the other two. When we get to Wigmore Castle, then Baron Wigmore will pay you. Until then your pay will come from the funds we have gathered as a company. You will all need a cloak, but that will have to wait until we find a market town. We have spare weapons; help yourselves to swords and daggers. As for arrows, you will need to learn how to fit bodkins and war arrows. You have used hunting arrows, and our prey is men! Welcome to the company of Gerald War Bow."

Each one of the four was different, and none were like my other men. What they all had in common was the ability to pull a bowstring, but their weakened condition meant they would need fattening up until they could be of use. We redistributed the war gear so that each of them rode. Peter found it amusing that he was no longer the novice rider and that his advice was sought by archers, a couple of whom were little older than he was.

The first part of our journey from Nottingham was fraught with danger, for we had to pass along the road which divided the land of de Ferrers from the land of de Montfort. We avoided every town and used farms that allowed us to pay for the use of their barns. We kept from the main road when we could and took greenways, tracks, even fields. Inevitably we had to use the main road occasionally, and each traveller we met was a potential enemy. Even if they did not know who we were they would talk, and our enemies would hear of a company of archers heading south and west.

We kept the new men in the middle of us. They were still weaker than we were and unused to travelling abroad. Peter proved a godsend, for he rode amongst them chattering like a magpie. Even the dour William of Matlac had to smile at his questions. I hoped that by the time we reached Burton we would have left pursuit behind.

It was not a pursuit that greeted us but a confrontation – and it was my fault. A blizzard blew up as we neared the tiny village of Walton on Trent. There was no inn and no barn. A yeoman told us that if we pushed on to Lichfield, we would find an inn. Lichfield was a cathedral city, but it was not large. The Bishop of Coventry was the lord of the manor and there was no castle. The new men were shivering, and we hurried on through the darkening gloom of a short November day. There was one inn and, when we dismounted, we saw that there were horses stabled there already. There was still room for ours and so, while the horses were stabled, John and I went in to acquire some rooms. There were just two left and neither was large. We would be cosy.

The inn was a popular one and, after we had put our war gear in the rooms, we went down to partake of the food. The landlord was apologetic. "Sorry, but these men have just had the last of our food. We can cook more, but you will have to wait."

I looked and saw there was a group of men wearing the livery of the Templars. They were sergeants at arms and not brother knights. Their eyes narrowed when they saw us, for they knew us not. I remembered that Lord Edward had broken open the gates of the Temple in London and stripped their headquarters of treasure. The Templars were now, most definitely, Montfortian! I did not wish any trouble, and so I smiled and said, "Is there another place you can recommend, landlord?"

He was unhappy at losing the trade but pointed towards the centre of the town. "The Prancing Horse is not bad, but their ale is not a patch on mine!"

"Then when we have eaten, we will return here and give you judgement on your beer."

Once outside we huddled in our cloaks. We would need to buy the new men cloaks at the market before we left in the morning.

John of Nottingham sidled up to me. "I think those archers recognised us as Lord Edward's men."

"How? We are not wearing our livery."

"When we headed to Wales, we rode through a column of them, do you remember? They were heading for London. Lord Edward made some disparaging remarks about them as they passed us. They studied our faces and those of Captain William and his men. The scrutiny we had from those Templars makes me think that they recognised us. Jack of Lincoln has a memorable face, and how many other captains of archers are as young as you?"

He was, of course, correct – we did stand out. I hoped the Templars would be abed before we returned, or perhaps we could avoid the drinking area and go directly to our rooms. I needed no more enemies!

The food in the Prancing Horse was hot and it was filling. That was all that we asked. The beer, too, was adequate, and the meal allowed us to get to know our new archers a little better. William was the quietest of the four, and I could understand why. I had been a little like that, after my father was killed. Men said that I had become less morose and perhaps he would, too. We were going to leave when a sudden flurry of snow drove us to have another jug of ale. Peter, of course, had just watered beer, but he seemed happy to sit and listen to archers speak of their trade.

When we did leave, the snow had stopped, and we crunched on freshly-fallen snow. It was as we reached our inn that we met trouble. Eight of the Templars, with swords in their hands, blocked our way.

The leader stepped towards us. "You did not think we would forget you, did you? Taking off your livery and keeping your bows hidden does not disguise you. You are Gerald War Bow and the captain of Lord Edward's Archers! He dishonoured us, and we will now punish you."

I could smell the ale on his breath. These men had been drinking heavily. I held up my left hand while keeping my right on my sword. "Friend, you do not want to make an enemy of Lord Edward. When he becomes king, you will need him as a friend."

He laughed. "He is in Wallingford Castle, and long may he remain there. We will not kill you, but you have pulled your last bows, for tonight you lose your fingers! At them!"

He thought to take us by surprise, but all the time we had been speaking, my men had been spreading out. I discounted my four new men for they were still weak, and Peter was too young. Eight against six were not normally good odds, but we had a few things going for us. They were mailed, which would slow them down, and we archers were all as good as most men at arms. If you added the fact that we were much stronger, then the odds were about even.

Despite the odds, I felt confident – for the leader said that he only wished to mutilate us. When you fought, you fought to kill! The leader ran at me and swung his sword at my head. Had he hit me then I would have been dead. So much for just punishing me! I sidestepped his swinging blow and brought the flat of my sword to smack hard into the back of his coifed head. He fell as though poleaxed. I spun around, for another ran at me with his sword held in his right hand and his left supporting the blade.

I did the unexpected. The wet snow was slippery, and I hurled my legs at him and slid beneath the blade. With my sword held above me, the blade rapped his knuckles and then slid between his legs. He squealed as my sword sliced into his unprotected flesh. The scream brought burghers to their doors. More, it made the other Templars stop – for John of Nottingham and Jack of Lincoln had laid their enemies cold, and there were now the swords of all my company, including Peter, pointing at them.

137

I pointed my bloody sword at them, too. "You are staying at our inn?" One of them nodded. "Not any longer." I walked over to the sergeant I had laid out and placed my sword's tip into the palm of his hand. "Go and fetch your horses. Do not delay, or your sergeant here will lose the use of his right hand. Pay your bill and leave."

John of Nottingham saw them hesitate. "We are archers, and we are the best. If you come near us again then we will use our bows, and it will not just be bloody cockscombs you will suffer."

One of them shook his head. I guessed that drink had fuelled their decision to hurt us, and now they realised their folly. "Come, we have to be in Leicester tomorrow anyway. Let us go now!"

The sergeant came to; the one who had been sliced along his groin was still moaning, but his wound had been tended to by one of his fellows. The other two had also been raised to their feet. I shifted the sword to point it at the sergeant's throat. "Your men are getting your horses and you will leave. I hope we do not meet again, for if we do then it will go badly for you. It is a long time since you fought in earnest. Enjoy the riches of your order and stay out of politics. You will live much longer."

He gave the slightest of nods. The clip-clop of their horses made me stand back and gesture for the sergeant to rise. They mounted and headed north. We watched them leave and then waited until the muffled sound of the hooves disappeared in the distance.

Mark the Bowyer shook his head. "I would never have believed that archers could take down mailed Templars!"

"They were slow, they were drunk and they were overconfident. By the time you are trained, Mark the Bowyer, then you will think nothing of taking on a man at arms with a sword."

We were not troubled again, and the next day, after buying cloaks and some food in the market, we paid our bill and left. However, I was unhappy for we had been noticed by too many people, and the lands of de Montfort and de Ferrers were very close, still. The Templars were heading for Leicester, and they would report the incident. They would couch it in different words, to make out that we ambushed them. That would preserve their reputation – but they would tell the earl's men of the fight, and we would be sought.

We rode south and west on the freshly fallen snow. We were the only ones attempting the journey, so we rode on virgin snow. John of Nottingham hung back in case we were followed.

We arrived at Wigmore Castle two days later; we had encountered no more enemies. Sir Roger was not at home. He had been summoned to a meeting. It sounded like a secret one, for those at Wigmore Castle were all close-mouthed about it. I knew not where the meeting was held, nor who else was at the meeting.

Surprisingly, Lady Maud invited me to dine with her and her young daughters, Isabella and Margaret. Roger's sons, Ralph and Edmund, were with their father. I was intrigued, for I was a lowly archer and she a high-born lady, but I knew that I was being shown great honour. Lord Edward would never even contemplate dining with an archer. It was fortunate that I had bought some decent clothes, which I wore. I just hoped that I would not make some mistake that would embarrass me.

Lady Maud de Braose came from a long and noble line. Like her husband, she was an implacable enemy of the Welsh, whom she hated with a passion, but she also hated Simon de Montfort and his sons Simon and Henry. Her daughters were old enough to know how to flash their eyes. Both were pretty and soon would be married to powerful men, for that was the way of the world of nobles – Lady Maud kept the two girls in check with a flash of her own eyes. The food we ate might have been good but I tasted nothing, for I thought about each word before

I spoke it. My hostess was a clever woman, and she used her words like weapons to probe, and her eyes searched my face for evidence of lies and untruths. I believe that, had it been allowed, she could have donned mail and fought alongside her husband. Certainly, she knew about war and, surprisingly, she also knew of me. We made talk about the weather and the journey we had made from the north. She raised her eyebrows when I told her of the encounter with the Templars. The food came and went. A single servant poured our wine and ensured that the other servants brought in the platters when we needed them. We finished with cheese.

"Yours is an interesting story, Captain. To command not only a company of archers but archers belonging to the next King of England is intriguing. Did I hear that you saved Lord Edward's life in Poitou?"

"Yes, my lady. It cost my friend his life, but it gained me this position."

"And you led archers in the battles in Poitou as well as against the Welsh?" I nodded. "I hate the Welsh but I know that they are good archers. Men say Gerald War Bow is better."

I shrugged. "I have a good eye and a good arm. My bow is the best, and I find archery easier than most men."

"And you have not answered my question."

"I did not know you had asked one, my lady. Forgive me, I am just a simple archer who is unused to such surroundings."

She laughed. "You are anything but simple." She turned to her daughters. "You two have made eyes enough at Captain Gerald. Go to your rooms and pray to God to help you become less vain, for vanity is a sin!"

They both nodded and said, in unison, "Yes, my lady!" They left without a murmur. Lady Maud ruled the castle and, I suspected, her husband too.

She had her servant pour us wine and then dismissed him. "My girls have good taste. You are a handsome fellow although the stitches give you a roguish look. I will have the doctor remove them, for I think you are more handsome without them."

She studied me. I was uncomfortable, for it was the sort of attention a wolf gave a sheep before it pounced. "I think I can trust you. In fact, we have to trust you, for you are vital to our plans to rescue Lord Edward." She had put into words that which I suspected. "What I tell you this night is between us alone. Do not tell your men. Not yet, anyway."

"They are clever men, my lady. They may discover…" I waved a hand, "…whatever it is that I am to do."

"Of course. You deserve to know our reasoning." She drank some wine and then, placing the goblet on the table, spoke again. "You, Gerald War Bow, can go where we cannot. You can hide in woods. You can sneak into a castle. We would have you go into Wallingford and tell Lord Edward that we are planning his escape."

"Is that not a little vague, my lady? Escape how? And when?"

"You are clever but fear not, all will be in place soon. My husband is, even now, making arrangements."

"Wallingford is many miles from here, my lady."

"It is more than a hundred, and the situation is not ideal, but we work with what we have. With snow on the ground, we cannot attempt anything. As much as it pains us, we cannot see this plan succeeding before March."

"Then we will be sitting here, being paid without having to do any work."

She snorted. It was not a particularly ladylike act. "Money? This is not about money; this is about who rules England, and we would have the rightful king and his son, not some pious, self-serving, failed crusader who wishes to rule without the right! Do not worry about money. You will earn it when the time comes."

I shook my head. "My men and I are unconcerned about money. We were well paid for our last job, and we just wish our lord to be freed. We are Lord Edward's archers, but it does not sit well to take the money and not earn it."

"You are an interesting young man."

She seemed reluctant to end the conversation, and we spoke until the jug of wine was empty and she summoned her ladies to take her to bed. She held her hand out for me to kiss; I had never touched hands as soft.

I retired feeling bemused. I had spoken at length to a lady for the first time in my life. I was surprised, for she seemed little different to many of the strong women I had met when growing up. Ada and Gurtha had been made of rougher cloth, but they still had the same steel in their eyes. I still remembered with fondness the two old women who had lived in the Welsh woods close to me and my father. Called witches by some, I had found them to be kindness personified.

We spent the next morning making our new quarters comfortable. The castle was not large, but they had a good warrior hall. The sergeant who had shown us to the hall had indicated which part we were to use, and though it was not as large as it should have been, it would do. We stored our arrows close to our beds, for they were important to us. We made sure that the horses were comfortable. Peter would see to them each day, but there was an ostler too, and a horse master, Alan of Ludlow. He showed his knowledge when he stroked Eleanor. "A fine courser. I am intrigued how you came to own her."

"Knights and gentlemen may ride such fine horses, but my bodkin arrows can pluck them from their backs; the fortunes of war. Knights take for ransom; we take to live." He nodded.

We had donned the livery of Lord Edward when we rose, and our next task was to seek clothes for our four new archers. We found a seamstress, a widow who lived in the village. She was able to make what we needed, but we would have to buy the cloth from Ludlow. It was just eight miles away and held a market twice a week.

I realised that the freedom we had enjoyed in Easingwold would be lacking. We would have to ask Lady Mortimer's permission. That turned out to be easier than I expected. When I asked her, she looked pleased. "I need to visit the market, and the men at arms who guard our home are dullards! We will go on Friday," she said.

I discovered that Lady Maud could ride, as could her daughters, and we were not held up. The snow had stopped falling but the land was a blanket of white. The roads were slushy black lines that snaked through the snow. When we had arrived, both times, Castle Wigmore had been cloaked in either night or wet. The clear day now afforded me the opportunity to see its position. It stood on a high piece of ground in the hills which rose, like main defences, towards Wales.

Lady Maud saw me turning and smiled. "Aye, the Welsh are close. Many people wonder why, with Ludlow so close, our castle is needed. The reason is simple: it is the Welsh who wish to reclaim this land, and their king is our implacable foe. Lord Edward should have finished what he started when he went into north Wales and ended their threat. You will earn your money, archer, if the Welsh choose to do that which they always do and raid during the depths of winter. They like to eat mutton, and our sheep are easier to take than they are to breed."

As we approached the castle of Ludlow, she pointed to it. "There is no lord at the moment." She leaned over to speak quietly to me. "I have hopes that when King Henry is secure once more then my husband may be given it. The castle and hall are much more comfortable."

"My lady, if there is no lord then who guards the walls?" I saw that they had new town walls.

"The men of Ludlow. It was they who applied for the right to have a wall, and they pay murage. They are good men and, in times of danger, we help each other." This was a noble who understood the need to have the ordinary people on her side. She was the antithesis of King Henry, who seemed to simultaneously fear and disparage the commoners.

I stayed with the ladies and kept Jack of Lincoln with me. I gave a purse of coins to John of Nottingham, and he and the other archers bought that which we needed. I was able to see the effect Lady Maud had, as she swept through the town. It was as though the Queen had come to Ludlow. There was much bowing and scraping, but there appeared to be no rancour about it.

While she chatted to some ladies of the town, the owner of the shop confided in me. "You are new here, archer?" I nodded. "People are very fond of Lady Maud. Her family, the de Braose family, have always kept us safe from the Welsh. You will find that you will earn your crust here."

I was learning that the Welsh were feared even more here than they had been along the Clwyd. Here, the rebellion was a distraction that made the lives of the people more parlous. We rode back with laden horses. We had bought some spare cloaks, for I knew that we would need them as we headed west, and it was confirmed when an icy wind blew into our faces. Our cowls and hoods were pulled tightly over our heads. Winter would be harsh here. Along the Clwyd, there had always been temperate air from the sea, while here, we were in the heart of the land.

As we rode back, I learned of Lady Maud's hatred of de Montfort. It seemed he had slighted her family, and she was not one to forgive. Simon de Montfot had made the mistake of not going to the aid of Lady Maud's father, and as that had cost the Braose family money, the grudge was born. The fact that he was French also seemed to make her angry – that her family came from Norman stock seemed irrelevant! She told me of the punishment she would inflict on de Montfort if she was the king. "His actions are nothing less than treasonous! I would have him hanged, drawn and quartered. I would have his head on the walls of the Tower until all flesh was gone and even then, I would leave it there as a reminder to all of the folly of treason. He is a foreigner, an intruder, and he seeks to undermine the king and his realm!"

I suspected that her punishment would be to avenge the insult her family had suffered rather than the slight to the king.

Baron Mortimer did not return to us until the first week in December. By then all of my men wore good livery, and we had settled into a routine. We took our share of the watches. Once the baron returned that duty became less arduous, as there were more men available.

I had come to know the garrison. It was smaller than I had expected. There were just four archers and four men at arms under the command of an old sergeant, Walter. Sir Roger had another four men at arms with him. Our arrival meant that the garrison had almost doubled. Our offer to share the watches meant the garrison accepted us as friends rather than intruders. I wondered about the armour we had brought and discovered that the plate was for the baron and his sons, while the hauberks had been for the men at arms. I shuddered to think how the garrison would have managed if they had been forced to fight in a battle against de Montfort. I discovered that Sir Roger previously had a much larger company, but they had died at Lewes.

If I expected to be summoned as soon as he arrived, I was to be disappointed. He smiled at me and welcomed me to the castle, but he did not tell me anything more. I knew he had been to speak with other royal supporters, which explained his lengthy absence and I knew, from my words with Lady Maud, that I was part of a plan to rescue Lord Edward, but he spoke not a word to me.

Perhaps it was the imminent arrival of the Christmas celebrations, or it might have been that their plans were not yet set in stone. Whatever the reason, I was left with the worry about the task which I knew awaited me – but my men enjoyed the celebration that was Christmas.

CHAPTER 10

The Welsh struck in the first week of January. They raided the farms that lay to the south and west of us. Refugees reached us late one day. I was not on duty but was summoned along with Walter. Baron Mortimer looked angry and Lady Maud, murderous.

An older man with a bandage around his head was the spokesman for those who sought refuge in the castle. "The Welsh have taken animals from our farms. We ride tomorrow. I wish to be on the road before dawn. Every man rides!"

Walter said, "Who will protect the castle, my lord?"

Lady Maud snorted. "You are an old fool, Walter, do you think we cannot defend our castle against the Welsh? We have Gerald War Bow's boy, Peter, we have the servants and Alan the horse master. You just recapture the animals and kill all the Welsh that you can!"

Walter recoiled under her torrent, and I saw Sir Roger and his sons smile. "Yes, my lady, I will go to the men."

I turned to leave but Lady Maud said, "Stay a moment, Gerald." I stopped. "You should know that Builth Castle, whence the raiders rode, belonged to my family. One day, we shall own it again. I believe that you were sent to us for a purpose. You lead our archers, and tomorrow you will show the Welsh that we can now match their archers!"

The baron said, "They will have left clear tracks in the snow, and they will move slowly. It will take them all day to reach Builth. You and your archers should catch them and hold them until we can reach them with our men at arms."

"Are your archers mounted, too, my lord?"

"Aye, but their horses are not the equal of yours. They will keep up with you or I will know the reason why."

I was dismissed. It was interesting that my main orders had come from her, and not her husband.

I told my archers what was needed. Peter was both upset at being left behind and excited at the prospect of guarding the ladies. Jack of Lincoln laughed, "It would take a brave Welshman to beard the formidable Lady Maud."

He was right. "Tom, you will be the scout tomorrow. Take William of Matlac with you." I remembered the fate of Stephen Green Feather. It was always better to have two scouts. I also needed to improve the skills of my new men, and this would be a start. The archers of Wigmore castle were bowmen, rather than archers. They did not use the war bow and none had a sword. They had helmets and they had leather, metal studded jerkins. That might help them to survive. I told John of Nottingham the four of them would ride at the rear.

I did not get much sleep, for I had much to plan. I rose before dawn and, waking the others, headed for the stable. The horse master was there already, feeding oats to the horses. "There is no grazing out there, Captain, and this cold saps energy. You have a long day ahead of you."

I nodded and pointed to our saddles. "We each have a bag of oats for just such a day. We care for our horses, horse master."

"I can see that you do. The castle archers you have with you will be riding poor horses. They only ride occasionally, and the horses they have are at the end of their lives."

My heart sank. They would struggle to keep up with us. As soon as my men had all arrived, we mounted. The four garrison archers struggled even to mount. I rode over to Evan, who was the senior archer. "Time is of the essence today. If you fall back then just follow our trail. The baron and the men at arms will be along soon enough, but we have to catch the Welsh quickly."

"Aye, Captain. It will not be for want of trying, but these horses…"

I nodded. "I know. The horse master has spoken."

It was dark when we left, but the snow gave some light, and we were able to follow the trail left by the refugees who had fled to the castle. We found the first farm that had been raided; it had been ransacked and the farmer slain. The trail led to the next farm, and then the next. Each farm had been systematically looted, and every old animal had been butchered; we found the bones and skins. The farm dogs had been slaughtered.

I had studied a map at the castle when I first arrived. It was a crude one, but I noticed that Builth lay to the west by south-west, rather than the south and west course we were following. I guessed they would sweep around in an arc and head back to Builth along the road.

"Tom, let us head more west by south and see if we can cut them off. Follow the trail they took to reach here." There was a trail which led across country, and with snow on the ground it would be as fast as the slippery cobbles of the road.

Evan said, "You are the captain, but if you lose them, then the wrath of Baron Mortimer will be terrifying to see."

"As you say, I am the captain! You four wait here and tell the baron what we intend."

It meant we could now travel faster, and I was sure that I had made the right decision. We were rewarded an hour later when, after following their trail, we found their campfire. It was still warm, and the trail that led from it could be clearly seen. They had raided and then camped here. A trail of animal dung and footprints led due west towards the road. "Tom, go carefully and use your ears. They are afoot, and if we can catch them, they will not escape. Our task is to hold them!"

"Aye, Captain."

The animals were not co-operating with the Welsh. I could see they had some cows with them, which had wandered off into the trees before returning to the trail. It was clearly cows, judging by their dung and their hoofprints. We descended a little and passed through tilled fields. I was not sure where the Welsh border lay, but suspected we were close to it. We did not see any farms so there could not be many people around.

Tom and William awaited us when we finally reached the road. "Captain, they are a little way ahead of us. They have armed men at the rear. We can catch them now, for I am guessing they are less than a mile up the road."

"Robin, you wait here for the baron." I saw that the fields to the right of us and the road were flat, but there was a piece of dead ground about a hundred paces from the road. "We will ride along the dead ground and try to get ahead of them and hold them up. String your bows!"

The bows had not been used for some time, as we had enjoyed little opportunity for practice. It was reassuringly hard to string them. I hung mine from my saddle. Robin nodded and I took the lead. Tom had been the scout, but now it was my turn to lead.

The snow was virgin and absorbed the sound of our hooves. The ride kept us warm, but I suspected the Welsh would be colder. Their feet would be in contact with the cold ground; cold would rise through thinly-soled boots and shoes, and they were moving at the slow pace of cattle and sheep. The ground to our left rose, and I realised that the dead ground was leading us to a shallow valley with a stream or small river at the bottom. When we reached it, I saw that it flowed towards the road, and that meant either a bridge or a ford. More importantly, it meant the animals would stop. They always did when there was water.

We waded across the stream, and I led us across the slope in an oblique line. I knew that we risked the Welsh spotting us, but it did not matter now. We could cut off their escape, for we were on the Welsh side of the river. Eleanor laboured up the slope, as the snow was thicker. She and the other horses could rest once we reached the road. We would dismount to fight.

There was a hedgerow along the road which meant we had to seek a gate. Once on the road, I turned to head back to the crossing over the water. The steam from our horses would be visible to the Welsh, but they might think that we were their own men, for we were approaching from the Builth side. We turned a bend and I saw the Welsh and their animals. They were 300 paces from us and approaching the stream. They saw me and I heard them shout. I dismounted and, tying Eleanor to a tree, took out a handful of oats to feed her as my men also dismounted. The Welsh approached slowly and we had time to prepare.

I chose a war arrow and peered towards the Welsh. There were more than thirty of them, all armed. I saw some with bows while others had spears and swords. Most had helmets, and those without bows had shields. My guess was that these were not brigands but served a Welsh lord who had sent them on this chevauchée. The Welsh stopped when they saw the line of men at the top of the slope.

"A stand-off, eh Captain?"

"Not for long, David, the baron and his men at arms will come soon, and we will seem an easier prospect than mailed men. For the moment, we watch."

I saw a debate going on amongst the Welsh, but while the leaders debated close to the old bull and four cows they had captured, I saw ten Welsh archers head towards the road. I pointed my bow. "There are our first targets. Spread yourselves out and choose a Welshman to hit."

We had the advantage of height and the fact that we were on the road. Already, the snow had turned to slush beneath our boots, and I was glad that I had paid for better boots. The Welsh archers were struggling through the snow which was knee deep in places, and they congregated towards the road where the snow was thinner. The ford was 180 paces from us, within our range. In the distance I heard a horn, which told me the baron had reached Robin and was letting me know.

The Welsh archers hurried as they heard the horn, for they knew what it meant, and I shouted, "Loose!"

The Welsh leaders then took their knives and slew the bull and the cows. It was a vindictive act to deny us their milk and offspring. It hardened my heart. I had intended to wound the Welsh archer, but now, I aimed for his chest. He was pulling back on his bow when my arrow threw him to the ground.

My archers had also aimed well. Two Welshmen had taken shelter behind a tree, and as soon as they emerged, they were dead men. I saw the baron and our men galloping down the road. The sheep fled in panic at the sound of the hooves, getting in the way of the Welshmen, who were heading for the road. They flooded over the ford, but there was little order or organisation to their flight; they were just escaping the mounted men. Mounted men at arms, not to mention the baron, his squire and his two sons, all of whom were armed as knights, were a daunting prospect.

I ignored the archers who had crossed and aimed at the leader who had ordered the slaying of the bull. My arrow hit him but did not stop him. He wore mail beneath his tunic. Cursing myself for my poor choice of arrowhead, I drew a needle bodkin. He was now less than a hundred paces from me. I saw his bearded faced beneath his round helmet. He looked on his death as the arrow sped down to tear through his mail, into his chest and out of his back.

I took another bodkin. If one man had mail then the others might too. I sent an arrow at the man next to the dead leader. He had a shield and was urging his men on. They were falling like flies as my men sent arrow after arrow into men struggling up either a slush-filled road or wading through knee deep snow. My arrow hit him in the neck and even though he had a coif, he fell. Men grabbed shields from the dead to defend themselves as the baron and his horsemen tore into them.

Behind me, Lewis Left Alone shouted, "Captain, I hear horsemen behind us."

They had to be Welshmen and were probably from the castle. "Turn, and have bodkins ready!" The baron and his men would have to deal with the raiders. This was a more serious threat. "Follow me and spread out behind whatever cover you can find!"

We ran back to the horses and stood beyond them on the Builth Castle road. I saw the horsemen. There were eight of them and they were men at arms, led by a knight. I picked out a bodkin. The Welsh knight shouted something and lowered his spear. He held his shield tightly to his body. He was not helped by the slushy nature of the road which meant his horse's hooves slithered and slipped on the surface. I waited until he was seventy paces from me before shouting, "Release!"

My bodkin hit him in the left shoulder. He dropped his shield to expose his side, which Mark the Bowyer sent an arrow into. His quick-thinking squire, who had managed to avoid being hit, grabbed the knight's reins and led him back up the road. Four of the horsemen followed him, but two others lay dead. One had been hit by four bodkin arrows.

"John, take the new men and keep watch here. The rest with me!"

By the time we reached our first position, the battle was over and the baron was disposing of the wounded. I turned and headed back to the dead men at arms. "Search the bodies and collect the horses. It is over and we can go home!"

I truly thought it was over, but it was not. The baron and his sons rode up to me, his face effused with the joy of victory. The enemy had been routed and most of the animals recovered, but the smile left him when he saw that Welsh nobles had led their men against us. "We have been too gentle with our foes. There are four Welsh farms between here and our castle. We will take payment for the cattle killed! The Welsh will have the hard winter, not my people."

And so we rode, not directly home but along a small road which passed the four farms which were in Wales. We had little to do save to watch. He and his men at arms, as well as his four archers, took every animal and sack of grain the farmers owned. When one farmer objected, the baron's sons beat him. It was unnecessary. I had grown up around people like the Welsh farmers. What had been done to the baron's people was bad, but this was worse, for it was entirely vindictive. We drove the cattle, sheep and fowl back to Wigmore Castle. Darkness fell, but by then we were back on the baron's land and a road which was dark against the white snow.

The baron asked one of his men to fetch me as we neared the castle.

"You did particularly well, Captain, although it was dangerous to anticipate the Welsh route. What would you have done if you had failed to find them?"

"I knew we would find them, but if they had evaded me, we would have been closer to the Welsh castle. My way was the only way to catch them and retrieve the animals."

He nodded and watched my face. "You disapproved of my actions with the Welsh farmers?"

"It has nothing to do with me, my lord."

"You would not have done what I did?" I remained silent. He sighed. "We live on the border here. You have seen my garrison. It is small, and more often than not the Welsh are able to raid at will. Our people have suffered greatly in the past. Simon de Montfort's rebellion has taken men away from the border, and what happened yesterday is a foretaste of what might happen more regularly. I lost men at Lewes who might have defended this land against the Welsh. When you have lived here longer, then you will understand."

I said nothing, but I doubted I would be there for long. As soon as Lord Edward was rescued, then I would return to his service. Until then I would follow orders, but I would not enjoy them.

We feasted well, and then the snow began to melt. It was a gradual process. The air did not seem any warmer but it must have been. The melting snow brought more misery, for the castle wards were turned into mud baths, and it was hard to keep anything clean. Worse, we still could not ride to Wallingford, as the roads to the south of us were still affected by snow. We practised. We used the butts, and we worked each day to improve our skills. When our shoulders ached, we used our swords. The men at arms of Wigmore were, at first, sceptical about our sword skills, but when I laid two on their backs in my first bouts, they changed their opinion. The baron's two sons were also interested in the bouts, and they joined us. Both were strong youths and had skill.

The damp months of January and February passed productively. Over those weeks Baron Mortimer began to hire men at arms to replace those he had lost at Lewes. The mood in the land was changing, and men who had hidden now emerged, and swords for hire sought a lord behind whose banner they could fight. Baron Mortimer went around his manors to speak with the knights who lived there. He was preparing them for war, too.

I was not invited to dine again, but Lady Maud made a point of speaking to me every couple of days. I could see that I intrigued her. It was partly due to my age, for I was just four or five years older than her sons, but while they were still boys, I must have appeared mature. I deduced that from the way she spoke to me, as she seemed to enjoy confiding in me. It was from her that I learned that I would be riding to Wallingford in the first week of March. I was to find my way into the castle and try to speak with Lord Edward to tell him that we had plans to free him. I knew it was risky, but it had been almost a year since his capture, and there had been no attempt to rescue him. Lady Maud, her husband and the other lords thought the time was ripe.

The real reason for the decision became clear when Gilbert de Clare, the Earl of Gloucester, came to visit. He had changed sides and was now an enemy of de Montfort. He arrived at the castle after dark, and cloaked. He was disguising the fact that he had turned coat. I only knew of his arrival when I was summoned to his presence, as it was a secret meeting. Two of the baron's most senior men guarded the door. Inside were just the earl, the baron and Lady Maud. This was, indeed, clandestine.

Gilbert de Clare was a dangerous man. His support of Simon de Montfort had enabled the Earl of Leicester to defeat King Henry at Lewes. I liked not the fact that he had changed sides, but I was merely an archer, and my avowed intent was to rescue my lord and return to his service. The fact that he was the same age as I unnerved me a little, though he seemed pleased to see me.

"This is the man then, the famous archer? I would say he appears little more than a boy, but I know men say that behind *my* back. Can you do it, archer? Can you get inside an enemy castle and deliver a message to Lord Edward? Can you help effect his escape?"

"So far, my lord, I have been told little other than I have to get into an enemy castle and speak with Lord Edward without anyone knowing, and then escape. What do I need to tell him?"

I spoke in a matter of fact voice. I saw Lady Maud smile, and then the Red Earl burst out laughing. "Well he has a sense of humour, I will say that for him."

The baron said, "You are right to mock us, Gerald. I know that we ask much of you, but all who know you speak highly of you. Your fame precedes you."

"And that fame will make it hard for me to enter the castle, for many men know my face, my lord. However, leaving that aside, I take it that I do not enter the castle merely to chat to Lord Edward? I assume that there is a plan?"

The baron nodded. "We believe that he is allowed to ride each day with Henry of Almain and a company of guards. We wish him to do so every day for a period of, perhaps, seven days. Each day he should ride a little further so that by the eighth day the horses will be tired. We will have fresh horses ready, and we will know their route, for we will have watched for seven days. You and your archers will ensure that when he escapes, there is no pursuit."

I nodded. It was an audacious plan, but it had merit, and I saw how it could succeed. "So, Lord Edward would determine when the rescue will take place?"

"That is the beauty of it." He patted his wife's hand. "And it is all from the mind of Lady Maud. The hard part, as you so rightly say, is getting into the castle. How will you do it?"

"To speak truly, I do not know yet, but then I have not seen Wallingford. I would need to scout out the castle and take a couple of days to formulate a plan. I should go now, and then I can return here and tell you what I have devised." They all agreed it was a sound plan. "I will take just three of my men, for it needs to be done in secret, and a larger number would merely attract attention."

"You have thought this out well, archer. I can see that your choice was a wise one. I confess that I thought I had made a wise choice when I sided with de Montfort, but he is a damned Frenchman who rewards only his family and his French friends. I was a fool to believe in him!"

I now had a better insight into the reason for the Earl of Gloucester's change of coat.

I told my men that I would be leaving. The three men I chose to accompany me were obvious: John of Nottingham, Jack of Lincoln and David the Welshman. Leaving Robin of Barnsley in command, we left on the last day of February. It was over a hundred miles to the castle, but we had company until Gloucester, as Gilbert de Clare accompanied us. He seemed keen to talk, mainly about my service with Lord Edward. He seemed fascinated by the future King of England.

As we neared his town I said, "My lord, I hope you do not take offence, but you seem to admire greatly a man you fought."

"It was not him I fought against. Do not forget that Lord Edward once also favoured Simon de Montfort, the Frenchman and his honeyed words that deceived the two of us. It was his father I fought. I had lands taken, and I petitioned to have them returned to me. King Henry rejected my petition. To speak bluntly, I would have Lord Edward as King of England in a heartbeat, but that is not the way it works. His father, faults and all, is still the king. I will have to hope that you rescue him, and that I can persuade him to have his father return my lands."

CHAPTER 11

It was easier riding once we parted, for we travelled quicker, and I did not have to worry about my words. We only had swords and two bows with us, though I did not think we would need them. It was another reason for my choice of men – these three could handle themselves in a fight. We had a story already: we were heading for Southampton to take ship for Gascony. Men were always needed to fight over there. I had a purse to pay for inns, and we wore simple garb which did not identify us as Lord Edward's men. I had allowed my beard to grow as a result of the wound to my face; I did not like the beard and I would have shaved it off were it not for this task, but now it provided an effective disguise as it hid my face and made me look a little older. It had been a risk taking Jack of Lincoln, for he had his split nose, but there were many such men in England.

We found an inn at Brightwell. There had been a castle there, but Henry II had pulled it down and there was no longer a lord of the manor living in the village. We were just one mile from Wallingford. We feigned an injury to Jack of Lincoln, so the innkeeper did not seem suspicious about our remaining there for three days while he 'recovered'. It gave us the opportunity to travel the area.

I went with David the Welshman towards the castle, having left my sword in the inn. I would not gain the castle through force of arms. I needed a cunning plan, for I was not sure how I would gain access. We could stay another two or three days and not arouse suspicion. I decided that the first day we would merely scout and try to discover weaknesses in the castle's defences; we were not trying to storm the walls but sneak inside.

The innkeeper had said there was a town close to the castle although the Black Death, which had arrived in the town sixteen years earlier, had decimated the population. He told me there was an inn. I made up a story about a fictitious friend who might have served in the garrison as an excuse to visit.

My plan had been to go into the town and drink; that way we could talk and then go outside to marvel at the magnificent castle, which had been a bastion of Matilda in the anarchy. Men at arms and archers were renowned for their appetite for drink, and they might let something slip whilst in their cups. However, as we neared the castle and town, that plan changed. There was a great deal of activity, and the gates of the castle were wide open. Not only that, there were people moving freely between the town and the castle. It was too good an opportunity to miss.

"David, I will try to get into the castle. Follow me as though you do not know me. Go to the alehouse and drink."

"Are you sure, Captain? If you are taken prisoner then it will not help Lord Edward."

I understood his concern, but we had been sent an opportunity, and it would have been foolish to ignore it. "I will be careful, but this plan necessitates my gaining entry, and this looks to be the best way."

He nodded and I hurried ahead towards the town. I saw men toiling with sacks, boxes and barrels. They were carrying them into the castle.

To me, it looked as though they were preparing for a siege. I saw a man carrying six live fowl. He was struggling to control them, and they were batting him with their wings as they tried to escape. I daresay that, stupid though they were, they had enough sense to know that they were going to their doom.

I was just ten paces from him when two of them escaped his grasp. They landed and, having had their wings clipped so that they could not fly away, ran back towards the town. I whipped off my cloak and threw it over them. In the dark, they stopped, and I was able to grab the cloak and wrap them within.

The man smiled and transferred one fowl so that he held two in each hand. "Thank you, friend. If you would carry them with me to the castle kitchens there is a beaker of ale for you in the tavern in the town."

"There is no payment necessary, for I am bound for the castle anyway. I seek my cousin."

"Then this is well met."

A suspicious sentry saw my cloak as we approached. "What is this, Rafe? What does your friend hide in the cloak?" There was an obliging cluck from within and the sentry grinned. "Ah, I see your friend knows how to transport hens! Pass."

And with that, we were in. God smiled on our venture, and I said a silent prayer of thanks for the simple ruse which had allowed me inside the outer ward of the castle.

Of course God smiled on us, for I was helping the son of the appointed king! I asked, once we were in the outer ward, "What goes on this day?"

"I know not save that the castellan asked for food and drink as a host of mighty lords and princes arrive later today."

The sentries at the inner ward appeared quite relaxed and lounged against the walls of the inner ward; they appeared to be looking inward rather than outward. As we went through the gate towards the keep and the kitchens, I began to look for Lord Edward.

At the gate, the scrutiny was also on those emerging. That made sense, as they would not want Lord Edward walking out with the tradesmen. There appeared to be little security in the inner ward, and I wondered if they were preparing for the feast. I was intrigued. A man, probably the steward, with a wax tablet, stood at the door to the kitchen, presumably checking off the items as they arrived. He looked at the man now identified as Rafe, and frowned. "There are supposed to be six fowl."

Rafe said, "My friend here has them in his cloak."

Seemingly satisfied he said, "Take them through the far door. Abelard will butcher them."

The kitchen was a maelstrom of activity. People who had come before us were placing their goods on tables and hanging them from hooks suspended from the ceiling. We had to squeeze through past an innkeeper who had just delivered a barrel of ale. He nodded to Rafe. "Another two barrels and I am done."

"I hope you have some left, John, I owe my friend here a beaker."

The man leaned in and said conspiratorially to Rafe, "The stuff I have delivered is not of my best. It is young Simon de Montfort who arrives, and he will drink wine. The beer is for their servants and soldiers. *They* matter not!"

We entered the butcher's room, and I saw that the ale cellar steps led down from it. The butcher looked up from the haunch of venison he was jointing and recognised Rafe. "Fowl?"

Rafe nodded.

"I will deal with them now, for we have no cages in which to keep them. This was hurriedly arranged. We only discovered that we had to cook for thirty guests yesterday. Thank the Good Lord that they leave on the morrow!"

I was intrigued. Young Simon de Montfort had been captured at Northampton by Lord Edward. Had he come to gloat? If so, he had waited a long time to do so.

Rafe said, "Friend, give him yours first, you have been of invaluable service to me."

I reached under the cloak and grabbed one by the neck. Drawing it out, I handed it to the butcher, who grabbed it in one hand and brought the cleaver down with the other. He held it for a while and grinned. "Some of these lose their heads and do not know they are dead!" He laid down the carcass and I handed him the second. That was dispatched as quickly.

Rafe said, "When you have completed your business, I will see you in the inn."

I draped the cloak over my arm and squeezed out of the room as a second barrel of ale was brought to the cellar, slipping out unnoticed by the steward, who turned to direct a man carrying onions to the vegetable store.

Once in the inner ward, I pressed myself against the wall so that I could not be seen from the door of the kitchen. The sentries on the walls were not looking within the ward, and I scanned it. There were stables, and men were entering and leaving. There were four men guarding the gate to the hall, as well as four at the gate leading to the outer ward, scrutinising the tradesmen leaving the castle. It looked hopeless – and then I spied Lord Edward and Henry Almain as they left the stables.

They were walking, and appeared to have no guards, although I saw the four men at the gate stare at them. They were under scrutiny. If they headed for the hall then all was lost, for there was no way I could gain entry there. I began to move directly to them. If I could, then I would attract the attention of Lord Edward. My plan to speak with him had involved hiding in the grounds and then finding his chamber which would, no doubt, be guarded. Now that I was in the castle I could see the plan was doomed to fail before it had begun.

Then, I realised that Lord Edward and his cousin were not heading for the hall, but for the wall of the inner ward. Lord Edward was a bundle of energy; he enjoyed exercise. I assumed that he had been forbidden to ride this day and was walking around the walls instead. I had a chance.

I turned to head obliquely for the gate leading from the inner ward. I had to time my approach so that I was near them when they were far enough away from the four guards at the gate. As the two prisoners approached the gate, I saw the four guards stiffen. They only relaxed when the two had passed. They were now thirty paces from me, and I saw Lord Edward look up at me as I was nearing them. Recognition dawned on his face. Despite my beard, I had not changed enough to fool someone who knew me well. He said something to Henry of Almain, and they slowed. I saw Henry sit on the edge of a water trough and take off his boot.

Lord Edward grinned when I neared him. He spoke to me, although it was quietly done. "You have given me hope, Gerald War Bow!"

"Lord, I must be quick. There is a plan to rescue you!" I quickly gave him the plan, acutely aware that the four guards at the gate were watching us. Even while I was speaking, I knew that I would need to concoct a story to get by them, or I could be incarcerated too.

"That is a good plan, but we must hold it in abeyance. Simon de Montfort's son comes this night, and tomorrow I am to be taken to London. There, we will be in the Tower."

Henry Almain had donned his boot and moved towards us.

"Have my friends keep watch. While I am in the Tower I cannot escape, but if I am moved then we put this plan into operation." I nodded and he smiled. "Thank you, Gerald, for your loyalty. It will not be forgotten, nor will the ills we have suffered. Tell those who plan this that I mistrust many of my nobles, but you I trust. If I do not see you when I am rescued then I will not go, for I will fear a trap."

Henry Almain said, "You had better go, archer, the guards are suspicious."

I headed for the gate and saw the four guards fingering their weapons. I had decided to play the country bumpkin. The sergeant drew his dagger and placed it at my throat. "Harry, search him and his cloak."

As the cloak was taken from me and hands groped me, I adopted an astonished expression. "What is wrong, sir? I have delivered fowl to the steward."

"And what were you saying to the prisoner?"

I grinned, making myself look simple. "Sir, I know that you great soldiers get to meet lords all the time, but I am a poor yeoman. How many times will I get the chance to meet the future King of England? When I get back to my village I will drink for a month on the strength of these stories!"

The man called Harry shook his head when he had searched me. The dagger was withdrawn and the sergeant asked me, "What did he say to you?"

I screwed up my face and said, "That is the strange thing, sir, he sought my opinion. He asked me what the ordinary men thought of the way his father, the king, had been treated."

The sergeant's eyes narrowed. "And what did you tell him?"

I shrugged. "That we thought what our lords told us, for to do else would be foolish."

He nodded and gestured for me to leave. "If you come back here, I will be watching for you."

I grinned again. "Do not worry, sir. When I have had the ale I am due in the tavern, I will head home while the story is still fresh in my head. I would tell my father the words Prince Edward used!"

The sergeant laughed. "He is not a prince and will never be a king. The days of kings in this land are over!"

I had to go to the alehouse, for to do other would have aroused suspicion. The man called Rafe was waiting for me within. "Did you find your cousin?"

I spied David in the corner and shook my head so that he would not try to join me, then turned my signal to David into a negative answer to the fowl man. "He was sent ahead to London. A shame, for I hoped he might get me a position at the castle."

"And tomorrow the castle will just have a tiny garrison. You came too late, my friend, for it has been well garrisoned since last summer. What will you do?"

"Head for London! It seems that is where men gather now."

"Aye, the Earl of Leicester rules this land now, and he has the support of the men of London. You do right, friend."

When the ale was done, I left. I was just 300 paces from the alehouse when David caught up with me. "Well, Captain?"

I told him and he said, "Then this was a wasted journey."

"The opposite, for Lord Edward thinks he will be moved from the Tower eventually, and when he is then this plan succeeds. We will have to stay one more day, but then Jack can have a miraculous recovery and we return to Wigmore Castle."

We were still heading for the village of Brightwell when we heard the arrival of the young de Montfort. He was enjoying his moment, for he had banners, heralds and a veritable wagon train with him. I knew not why the castellan had laid in supplies, for it looked as though Simon de Montfort had brought enough to feed the county.

We left the next day and, with brightening skies, rode harder than we had when we headed west. It was with some surprise that we met the Earl of Gloucester and his household knights. They were heading towards the London road. He reined in but waved away all of his men and mine. I would tell my men all, that was my way, but the earl was a plotter and a secretive man.

"What have you learned, archer?" He was blunt to the point of rudeness.

I told him of the imminent departure of Lord Edward and he looked downcast. "So, it all begins to make sense. I was summoned to Westminster for a meeting on 11 March at Westminster Hall. Now events come to a head. Our plan, it seems, was conceived too late. You had best make all speed to Baron Mortimer. He will need to know that our plans are in tatters."

And with that, I was dismissed.

We rode as hard after the meeting with the earl, for we now had a better idea of the purpose of the removal of the prisoners. When we reached the castle the baron and Lady Maud were waiting for me in the inner ward; they must have seen our approach. "The Earl of Gloucester has been summoned to London. Our plans lie in ruins unless you can tell us that you delivered the message."

I said, "Shall we speak indoors, my lord?"

Lady Maud smiled. "Lord Edward's archer seems to understand the situation better than we do. We will do as you ask, Captain."

Once in the Great Hall, all were dismissed save for their sons. "I met with Lord Edward, and he approves of the plan but…" I paused, I was learning how to be a storyteller, "he left the following day for London. I believe that the Earl of Leicester has called this meeting to announce something which involves the king and his son."

The baron paled. "Execution? Regicide?"

Lady Maud dismissed that with a wave of her hand. "If that was the case then it would be done in secret. The fact that all the great nobles have been invited tells us that there is still hope. Continue, Gerald." There was the hint of censure for her husband in her tone.

"Lord Edward believes that he will be sent to the Tower before being moved somewhere else and, when that happens, we are to be close to hand, and he will follow our plan as it was intended." They both nodded. "There is one more thing. Lord Edward no longer knows whom to trust. If he does not see me at the rescue then he will assume it is a trap."

The baron became agitated. "But we have risked all for this plan!"

Lady Maud smiled and nodded. "Husband, put yourself in Lord Edward's shoes. Can he trust de Clare? John de Warenne abandoned him at Lewes. Of all the leaders only you and Henry of Almain, also a prisoner, are to be trusted, but you are too easily recognized, and if you were seen close to Lord Edward's next gaol then they would guard him even more closely. I can well understand him trusting this archer. Have we seen anything in his behaviour that suggests anything other than loyalty?"

"You are right."

"And remember this, when Edward is king it is the likes of us who will reap the reward of estates and lands, not Gerald War Bow." Her husband had not thought it through to its logical end. Lady Maud smiled. "However, Gerald, I shall not forget you, and I will make certain that you are rewarded."

The next two weeks were dull, and that was a relief. We were stuck on the edge of England, far from the events in London. We had little to do except to practise. The new archers had built in strength and could now send an arrow almost as far as the rest of us. Peter had improved. Within two years he would be able to handle a much longer bow. We ate well, we slept and we prepared for the rescue.

It was the last week in March when life became a little more interesting. The Welsh at Builth Castle had not been happy with our treatment of their farmers. I learned that the knight I wounded was a local baron, Iago ap Rhodri. Baron Mortimer kept men watching his borders, and his farmers, grateful for our intervention, told us much about their activities. The baron heard that Sir Iago planned another chevauchée. It was ill-conceived, for it was common knowledge along the border. Knowing that the Welsh planned to raid, Sir Roger worked out where that raid would begin. The best place for horses and horsemen to advance was towards the stream where he had been wounded in winter. Accordingly, the baron called out the fyrd. They owed him forty days' service, and as he had not used them in winter, he used them now.

It brought us forty men. Unlike the English variety, these Welsh men knew how to use a bow, and more than three quarters brought their own. While their other weapon skills were poor, their archery was good. We mustered on the ridge which lay on the English side of the small river. Technically it was Welsh territory, but the farmers who had farmed that side of the river had been forced to flee by our attack.

I had worked during the winter with Evan who led the baron's archers. The baron had hired more, and we now had a sizeable company of archers. I would command them all. When I had first arrived, Evan had been sceptical of me, but that was due to my age. Now, as we waited for the raid, we sat together. He was happy for my company; we spoke and chewed on liquorice roots.

"What you have to understand, Captain, is that this is not England. It is the Marches. Kings and princes might make peace, sign treaties and accords, but here they don't matter at all. We raid them and they raid us. It is a way of life. We usually win, but there are English slaves in Wales as well as Welsh slaves here in England, and it does not sit well with us." He turned to look at me and offered some advice. "When you aim, aim to kill. There is little to be gained from taking a hostage in any case. The Welsh are poor as church mice. The baron, he might take a prisoner, but not for ransom, he would take a hostage just to keep them honest!"

The Welsh came at dawn. Perhaps they thought they might sneak across the border and raid us while we were asleep. We were all awake, although many men lay down to rest.

Evan had brought dogs and they growled. He hissed, "Stand to!" The message was passed from man to man, the stream covering any noise we made.

The archers and the fyrd had rested in the clothes they were wearing, but the men at arms, the baron, his sons and his squire had to don mail. We lined the ridge with strung bows but no arrows nocked. We were behind the fyrd because we had a longer range and could release above the men armed with hunting bows. When the men at arms were mailed, they would form their lines to the right of us. The fyrd knew they had to bear the brunt of the attack, but we knew we had the advantage; the enemy would not know that we were here and waiting for them. I heard their horses, for one neighed as it was pulled back when it descended the slope. I hoped the baron would hurry – for if he was not present then I would have to give the command to release.

"Nock!"

The professional archers nocked war bows while the fyrd nocked their hunting bows. Their arrows would not pierce mail, but the Welsh would bring their fyrd, too.

I heard jingling mail behind me. The decision would now be the baron's. "Can you see them, Captain?"

"No, my lord, but from the noise of their hooves I think they are descending the road to the water."

"Is that in range?"

"It is."

"Good, then when you hear them in the water, order the arrows. Give them five flights and then we will attack. Evan, lead the fyrd and our archers to follow us."

It was not the plan I would have used, but it seemed a reasonable one, and the baron knew his enemy better than I did. An archer learns to feel an enemy, to sense when they are close. My senses told me that they were almost at the water. I took a risk. "Draw!"

My men could hold their powerful bows longer than the fyrd. I could not risk a premature arrow. I heard the first splash and then a second as the Welsh entered the water.

"Release!" Even while the arrows were in the air and starting their descent I said, louder this time, "Draw!

I did not wait more than a moment for the next command. "Release."

The arrows of the fyrd were irregular in comparison with ours, but it did not matter. Men lifted shields and then moved forward when the arrows had struck. The tardy fyrd kept the arrows falling. I heard men scream as war arrows tore into flesh and the chink as arrows hit helmets and mail. For the mailed men we would use bodkins – but

I would not waste a valuable arrow on speculation. When I saw mail, *then* I would use a bodkin.

A Welsh voice shouted something I guessed was, 'Charge!'

I sent two more war arrows at the mass of men who were still just a shadow moving towards us and then drew a bodkin, for I saw, charging up from the water, mailed men. My company all had bodkins nocked. Mine went into the chest of one of the knights. My arrow had a flat trajectory, and as he was struggling up the bank, he laboured to get his shield up. His cantle held his dying body in the saddle. We had each sent our five arrows, and so I dropped my bow and drew my sword.

Evan shouted, "Men of Wigmore! For England and King Henry!" He drew his sword and hurtled down the slope. We had stopped their horsemen, and the baron was charging into their flank. It was a battle fought in the dark, for dawn was still a little way away. It would be all too easy to slay a friend as well as foe.

I shouted, "My company, stay together. Peter, watch the horses." With sword and dagger, I headed down the road. A horse loomed up out of the dark and I instinctively raised my blade. I saw it was the warhorse with the dead knight I had killed still upon its back. "Peter, here!" He arrived next to me and I handed him the reins of the warhorse. "Keep this safe." He grabbed the reins and began talking to the wild-eyed horse. I hurried down the slope, aware that I was now behind my men. I should have led them.

While the baron fought horsemen, we were charging through the Welsh fyrd. Despite Evan's words, I could not bring myself to be ruthless. The Welsh were tough, but their weapons were poor. I brought my sword down on a farmer wearing an old helmet. He tried to block it with his own sword but my blade smashed his in two. Even as he stood looking in horror at his broken weapon, I punched him in the face. I used the pommel of my sword and rendered him unconscious. I saw that Evan and the garrison archers had no such compunction, and two youths were slain as they tried to take on men wielding swords while they just had daggers. I was glad when a Welsh horn sounded and they fell back.

Dawn was just beginning to break, and I saw that twenty Welshmen were either dead or wounded. The wounded were being helped back by their friends and family. I sheathed my sword. Evan and the other garrison archers ran after them.

Geoffrey, son of Martin asked, "Do we follow them, Captain?"

I shook my head. "We have done enough this day. Find our arrows. If you slew a knight or a man at arms then what he has is yours. I slew a knight, and we will share in the proceeds from him and his mail."

I guessed, although I did not know, that the knight I had slain was Sir Iago. I knew, from Evan, that he was the richest knight in these parts. We would do well out of this, but the slaughter of farmers made my stomach turn. I did not enjoy it.

We returned to Wigmore at noon. The garrison and the fyrd were in good spirits. This was another victory and I knew that not only Evan but also Baron Mortimer regarded my archers and me as good luck. Men, even Christians, were always superstitious. *I* put it down to the fact that we were good at what we did.

Lady Maud was even more overjoyed, and she organised a feast for the warriors who had won, on the day following the slaughter. This did not include the fyrd. They had dispersed to their homes, but they were richer by the coins they had taken from the dead as well as the weapons and, in some cases, even boots and belts.

It was a raucous feast but I was largely silent. John of Nottingham leaned over. "Why the long face, Captain? We won, did we not? And none of our men were even scratched. We are all richer. When we lost at Lewes many men would have been downhearted, but we knew that you would find a way to enrich us and you have. And now there is every prospect of being reunited with Lord Edward. From what you say he is already in your debt. The future looks bright."

"I know, but the hardest part is yet to come." I lowered my voice. "The Earl of Gloucester knows our plan. He is in London with the Earl of Leicester; what if he tells our enemy of the plan?"

"Why would he do that?"

"Because he seeks the lands that his family lost, and he will do anything to get them back. He fought against Lord Edward before. What if he chooses to do so again? This plan only works if the enemy knows nothing about it. Even a hint of the plan will mean we cannot rescue him, for they will stop him riding abroad. I will have to get close to wherever Lord Edward is being held. What if it is in the lands controlled by de Montfort or de Ferrers? Do you think I would succeed, then?"

"Captain, you will not be alone. We will be with you."

I shook my head. "And that does not make me feel better, for it means I put all of you at risk. Had we begun our plan but a fortnight earlier…"

"Then it would have failed." I looked at him. He shrugged. "We only got into the castle because of the feast. If they had not been coming for Lord Edward then you would not have even got close! This was meant to be." He held up his beaker and drank some. "It is half full, Captain. Let us see what happens when we throw the bones."

I nodded. "Aye you are right. We are still alive. We are rich, and there is always hope."

CHAPTER 12

In the last days of April and the first days of May, that hope became tangible. Two things happened within a seven-day period. The Earl of Gloucester finally broke with Simon de Montfort. He and his allies left London for Gloucester. He had not received that which he thought was due to him and he left. I did not trust the earl, and my view was that, had he reaped a better reward from the Earl of Leicester, he might have betrayed us. Simon de Montfort was the architect of his own downfall, for he ignored de Clare and that would cost him.

A day later, we heard that Simon de Montfort was heading for his manor at Hereford. Not only that, he had the king, Lord Edward and Henry Almain there with him. The only royal prisoner he did not have with him was Richard of Cornwall, who was still held at Kenilworth. When the baron told me, I could not believe our good fortune. Hereford was just twenty-four miles from Wigmore and twenty-eight from Gloucester. He was close enough to touch, and our plan, suddenly, had a chance of success.

I was confused about what seemed like a military blunder, until the baron explained to me that Simon de Montfort was a supreme strategist. The Marcher lords were his enemies, and if the Earl of Gloucester led them then he could have a rebellion on his hands. He would place himself on the Severn so that he could control any attack and snuff out any opposition to his rule from the borders. His three prisoners were his surety.

"We have him, Captain Gerald! You need to take your men as close as you can get to Hereford. Roger de Leybourne is one of Lord Edward's friends. He will try to see Lord Edward at Hereford."

"Is it likely that de Montfort will let him close? At Wallingford, they had my lord closely watched."

The baron smiled. "He is not as closely guarded, and de Leybourne will stay with him. It will make them less suspicious and mean that even if they arrest de Leybourne, he will still have a chance to speak with Lord Edward and let him know that you are ready. The rescue will be within seven days of the day of his arrival. So, you see, this is even better. Leave tomorrow, and when de Leybourne arrives you can watch and follow." A shadow fell across his face. "Of course, if you are seen when following Lord Edward and his guards then the plan fails, for they will lock him up again."

It was my turn to smile. I knew Lord Edward and he knew me. "Do not worry, my lord, they will not see me. And when I have him safe, where do we take him?"

"De Montfort has men watching the Earl of Gloucester's castle. The earl is not there, he is at Ludlow. You take him to Ludlow." The baron had bought the Welsh knight's horse from me. He smiled. "You can take the Welsh knight's warhorse for Lord Edward and the other knight's horse for Henry Almain. They should be able to evade capture on those two mounts."

Now that the game was afoot we were all keen to start, and we rose before dawn so that we were riding by the time that the sun came up.

I had met Roger de Leybourne and would recognise him, and knew him to be loyal to the Prince. I knew not how he had inveigled himself into the enemy camp, but he had, and I was grateful that we had an ally whom we could trust. The baron had said that he would be with Clifford, a noble with influence along the border, too, and I also knew him. As Gloucester was being watched, Roger de Leybourne would tell Lord Edward to head north. We needed somewhere we could watch the castle and yet stay hidden.

It did not take long to reach Hereford, and we had time to search for somewhere to hide and yet keep watch on the road north. We were lucky and found a wood. It was one of the smallest woods I had ever seen, and there was no water, but there was a ruined farmhouse. The half-wrecked barn provided cover and some shelter for the horses. We would fetch our water from the River Wye.

I was the one who knew de Leybourne and Clifford, so I had to be on watch throughout the daytime. We knew it would be daylight when they arrived, and so I had sleep each night. My men took it in turns to watch with me and to care for the horses. The refuge would only be temporary. Once Lord Edward began to ride, we would need to anticipate where he would be by the eighth day. Our camp would be moving ever northward as we kept pace with Lord Edward's rides.

What we saw, at the castle, was the army Simon de Montfort was gathering. Although his knights were quartered in the town, his men at arms, archers and crossbowmen were camped by the Wye. He was preparing for war, for he did not trust his former ally and supporter. De Clare had changed sides too often. While de Montfort held the leaders of the royalist cause he would destroy his enemies in the west. With the Midlands, London, the east and the south under his control, there would be no opposition to him once the Marcher Lords were defeated.

By my reckoning, it was about 20 or 21 May when I saw the two young riders, de Leybourne and Clifford, gallop up to the castle. Dates meant little to me. The high and the mighty seemed overly concerned with such matters. We knew church days and holidays, and the rest was determined by the weather. The weather had changed over the last couple of days to become warmer, almost hot, and we simply knew that it was getting closer to summer.

Lord Edward and Henry Almain had ridden forth on each of the days we observed, but they had merely ridden for a mile or two and then returned to the castle. I saw that when they did ride, they had an escort of eight men, half of whom looked like young nobles although they were all armed. I observed that none of the riders, including Lord Henry, wore mail. Lord Edward and his cousin were weaponless. That, I would have expected. I saw that two men rode before the two captives, and two hung much further back than their companions. We might have six escorts to deal with when we attempted to rescue the two men; I had enough archers for that. We had bows and we had a reputation. On the day we rescued Lord Edward we would wear his livery.

That night I went over the plan with my men. "Tomorrow I ride with Tom. We will follow Lord Edward. When they reach the end of their ride Tom will come back and fetch you, while I find somewhere to camp. John, I leave it to you to ensure that you are not seen when you join us. You are woodsmen and you can ride in the dark. Secrecy is all. Lord Edward will keep to the same route each day, it is just that he will extend his ride each day."

They nodded their agreement.

I went over to Peter while food was prepared. "You know what you must do?"

He nodded. "Aye, Captain, I am to keep Lord Edward's horse close by me. I must make certain that he is well fed and watered." He smiled. "War Bow is a good horse, Captain."

I smiled back at him. "He is named War Bow?"

"I knew not his name when he came to us. At Wigmore Castle they did not speak to the horses. It is good to speak to the animals, I gave him the name and War Bow seems to like it." He suddenly looked worried. "I hope that you do not mind."

"I am flattered, that is all."

I had Eleanor saddled before dawn, and Tom and I waited in the woods. The plan hinged on remaining hidden until the day of the rescue and ensuring that the spare horses were in place when we needed them. Tom also had a good horse; it was a palfrey but a sound one. We had been lucky in war, and we had managed to acquire better horses than other archers.

Lord Edward and his companions must have breakfasted well, for they emerged late. I saw that Clifford and de Leybourne were with Lord Edward and Henry Almain. That had resulted in an extra four guards; it was something we had not planned for and showed that de Montfort was being careful. Our vantage point was half a mile from the main road north. I knew that Lord Edward would keep the route simple, for he was a clever man. Lord Edward pointed north, and they took the road that passed by the end of the lane which led to the wood and the farm. Protected by hedgerows, Tom and I walked our horses down it slowly.

We were halfway to the main road when we heard the clatter of hooves and the sound of laughter. I now saw why Clifford and de Leybourne were there. Lord Edward would be expected to have conversations with his old friends; the talk was to let us know where they were. Until they left the road, we would be exposed. Once they headed for fields and woods then we would have more chance of concealment.

We reached the main road and headed down it. The steaming piles of dung told us, even had we not seen them, that the men we followed were ahead of us. Surprisingly, Lord Edward led them along the road for some time until we came to the village of Moreton on Lugg. We almost missed them, for I had become used to travelling on the road. Tom heard their laughter. "Captain, they are heading towards the river."

It was a little road which led to the river, and I knew we would be spotted if we followed along it. There were fields beyond the village and I took a chance. We turned through the village and rode between two cottages. I headed north and east; I would get ahead of them and reach the river. It was a risk, but Lord Edward had not done exactly what I had expected. We passed animals grazing in a field and then the ground dipped towards the river. The Lugg was not wide but there was a bridge. When we reached the river, I saw that the riders had dismounted and there was laughter coming from the bridge. We dismounted and I made my way through the tangled undergrowth next to the water, to get closer to them.

I saw that there were two guards on the bridge and two on the road leading to the village, and they were taking no chances. The captives were close to and between them and their horses. I saw that the four lords had wineskins and some bread. They were dining. I found a willow, from behind which I could observe them – they were fifty paces from me. While I heard occasional words, they were largely incoherent. I saw them put the wineskins in their saddlebags and mount.

I did not panic. There were two ways to go. They could continue over the river, in which case Tom and I would have to swim it, or they would return to Hereford. As soon as they clattered back up the tiny lane through the village, I knew we had somewhere to wait.

I returned to Tom. "They are gone back to Hereford." By my

reckoning, we had ridden just under four miles. Lord Edward would need at least a ten-mile gap between us and Hereford to ensure that we could reach Ludlow. "We will cross the river and look for somewhere to camp on the far side."

"Surely that is a risk, Captain? Suppose he comes to the village and carries on north?"

"Lord Edward came to the bridge for a reason. They left the castle later than normal, and they ate at the bridge. If he heads north it will be on the far side of the river."

We retraced our steps to the village and rode down the lane. The birds were already pecking at the crumbs that had been left by the bridge. We crossed over, and I saw that the fields on the eastern side of the river must have been prone to flooding, for they were neither tilled nor cleared. The willows, alder and elder made an effective wall close to the river. We left the road and I headed for the Lugg. If we only had to spend one night there, then it was possible it would hide us.

"Tom, ride back and fetch the others. You had better leave well before dark. If you ride through the village after dark you may arouse suspicion. When you come back make a point of stopping in the village and when you are questioned, as I know you will be, then tell them that you are from de Montfort's army and seeking better grazing for there are too many horses close to the castle."

He nodded and left me. It was always as well to have a good story, even if you did not use it. I had plenty of time, and so I rode north along the road. I came to a village which had a church. The church was so tiny, as was the village, that I doubted they even had a priest.

The river tumbled next to the church and there was no bridge. Horsemen could ford the river and that made this place interesting to me. Pushing on, I saw that the road, small though it was, paralleled the river. Eleanor was still fresh, and so I rode another three miles. I came to a ford in the river and found myself in a thick wood. There was a trail which led through it.

I forded the river and, while Eleanor drank, examined the trail. It was ancient, but there was no sign of horse dung. If Lord Edward could get as far as here then we had the perfect place to rescue him, for we would have trees to hide us and woodland trails to disguise our route.

I headed back to Moreton on Lugg. I estimated that the ford lay almost ten miles from Hereford. Twenty miles was further than might be expected for a day's ride. If they tried to reach the ford then it would result in questions from his guards or some punitive action to restrain them. I made the camp Tom and I had chosen and, as I took off Eleanor's saddle, I began to plan. If, as I expected, Lord Edward came towards the tiny church then I knew he would head for the wood. We could make a camp in the wood on the far side of the river where it would be easier to hide our horses. Tom and I could still watch the route Lord Edward would take, and we would not have to move. We would camp here for one night and then, if Lord Edward came this way, we could camp in the woods across the river. The more I thought about it the better the plan seemed. We would have the cover of the woods and the direction of our escape would be hidden.

My men rode through the village in the late afternoon. I heard John speaking to someone who came out of one of the houses. There was laughter, and then the horses continued towards me. Tom brought them through the woods to the water.

As they dismounted, Jack of Lincoln sniffed, "If I had known these would be my lodgings when I gained honest employment I would have stayed in the greenwood!"

He was right, the camp was primitive, even by our standards. "One night of roughing it Jack, and then, for the next few nights we can have a better and more secure camp. It all depends on if I have read the mind of Lord Edward. I believe he will take his guards further north little by little. If I am right then tomorrow he will stop at the small church and hamlet less than a mile up the road. For tonight, we have cold rations."

Despite his griping, Jack did not mind the conditions. It is the way with soldiers that they like to complain. You rarely find a happy soldier, at least, not on the surface.

Tom and I saddled and mounted Eleanor and Bess at dawn and we waited, hidden by the undergrowth. They arrived at the bridge earlier than I had expected, and I heard Lord Edward say, loudly, as they threw their crumbs to the waiting birds, "Let us ride to the church which lies up the road. I would go inside and pray alone for my release from this captivity."

I heard Henry of Almain say, equally loudly, "Aye lord, and I will pray too for my father."

I knew the words were intended for my ears. I heard the hooves as they clattered over the bridge, and then as they passed us, I realised that I could not see them which meant they could not see me, but I heard them as they chattered and laughed. It was only the words of the four nobles I heard while the guards were silent – they would be watching and listening for danger.

Lord Edward had revealed his plan to us, and so I did not follow immediately. The church lay down a lane. It was 400 paces from the village which, itself, was just 200 paces from the road. I was wary as we neared the village, but there were no horses to be seen. The two of us kept riding and passed the end of the road and the village. We were not seen. When we were a hundred paces from the village we stopped. As soon as they emerged, I would pretend to be examining my horse's hoof.

I heard the hooves and bent down. The horses did not continue down the road towards the ford and the wood but headed due south, back towards Hereford. As they disappeared we mounted. "Come Tom, let us examine the church."

The village was a sleepy one, with just six houses. Heads came from doors, for the road led nowhere save to the church. When I turned, the heads quickly ducked back within doors. They had learned to keep themselves to themselves.

I handed my reins to Tom and entered the dark church. It was small. There was a single candle burning, but it was a fresh one. I guessed that Lord Edward had lit it and made an offering in the offertory box. I knelt in front of the altar pretending to pray and, as I glanced to my right, I saw a tiny piece of parchment on the floor. I picked it up and stood. It must have been left there by Lord Edward. I hurried out: I would read it back in our camp.

My men had heard Lord Edward and his captors head back to the castle, and they looked at me expectantly. I opened the parchment. It simply said, '3'.

I showed it to them. Tom asked, "What does it mean, Captain?"

"I am guessing, and it *is* a guess, that they have brought the date forward, and we rescue him on the third day from now."

"Doesn't that complicate matters, Captain?"

Tom knew my plan already, having waited with me. "It could do, but I think we move the camp anyway. We will wait at the church tomorrow and the day after. That way we can see where they go. Then, on the day of the rescue, we will wait by the ford with the rescue horses. It is all that we can do."

We made a camp on the far side of the river. It was a better camp, and I charged Jack and Robin with the task of finding us the quickest way to take us to the Ludlow road. I spoke at length with John of

Nottingham. He was an older man and I needed his advice. After I had told him the way I expected events to turn out, he nodded. "Your reasoning is sound, Captain. The problem comes if they make a fight of it. The last thing we need is for Lord Edward to be hurt or, God forbid, killed in the rescue attempt."

I nodded. "I want you, Jack and David to have arrows ready on the day of the rescue. If any look to harm Lord Edward then pluck them from their saddles."

I knew for certain that Lord Edward had changed his plans when the following day the riders approached much earlier than on the other days. As they hurtled past the end of the village, where we were secreted, I saw that their horses were lathered. Lord Edward and Henry Almain were laughing. They stopped less than a mile from the lane's end. We watched them walk back along the road, leading their lathered horses.

I heard Clifford complain, "We will not be back until the sixth hour of the day! My stomach thinks that my throat has been cut!"

Henry Almain said, "We can always find an inn while the horses recover."

"And that is a sound idea. Perhaps my prayer yesterday in the church paid off, for after that fast ride I feel alive. We must do this again tomorrow but faster and further."

They were moving away from me, but I heard a voice – one I did not recognise. "Remember Lord Edward, if you try to escape you will be punished and your riding privileges removed. Do not forget that our horses are the equal of yours, and we will catch you."

"I know."

I was now convinced that I knew the plan. The horses had looked exhausted as they had passed us, but there were still too many guards. I hoped that Lord Edward had a plan to neutralize them.

The next day was almost a copy of the first, and we remained hidden in the lane. I had Geoffrey and Lewis hidden halfway to the ford. This time we heard one of the guards – from his voice I think he was one of de Montfort's knights – say, "The earl has said that you may ride no further north than the river, lord, for there is nothing north of there, save the woods."

Henry of Almain laughed. "And if we reach there, we will be so exhausted it will take us a whole day to return."

The guards said, "I know not why you ruin your horses, lord."

When we picked up Lewis and Geoffrey, they told us that the riders had galloped past them as though they were having a race.

"Tomorrow, I want the two of you to wait here. You are here to intervene if Lord Edward looks to be captured or does not make the rendezvous. If the rescue takes place, as I hope it will, then it will just be the guards who return. You two make your way to the river and cross. Follow us to the Ludlow Road."

"Aye, Captain." The two of them were now far more confident and assured than they had been when they had first come to me.

That night, we went through our plans carefully. We would have to ensure that Lord Edward was safe, and after that, we would see to his companions. In a perfect world we would save them all, but this was imperfect, and we would take what we could. I would have a horse for Lord Edward, Tom would have one for Henry Almain. William and Mark would have two spares for Clifford and de Leybourne. We had kept the last two spare horses for an emergency. If a horse broke down now it would cause trouble, for we would have used them for the young lords.

Lewis and Geoffrey left before dawn. They had spent the night going through their plans. They had their bows and war arrows and would disable the horses of the guards if they could.

187

I was awake at dawn. I was nervous. So much rested on my shoulders and I did not like it. My happy times had been when Roger and I crossed to France and were bows for hire. Life had been uncomplicated then. The moment my life became tied to Lord Edward it had changed, and the worst of it was that I could not now leave. I was Lord Edward's archer – our lives were bound together.

It was gone noon and they had still to arrive. I began to fear that the plot had been discovered. Perhaps the suspicious guards had mentioned something to the Earl of Leicester or someone could have informed on them. There was much treachery on both sides of this conflict. I stood holding Eleanor's reins and the reins of the warhorse for Lord Edward.

Tom gave me a wan smile. "They have further to come today, Captain. They are not yet late."

It was almost as though he had summoned them with his thoughts for I heard, in the distance, the thunder of hooves.

"It is time!"

I mounted and moved towards the edge of the river. If I crossed, then I would be seen by the guards, and I had to remain hidden. I would reveal myself – but I had to choose when I would be seen, or else Lord Edward would abort. I saw Lord Edward's head as it appeared on the other side of the river. I dug my heels into Eleanor and splashed across, leading the warhorse. We laboured up the slippery bank; Tom brought the second horse. As I rose to have a good view up the road, I saw Henry of Almain, his horse just twenty paces away. Their six guards' horses, lathered and winded, struggled to make the ford and were forty paces back.

Lord Edward saw me and urged his weary horse towards me. When he was four paces from me he leapt from his horse and sprung onto the back of the warhorse. He stood in the stirrups and, waving his hand, shouted, "Lordlings, I bid you good day! Greet my father well and tell him that I hope to see him soon, to release him from captivity!"

As Henry of Almain mounted the second horse, Lord Edward wheeled the warhorse and I saw that he was grinning. "Well done Gerald, we did it, and I shall never doubt you again!"

CHAPTER 13

All of our horses were fresh and we galloped off. John and my rear-guard waited long enough to see the guards dismount – for their horses could go no further – then they joined us. So far, the plan was working, and the exhausted guards would struggle to get back to Hereford.

Robin led us, for he had scouted out our escape route. Lewis and Geoffrey caught up with us when we were a mile into the trees, and their smiles told me that we were not pursued. We bent over our horses' heads, for we did not want to waste this God-given opportunity. When we left the forest, we hit the Ludlow Road. We had fallen into our normal formation: Tom was at the fore with Robin, John and Jack at the rear. Lord Edward was desperate to talk, I could see that, but the pounding of the hooves and the fear of pursuit kept him silent. It was only when we neared the town and castle of Ludlow that we allowed our horses to walk and for us to talk.

I let Lord Edward begin, although I had many questions. "You found my note. I knew that you would. Do not worry, Gerald, I never once saw you but, you know, I sensed that you were close and could hear me. Strange, is it not? Clifford and de Leybourne complained that they could not keep up and stopped. Four of the guards remained with them. I expect them to follow soon."

"Will they not be held and punished, my lord?"

He laughed. "When I mounted this fine horse – you must tell me whence you had him – I looked back and saw the four guards coming to join the others. Clifford and de Leybourne will have gone back to Moreton on Lugg and rejoined the road to Ludlow there. Their horses will need to be conserved but they will get here." He patted the horse. "Well, where did you get this fine horse?"

"He now belongs to Baron Mortimer, but I slew the knight who owned him."

He nodded. "And that is what I should have done at Lewes, instead of chasing the scum of London. I have learned a harsh lesson, Gerald, and I am much humbled. Now we can take back our country."

"But your father is still a prisoner, my lord!"

"And he is king. If de Montfort wished to commit regicide he would have done so long ago. The king is safe. The Earl of Leicester thinks that the dogs he has raised as a parliament of the common folk will bark loudly enough and drown out our voices. They are wrong, it is a parliament of paper he has made, and that can be torn down." He turned to look at me and both his tone and his words were murderous. "When next we fight de Montfort and his cronies it will be the last battle, and I will eradicate the rebellious heart of de Montfort and all those like him."

*

The gates of Ludlow were open, and I saw a host of lords waiting for us. Mortimer and de Clare were at their fore, and there was joy on their faces. They crowded around and greeted one another like old friends. Old divisions between de Clare and Lord Edward were a thing of the past; they had a new start. I thought that we were forgotten; as the gathered knights and barons all clamoured around Lord Edward, my archers and I were pushed to the side.

"Let us take the horses to the stables." I was not convinced that there would be any room at the stables, for there seemed a mighty host in the castle already. News of the planned escape must have been more widespread than I thought! Strangely, I did not mind being ignored because I did not like being the centre of attention. I was just pleased that it had all gone well and I had lost none of my archers. To me, they were family, even the new ones. Like John and the other older archers, I viewed Peter as a young brother. All of the archers were protective of him.

When I reached the stables, I was in for a surprise. The ostler said, "Your stalls are kept for you, Captain. They are upon the orders of Baron Mortimer. This is his castle, now."

"Thank you, ostler." This was a case of you scratch my back and I will scratch yours. I had rescued Lord Edward, and the baron's reward was the castle and manor of Ludlow. Giving me some stalls was a small price to pay. I was learning this game of barons and knights. "Where do we eat? For we have had a long day."

He pointed to a building attached to the great hall into which the great and the good had retired. "The warrior hall, sir."

All the saddles were removed, and we then brushed and combed our mounts. We gave them water and feed, for they deserved it. I also fed the two horses Lord Edward and Henry Almain had used. By the time we had finished it was dark, and the men waited for me outside the stables.

"Archers, you have done me great honour over the last days. We have shown Simon de Montfort that he cannot bend the will of all the people to his view of the world. Lord Edward is our master once more. I thank you for following one so young."

To my surprise and great embarrassment, they began to clap their hands. They said nothing, but their smiles and their eyes bespoke volumes. I was happy. We picked up our war gear and headed across the inner ward. I knew that, no matter how crowded the warrior hall was, we would be better off than sleeping in a field.

We had almost reached the hall when a page found me. I did not know him, but I recognised his livery. It was that of Sir John who had once been Lord Edward's squire. The page looked nervously at me. He could have been no more than twelve years old, and I suspected he had barely begun his training. He grinned sheepishly at me as though waiting for an answer to an unspoken question.

"Yes, young master?"

"My lord, Sir John, says that you are invited to the great hall, for Lord Edward wishes you to dine with him."

Inwardly I cursed. A night with my men eating plain food and drinking honest ale appealed; I did not relish a high table with pretentious food and wine I did not enjoy. However, I was Lord Edward's archer and I would obey. "Tell him I will be along shortly."

"Sir John said I was to wait for you, Captain."

I shook my head and handed him my bag of spare clothes. "Then make yourself useful and carry that to my bed. Come, boys, we will take my war gear to the hall, and then I will endure a night the like of which you can only imagine."

Peter said, "That good?"

John of Nottingham laughed. "No, young Peter, that *bad*!"

When I reached the hall, it was clear that half of the knights and barons were already drunk. I saw Clifford and de Leybourne, who were surrounded by young knights and, from their arm movements, I took it that they were describing their part in the rescue. I recognised many of the lords. There were some power men there: de Warenne, de Valence and others, but closest to Lord Edward were de Clare, Mortimer and Henry Almain.

Sir John saw me first and headed over to me. He clasped my arm. We had fought together. Between us, there was no rank, although I called him, 'my lord'. He had been a squire, and me, just an archer. Such things are important to warriors.

"Gerald, it is not only good to see you, it is an honour. When the rest of us did nothing you, alone, sought to rescue Lord Edward."

I shook my head. "Baron Mortimer and his wife were the ones who devised the rescue. I was the instrument, but I am right glad that I did so. And how have you been, my lord?"

"Cooling my heels, as I sought a way to fight de Montfort. I am certain his lordship knows that you were right about the wood, the dead ground and the archers at Lewes. I too felt bad that I had not argued your cause more strongly."

I nodded. "But the king, his father, would still do things the same way."

"He would, but…" he brightened, "the king is still de Montfort's prisoner. When we go to war it will be behind Lord Edward's banner."

"Good." That was all I said, but inside me, I knew that the reckless charge of Lord Edward had cost us the battle. Had he learned in the year since Lewes?

"Come, let us sit. Lord Edward has asked for you to be close to him. He has much to say while we eat."

We went to the long table, which housed the greatest nobles who followed Lord Edward's banner. Sir John and I were the lowest ranked by a considerable margin. I was so out of my depth I was sure that

I would not be able to eat a morsel. There was food, wine and ale in huge quantities. I spoke with Sir John and learned of his wife and young son; Sir John had high hopes of a better manor after the war. I heard the same from all of the lords on the long table close to ours; each of them spoke of the war and the rebellion being almost over. I could also hear, from my left, the sound of arrangements and accords being made. Lord Edward was rewarding his allies before the battle began. He knew that de Clare was a key piece in this real-life chessboard. I saw his head close to Baron Mortimer. When they spoke of me, I knew, for both looked at me. Having had little sleep for the last few days, I was desperate for my bed, but I knew I had to wait until either I was dismissed, or Lord Edward retired.

I do not know if Lord Edward could read my face or he was ready to speak but, in any event, he soon rose from his seat. I saw men looking at him and wondering who he would honour with a private word. He came directly for me.

He leaned close to me and spoke so that only Sir John could hear his words. "I owe you more than I can say. Know this, Gerald War Bow, when I am king, and king I shall be, you will be elevated. Before that time, however, we have a great battle to fight, a battle you have already shown you know how to win. I know this formality is not for you and so, when I have spoken, you may rejoin my archers. Tomorrow, we start to reclaim England."

His fingers bit into my shoulder, for he was slightly drunk, and then he stood. "My lords, we have amongst us someone who is from common stock but know this – stand, please, Gerald." I stood. "Gerald War Bow is a warrior and a *great* warrior. I can give him no higher praise. Along with my good friend, Roger Mortimer, they have taken me from a dark place and brought me into the light!" He spread his arms and the hall erupted, as drunken lords banged the table. I stood and bowed. I walked out with a red face. Many lords would say it was wine, which was too strong for a commoner, but I was simply embarrassed!

The next morning more lords arrived, and my archers and I practised. We used the green, for both the wards were filled. It was there I saw Captain William and Ralph Dickson as they rode towards the castle. They stopped close to us and dismounted. Both looked much older than the last time I had seen them, a year ago, before the battle of Lewes. I grasped Captain William's arm. He beamed. "Good to see you, Gerald! I see you have prospered."

Shaking my head, I said, "We have survived, but now that Lord Edward is freed then we can prosper once more. Where are the rest of your men?"

His face fell and his smile disappeared. "This is all that I have left: Sergeant Ralph and myself. It may be that Lord Edward will not need us."

"He has learned from Lewes, Captain William, and he knows he will need you. There are many men at arms heading here in prospect of battle. You will find more."

He nodded and took his reins. "We will go and see Lord Edward. We will talk later, for I can tell that your tale is a better one than mine." He and Ralph walked their horses towards the castle keep.

"Is that a knight, Captain?"

"No, Peter, he is a man at arms, and he leads men who serve Lord Edward."

John of Nottingham said, "And there is a lesson for you, Peter. We all fought in the same battle, and Captain William led many men at the battle, but just two survived. Our captain may be young, but he has a mind for war."

That evening, when we ate in the warrior hall, we learned that most of Captain William's men had been slaughtered. The knights had been taken for ransom, but men at arms had no value save the mail they wore and the weapons they bore. Sir John had been the saviour of Captain William and Ralph. He had managed to escape with them.

"We have had a home this last year with Sir John. We offered to serve him, but Sir John is loyal and he said we were Lord Edward's men. He was convinced that all would be right."

Sir John had been a good squire and now he was a good knight.

Ralph grinned. "And, we have heard, Captain, that it was you and your band of cutthroats who effected the escape! That was well done!"

John of Nottingham and Ralph got on well with each other, and John was game for the banter. "For an archer it was not difficult, but for a man such as you lumbering around in mail, it would have been impossible."

There then followed a debate between Ralph and John on the merits of their arms. Captain William and I left and went to the inner ward. "You were right, Gerald, Lord Edward does want us to form another company for him. It will take time."

"And time is the one thing we do not have, William. I have spoken with Baron Mortimer." Captain William raised an eyebrow and I shrugged. "I have done him no small service and he seems to like me. He told me that the Earl of Leicester has sent emissaries to meet with King Llewelyn. That does not bode well. I think that de Montfort would give the Welsh back their marches just to have England his personal fiefdom."

The captain nodded. "And King Henry?"

"Is kept as close to de Montfort as it is possible. The Earl of Leicester has lost one Plantagenet, and he would keep the other close. The king's brother, Richard, is heavily guarded in Kenilworth too. So, you begin your search for men on the morrow?"

"Aye, I have gold from Lord Edward. I shall be choosy, for it is better to have fewer men that you can rely on than men like Tilbury who simply cause trouble."

Tilbury had been one of his men at arms. It had taken a mighty blow from Jack of Lincoln's fist to make him heed orders.

I was summoned not long after dawn. Lord Edward had returned from his incarceration a different man. He was like a pup that has suddenly changed to become a guard dog with a purpose. Once he had been under the sway of de Montfort, and now he would use his knowledge to bring down his former mentor. Lord Edward was with de Clare and Mortimer. I was not greeted as a hired bow but, almost, as a friend.

"Your men are ready and eager, Captain?"

"Aye, Lord Edward. Our horses are recovered, we have arrows and we are keen to serve you once more."

He smiled. "Sir Roger has told me of your exploits. It is good that you have remained loyal to me."

I was no fool. If I had become Baron Mortimer's man then Lord Edward, for all his smiles, would never have forgiven me. I gave a slight bow and Lord Edward continued. "I need to know where de Montfort is gathering his army. Ride south as far as Gloucester."

I looked at de Clare, who shook his head. "I fear de Montfort has taken my home."

Lord Edward put his arm around the shoulders of his former adversary. "Never fear, we shall take it back. Captain, I need to know how many men are in Gloucester. I want to know if we can take it and I trust your judgement. I will bring the army behind you. Hereford will fall too, and with Ludlow and Hereford as bastions here we can cut off de Montfort's tentacles one by one. I have called for my loyal barons to meet me at Worcester." I nodded. "But I need the main crossing of the Severn in my hands!"

De Clare added a word of caution. "My lord, young de Montfort, de Ferrers and all of de Montfort's allies lie to the east. If he can combine with those men, then we shall be outnumbered."

This was a new Lord Edward I saw before me. His recklessness was gone, and he appeared to be in control both of himself and his emotions. "Fear not, Gloucester, I have a plan, but first I need my archer to tell me how to take back your home!"

We had no time to lose, for Gloucester was almost fifty miles away. As we headed down the road, with our spare horses carrying our arrows and war gear, I thought about the major problem that not only we, but Lord Edward and his army, would face – the River Severn. It was a mighty river and, for many years, had been a natural border with the Welsh. Consequently, the bridges which crossed it were well guarded. We would have to choose our crossing point wisely.

I headed for Worcester. Lord Edward had already sent Sir John with a conroi of knights to hold the town. I daresay that had Captain Williams had his company, then they would have been with Lord Edward's former squire. We reached Worcester in the late afternoon. We could have hurried on, but I wished to see what I could learn from Sir John.

"Well Captain, it seems that the earl's son, Simon, is gathering an army in the Midlands and London."

"Then it seems our task is vital, for if Gloucester is fortified by the rebels then Lord Edward could be trapped here in Worcester."

Sir John smiled. "This is a different man from the one who left his father and charged after the Londoners. King Henry does not rule any longer. He may sit on the horse, but it is Lord Edward who holds the reins. He has lost his kingdom once and he will not do so a second time. He was a reckless youth, I fear, but now he will be a ruthless man!" He and I could speak openly, for we were both Lord Edward's men.

199

We camped outside Gloucester. There was irony in the fact that this was where King Henry had been crowned as a boy king. With sentries set around the camp, which was just a mile from the town's gates, I spoke to the rest of my men. "David the Welshman and I will change into ordinary clothes and enter the town. I intend to spend tomorrow walking the streets. Tomorrow evening we will return, and I will want two men to return to Worcester with the news we find."

"That is risky, Captain, you are known, and since the rescue, the bounty on your head will be even greater. Let me go."

"No, John, you could do the job, I know that, but I would recognise more of the lords than you. If I know who commands then that will help Lord Edward."

We slipped out at dawn and waited outside the town gates. My men insisted upon waiting where they could see the town gates and yet remain hidden. There were others there, for the town was secured each night. This would be our best chance to get inside the town. Our story was that we were swords for hire: we had taken a couple of shields from Worcester, plain, faded, red ones that looked to be the sort a down-at-heel soldier might carry. My sword was a good one and would tell any questioner that I was a warrior.

In the event, we were not questioned. The gates opened and the mob outside flooded in. This was not a town under siege. In fact, I saw few soldiers except for the ones on the walls. The castle was garrisoned but I did not recognise the livery.

David and I walked the town. We found that the bridge was well guarded; that was to be expected. We found a tavern close to the castle where we had ale and pie. We did not question, but we listened. Soldiers from the castle came here to drink and they were free with their tongues. David and I huddled in a corner, our heads down, and learned much.

The reason for the paltry garrison was simple: Simon de Montfort was heading for Wales. He was at Newport and preparing to meet with the Welsh king. The men of the castle believed he was going to defeat the Marcher Lords before turning his attention to Edward, whom he assumed was in Ludlow. There appeared to be a great deal of confidence and belief that de Montfort would be able to defeat the reckless Edward. They spoke disparagingly of the reckless prince who had thrown away the battle of Lewes. I knew better. I also learned that the garrison was fewer than sixty men. Some of it was deduction, but they said enough for me to be fairly certain of my estimate. Having learned all that there was to be learned, we left the tavern.

We were followed by armed men. I had no idea of numbers, but I knew that we were being trailed. Both David and I knew how to track animals. You listened for subtle sounds. I had heard the sound of metal. Ordinary folks had little metal about them – metal meant soldiers. As we had been close to the castle, I had to assume that we had been observed and someone had been suspicious.

David looked up at me and I nodded. He, too, had heard the noise. I lengthened my stride. It would not appear to those following that we were alerted, but we would reach the gate quicker. I saw that the two sentries who had admitted us now lounged on either side of the portal. The busy part of the day was over, and now it would be quiet until those using the market left. It was tempting to run, but the two sentries would simply cross their spears and halt us.

We were ten paces from them when there was a shout from behind. "Stop these two men from leaving! I think they are spies!"

The two sentries did as I had feared and crossed their spears. They would slow us enough to allow those in pursuit to catch us. I took another three paces towards the sentries when a commanding voice from behind shouted, "You two, halt, or I will have you cut down like a dog! There is a crossbow aimed at your back!"

I turned, but took another step back as I did so. I also put one hand behind my back to rest on my belt. I could reach the dagger there in a heartbeat.

I saw that there were four men wearing livery. One was six paces away and had a crossbow; it was aimed at my chest. It would be a quick death.

"What do you want with us? We have done nothing wrong, save have an ale!"

The leader was a sergeant at arms. He wore mail beneath his tunic and had his hand upon his sword hilt. I noticed such things, for when I fought, I had to know the weaknesses of my enemy. They were relying on the two sentries and the crossbow to hold the two of us. The other two had leather jerkins and both looked young.

"I want you to come with me to the Sherriff. You were in the tavern."

I laughed and shook my head. "When did it become an offence to drink ale? Would you lock up every man in England?" Behind me, I heard one of the sentries laugh. It was a sign that he was relaxing a little and saw no threat.

The sergeant at arms, however, was no fool. He drew his sword. "Aye, friend, men may drink ale, but they do not leave ale in their beakers when they leave, and they generally talk while they drink. They do not sit in a corner and listen to the words of the garrison. If you are innocent then you will be released, and if not," he leered, "then you will be mine!" His leer told me it would be a painful death.

I had to think quickly and rely on the quick wits of David the Welshman. The danger was the crossbowman, and then the sergeant. The crossbowman was now five paces away from me and had allowed enough space for the crossbow to have a direct line to my chest. I used the distraction of my right hand to draw my dagger. The sentries would see the movement and shout, therefore I had to be quick. I waved my hand to the right and began to speak: "I had…"

I saw the crossbowman's eyes flicker to his left. It was natural. In one movement I drew and threw my dagger at him. I was lucky; the dagger struck him in the cheek. It made him drop his crossbow and the bolt fell to the ground. The string released. Even as I drew my sword, David the Welshman had drawn his and rammed it into the sergeant's thigh as he swung at me.

"Run!"

The two sentries turned their spears to face us. We had the advantage, for we knew what we would do, while the sentries looked from one to the other. As a spear came towards my chest, I grabbed the shaft below the head and then slashed at the man's leg. His leather jerkin afforded too much protection for me to disable his body. David held his dagger in his left hand, which allowed him to deflect the spear and then step inside the sentry's guard. He hacked across the man's wrist. The half-severed limb bled heavily. He would not be able to hold a weapon.

We hurtled through the gate. Behind us, I heard cries as the guard was called out. There were men in the towers and in the castle, but they would take time to reach us. We ran for the woods. Suddenly two arrows flew into the air. I heard a cry and, turning, saw that one of the men who had chased us lay dead; his body had two arrows sticking from it. The others had halted. Ahead of me, I saw John of Nottingham and my men. I daresay that we might have been able to deal with the two men following without them, but this was easier.

John said, as we passed, "Jack and I will hold them while you fetch the horses for us, Captain!"

We had half a mile to run. I hoped that would be enough time for our men back at camp to have readied the horses. I whistled and, as I neared our camp I shouted, "Peter, horses!"

The horses were already saddled, and he led Eleanor and Bess towards us. I threw myself onto Eleanor's back and grabbed the reins of Bess. Tom and I turned and galloped back. Tom still had his bow in his hand, mine was in my case. I saw that John and Jack had been compelled to move deeper into the wood, since the garrison had crossbows on the town wall. There were two other men being dragged back inside the walls of Gloucester. We did not like to use our bows from the backs of horses but if we had to, we could. As Jack ran back to his horse, John sent an arrow towards the walls, while Tom used his bow to send a flight at the gate. It allowed John to throw himself into his saddle, and turning, we galloped.

There would be horses in the castle, and it would not take them long to follow. I shouted, "Take the Worcester road; we have learned all that there is to learn!"

Only David and I did not have a strung bow. If we had to turn to discourage our pursuers, they would be our best weapon. For that, however, we needed open ground. The wood did not suit us. The wood was not a large one, less than a mile in total length. We burst from the wood and galloped across the bridge over the small brook. There were open fields for the next mile or so, and then we would hit the hamlet of Twigworth. We had only recently travelled this road, and its features were clearly etched in my mind.

I glanced behind and saw half a dozen horsemen just emerging from the woods. When I heard them on the bridge, I looked behind and saw another eight following. I shouted, "Prepare to stop, turn and send a couple of flights at them. Try to hit their horses!"

There was a chorus of, "Aye, Captain."

I saw the hamlet ahead and shouted, "Now!" I wheeled Eleanor around and made as though I was going to charge them. I drew my sword and raised it. They slowed. It was not by much, but it was understandable. They wanted their fellows to join them and form a solid line. Nine arrows soared and then another nine. One man fell from his saddle and another clutched his arm. Three horses were struck, and two of them headed off into the nearby fields. As the last arrow fell, another man was hit in the leg.

"Ride!"

My men had not been as accurate as usual, for they were on their horses, but the eighteen arrows had generated a good return. We had slowed down our pursuit and made them wary. Each bend and rise in the road made them slow, and we increased our lead. Even as we galloped through Twigworth I began to plan how we would replace our horses. By the time we reached Norton, they had lost interest in us, and we reined in so that my men could unstring their bows and put them back in their cases. As they did so, I told them what we had learned.

John of Nottingham shook his head. "I was right though, Captain. Any of us could have done what you did. Why take the risk? Lord Edward thinks highly of you; do you think that we would still be employed if you were gone?"

"I am still captain, John of Nottingham, and my father taught me that a captain leads, and that means being at the front. All is well and I am whole!"

We were weary when we rode into Worcester. Lord Edward and de Clare were there. As we were stabling our horses, Sir John's page, Richard, found me. "Captain, my lord asks you to come to the hall."

He did not say great hall, for Worcester was still a timber castle. "He is there with Lord Edward and the Earl of Gloucester."

"Is Baron Mortimer with them?"

"No, Captain, he is gathering his men to join us here. Lord Edward thinks the cost of taking Hereford is unnecessary. Gloucester is more important."

It was a tiny hall, and I knew that this would just be a jumping-off point for an attack. The two men were poring over a map as I entered. Sir John waited behind them. They were eager for our information. This was one of those times a commoner was more valuable than a noble, for we could go where they could not. We could spy and gather information.

"Well, Gerald?"

"The Earl of Leicester is in Wales, my lord. I believe he is west of Newport. He appears to be talking to the Welsh! There is a garrison of less than a hundred in Gloucester."

Had I told him that I had rescued his father I could not have had a better reaction. "By God, we have him! John, I want every bridge over the Severn destroyed! Every boat must be either pulled to the eastern bank or demolished. We have him trapped, and his army is still in the east!"

"Yes, my lord."

I was ignored as the two men talked. "We retake my home, Lord Edward, and have men on the western bank to guard the bridge. All we need now is the armies of de Warenne and de Valence to join us and we can defeat him."

Lord Edward shook his head. "I want this victory to be a complete one. I do not want to leave any heads on this hydra. Where is the young Simon de Montfort, eh? We have time, for with every bridge destroyed we force his son to try to help his father. We take Gloucester and the bridge first."

De Clare nodded. "You have a better idea of strategy than I do, lord."

Lord Edward turned his stare to me. "You have done well, Gerald, as always. When we have taken Gloucester, I have a task for you and your men."

"Aye, lord?"

"Find the Earl of Leicester's son, young Simon de Montfort."

"But he could be anywhere to the east of us!"

"I did not say it would be easy, but know that he will have a large army, perhaps as many as 300 knights, and they will be heading west."

De Clare nodded eagerly. "And I know where he was the last time I was with the enemy. He was besieging Pevensey Castle."

"Then it is decided. We take Gloucester first, and when I know that de Montfort is trapped, you find his son for me." He smiled. "Now, get some rest, for you will be leading the vanguard tomorrow. Captain William now has a company, and you two will be with Sir John and his retinue. It will be my banner which leads my army to Gloucester. I want them to know that this is my time! I have waited long enough and now I will show them my teeth!"

CHAPTER 14

Our spare horses now proved to be invaluable, for we would need them if we were to scout out the road to Gloucester. I met with Sir John and Captain William after I had eaten. I told them all that there was to know. It was Sir John who offered a word of caution. "I know that Lord Edward is confident, but they may reinforce Gloucester. I know I would."

"I saw no sign of knights in the castle, Sir John, and the men wore the livery of the Sherriff."

He smiled. "Gerald, I am now a banneret, and that means I lead twenty of my own men. All it takes is for de Montfort to send ten bannerets, and the garrison you saw could grow from eighty or so to over 250. That would be a hard number to assault, especially as we cannot attack the riverside. Let us hope that they are not reinforced."

Sir John proved to be prophetic. It was when we were just north of Tewkesbury, where the Avon and the Severn run close together, that my men and I caught up with the baggage of a column of men. We knew they were not allies, for they had the familiar white crosses on their armbands. It was Tom who found them, and he rode back to tell Captain William, Sir John and myself.

Sir John had also grown and was a more confident knight. "Captain Gerald, try to get ahead of them and slow them down. Captain William, let us chase them down!"

That was easier said than done, for the River Avon was next to the road; however, I remembered that there was a large loop in the River Severn. The adjacent land was not built upon, for it flooded. The column would be slowed as they rode through Tewkesbury, and we had a chance to get ahead across the flood plain.

"Peter, stay close to the baggage with the spare horses and war gear. The rest of you, ride!"

We left the road and headed for the river trail. It was wide enough for just one horse, and it was perilously close to the Avon. When, however, we reached the larger Severn, the river took a loop, and we saw open ground before us. This was June. I would not have risked as much in winter, for it would have been a boggy and muddy morass. It was firm riding, and we headed for the end of the Severn loop. The Gloucester road took a turn to the south-east after Tewkesbury, and our only chance to hold them was at the point where the road turned. We were too late. The vanguard was already heading south and I counted ten banners. There were still men heading down the road, and so I halted us 150 paces from the road. We had no horse holders, and we just dropped our reins and took out our bows.

The time it took to string our bows almost proved costly. Horns sounded, and some sergeants at arms and crossbowmen detached themselves from the middle and came charging across the flat ground towards us. We were only saved by the fact that crossbows took longer to load than a bow.

"Release when you have a target!"

John of Nottingham was the first ready, and his arrow struck a crossbowman in the head. They were the more dangerous target. The twenty sergeants rode poor sumpters, and they would be waiting until the crossbows had thinned us out before attempting to charge archers. I heard the sound of battle from our left as Sir John and Captain William attacked the baggage train. We might not be able to stop the enemy getting to Gloucester, but we would stop some of them from doing so, and we would make sure that they had no supplies with them. I knew that my pursuit of Simon de Montfort's son would be delayed. There would be a siege and we would be involved.

I sent an arrow with a needle bodkin towards the sergeant who led the charge, and he tumbled over the back of his horse. I was fast and had a second bodkin nocked and ready in the blink of an eye.

I aimed at the next rider, as I could leave my men to deal with the crossbows. I hoped to discourage the sergeants. The second rider held his shield before him, and so I aimed at his right side and saw my arrow pierce his leg. It was a waste of a bodkin; I could have used a war arrow. I chose a war arrow next and aimed at the horse of the nearest rider. The arrow struck it in the shoulder. A warhorse would have carried on, but the sumpter wheeled and barrelled into the next rider, unhorsing him. That proved too much for the sergeants. The survivors turned and rode after their lords who were now racing for Gloucester.

Our own horses had wandered over to the river to drink, all save Eleanor who stood patiently close by.

"Robin, David, fetch the horses. The rest of you search the dead and destroy the crossbows."

We had slain eight men, and we used the broken crossbows to make a pyre. By the time Captain William found us, the battle of the baggage train was over and the column had disappeared.

"We have hurt them, Gerald. We killed all fifteen of their rear-guard and took their baggage and horses. There are twenty-three accounted for, and you will have wounded some. The crossbows you burned cannot be used against us."

I shook my head. "Aye, lord, but it is not a victory, and now we have a siege to prosecute."

"The fortunes of war."

We pushed on hard and, as we reached the town, we saw that the gates were still open and people were flooding into the town. Sir John was decisive. "Let us charge them and take the town! We can seize the castle before the garrison is reinforced with townspeople."

Sir John and his squire both had good horses, as did I, and we soon began to outstrip our men. I drew my sword. There was a press of men at the gate. As we approached, some fled towards us, but the majority tried to get inside the gates, and the men trying to close them had no chance. Once we were at the gates, our three snorting, biting horses helped to clear the way, the press of men diminishing as people moved away from us. I thought they might succeed in closing the gates, until Sir John made his horse rear and its hooves smashed into the gates, forcing them open. I dug my heels into Eleanor and swept down with my sword. The gatekeeper held up his spear but my blade sliced it in two and then ripped open his head. Sir John and his squire chased away the other guards, and so we had the gate.

As our men poured through, we galloped towards the castle. This time, they made no mistake, and the bridge was raised before we reached it. The ten knights who surrendered to us would not join the garrison. Sir John sent Captain William to secure the bridge over the Severn: with that in our hands and the rest of the Severn bridges destroyed, then Simon de Montfort was trapped.

We waited for Lord Edward and the Earl of Gloucester to arrive.

They reached us at dusk. We had made no attempt to speak with the garrison as that was a task for Lord Edward. We *had* managed to secure the town, and that had surprised even me. When Lord Edward saw the two of us at the gate he leapt from his horse. "And the castle?"

"Sorry, my lord, they secured the gate and, worse, there are now ten bannerets and their retinue within the walls."

The hint of a frown passed over his face and then he smiled. "The bridge is in our hands?" We both nodded. "Then this is better than we might have either hoped or expected. I will go and talk terms with them. They will refuse, of course, but there is an order to these matters."

We accompanied him. We had placed my archers and Sir John's men at strategic places in the town, but seeing the Earl of Gloucester striding along with us encouraged the populace to cheer us. He was, after all, their lawful liege. De Montfort had returned his title and lands to him, Lord Edward had confirmed it.

At the gate, Lord Edward took off his helmet and his gauntlets. "I am Prince Edward, son of King Henry of England, who holds the castle against your lawful liege?" There was a delay as someone was brought. Eventually, a face appeared on the gatehouse.

"I, Matheus Werill, High Sherriff of Gloucester, command the castle."

"Then open the gates and admit your lawful lord, Gilbert de Clare, and the Earl of Chester and heir to the crown!"

"I fear I cannot, my lord, for the castle has been taken over by knights who are loyal to the Earl of Leicester, and they will not surrender."

That puzzled all of us. Why were they not speaking to us? The Earl of Gloucester was famed for his red hair and his fiery temper and he spoke again, much to the irritation of Lord Edward.

"Are they cowards, that they will not face us?"

"I am sorry, my lord, but they seem to think that relief will be coming their way."

"Each day that I am kept waiting for the surrender will increase my anger. Think on *that*."

He turned to Sir John. "Have men cross the bridge and secure the other side."

"Yes, lord."

Surprisingly, Lord Edward did not evict burghers for their houses. Instead, we camped outside the town walls. I wondered what was behind that. The next morning, he held a council of war with his lords. As his two captains, William and myself were also invited. I could not get over the change a year had wrought in Lord Edward. He had come of age.

"My lords, gentlemen, by my reckoning, there are fewer than 200 knights and men at arms in the castle. They have not had time to lay in great quantities of food and fodder. We cannot build war machines as they would take time to build, and time is our enemy. Thanks to Sir John every bridge and boat on the Severn is destroyed. However, that still leaves the sea. The earl and I will cross the bridge to Chepstow, for I would have ships watch for Montfort. It may well be that he tries to cross by sea and join up with his son who, the last we heard, was in Pevensey. Until then, we prepare for battle. Keep a good watch on the castle and send word to me in Chepstow if and when they eventually surrender. When Sir Roger arrives, he is to command the siege. Until he arrives, it is your responsibility, Sir John."

We left the next morning for Chepstow. We had half of the army with us, and it was the more powerful half, for we had most of the knights and were all mounted. I knew that it was across the river from Newport, and I confess that I had feared that de Montfort would come by water. I still did not know how we would deal with such a threat.

We rode with Captain William's men and mine. We also had ten of de Clare's young knights and forty men at arms as well as Lord Edward's young knights. It did not seem enough, to me, to protect Lord Edward from harm. Two days later we reached Chepstow, which was still loyal to the king. I did not know that de Clare had kept men on the north side of the estuary. I had to admire the move because we had, effectively, cut de Montfort off from not only the Severn but also the River Usk. He would be trapped in Wales, and his only escape would be across the channel between Wales and England.

It was as we prepared that we had word from the siege. Baron Mortimer himself brought us news: Gloucester castle had succumbed. The garrison had departed the city swearing not to fight for forty days. I suspect that, had Lord Edward been there, the agreement would have been more draconian. This worked out well, for the knights who swore the oath were young knights with great skill in battle and were a grievous loss to the Montfortian cause.

De Clare had spies in Wales, and one managed to return to Chepstow to report that Simon de Montfort, at Pipton, had given away five royal castles to Llewelyn to form an alliance with the Welsh. That they were not his to give was irrelevant. It was a disaster, and Lord Edward looked as angry as I had ever seen him. With the west secure, for the Welsh would raid the Marcher lords, Simon de Montfort turned east. The rumour was that he was heading for Newport and, perhaps, England. I know that Lord Edward hoped for a battle, but de Montfort was far too clever for that; he would head for a reunion with his son. Pevensey was on the south coast, and de Montfort could sail to Southampton or Pevensey itself. In one clever move, he would have outwitted Lord Edward. It was then that the Earl of Gloucester showed he had the mind of a general. He came up with the idea of putting men in ships and sailing to stop de Montfort reaching England by sea.

With hindsight, it seems an easy enough plan – but it was a risk. Lord Edward once again showed his experience. "Aye, and we will march to Newport and confront him at the bridge of the Usk. Fill three ships with all of our archers." He turned to me. "Gerald, let us show these Welsh that my archers are their superior! Take my archers aboard one of the ships."

"Aye, lord." I was less than enthusiastic.

I had never fought at sea and the prospect frightened me, for I could not swim. Nonetheless, I obeyed. "We will only need war arrows. Peter, stay ashore and guard the horses." I saw the disappointment on his face, but if we were to drown, he would survive. The other archers went to the other two ships Lord Edward had hired, but I kept my company all together. We boarded a ship, which I can only describe as a pirate ship.

Captain William One Eye looked every inch the pirate from his black patch to his double-handed sword, but he welcomed us aboard. "Ah, Captain, you are just what we need. I have no archers. Mayhap you can remedy that fault. You shall have an easy time, for my men row!" His mild manner was at odds with his features. We set sail amongst a fleet of twenty ships, seventeen of which had been commandeered by the men of Bristol, and I was glad that ours was one of the bigger ones.

We headed downstream towards Newport. We would not be at sea, as the Severn was an estuary, but I still found the motion of the boat unnerving. I had been on ships before, but I had never had to fight from one. I felt, as I was sure my men did, a little lost.

The well of the ship was filled with the men who would row. They were a relic from the days when Vikings and Saxons rowed their ships to capture merchantmen. This, however, was not a dragonship. I had heard of those, and this was neither long nor narrow. It was almost tubby, with a high prow and stern. In the middle men were three to an oar, while nearer to the bow there was just one man to an oar.

The captain spoke to me, but all the time he was adjusting the tiller and glancing at the pennant flying from the mast. "Keep your men here, close to the tiller. Your job is to slay the men in their rigging and the men who steer their ship." He tapped his chest; he was wearing a mail hauberk. "I have my own protection, and I am hard to kill. I hear that you and your men are good, Captain Gerald. I hope so, for my crew and our two consorts are the best." He waved a dismissive hand at the rest of the small fleet. "The rest give us numbers, but it is we who shall win the battle."

"Captain, how do you know we can catch the enemy?"

"This is not the land, we are on a river – a mighty river at that. De Montfort, if he is going to sail, will have to sail on a high tide. This is just such a tide. He has to sail when the winds are favourable, from the north and east. Today is just such a day. We three ships are the only ones which are rowed and not at the mercy of the winds. He might try again tomorrow, but that will depend upon the wind coming from the same direction – and all sailors know that you cannot predict the wind. You can guess and deduce, but your Earl of Leicester is a creature of the land. We have seen, over the past days, ships gathering in Newport." He chuckled. "We are paid to do this, but we would still have gathered to attack them without the pay. This means that we are doubly paid!"

Just then, a cry came from the masthead. "Captain, ships putting out from the river at Newport!"

"Now it begins. Prepare your men." He used his left hand to cup around his mouth. "Not long now, lads, and I promise I will lay us alongside the biggest prize there is, and we shall be rich!" His men cheered.

"String your bows."

I began to string mine, and I saw the snake of mounted men riding down the coast road from Chepstow to Newport. Would de Montfort flee or fight? Either course of action suited Lord Edward.

As we strung our weapons, Jack said, "How does a man keep his feet and use a bow on a ship? I fear I will hit nought but the sky or their sail. I am a good archer, Captain, but this will be impossible."

I realised that I was the only one who had been at sea. I thought back to the first long voyage from the monastery to France. I heard the advice given to me by Dickon. "Keep your feet wide apart, and do as you would when hunting a deer that was running through the woods. Anticipate and lead the animal. We will not loose from a long distance. We will wait until we are less than one hundred paces from the ships and use our arrows wisely."

I saw my archers try to draw while spreading their legs; I did the same. I was offering advice, yet I had never done this either. Inwardly, I agreed with Jack of Lincoln: this was impossible. But I was the captain of Lord Edward's archers. I had to appear as though I knew what I was doing.

I found that the motion was not as bad as I had expected. So long as I did not move my feet, the sway, the rise and the fall, were all a little more predictable than I had expected. I found that it was possible to keep the bow relatively stable even though my body moved. I compensated with my arms. We were all strong, and our arms were our most powerful weapon.

I selected a good war arrow. The heads would be lost; there would be no chance of recovering either arrows or heads. We needed more, and I would need to find a source when we landed at Chepstow.

The captain put the tiller over and we began to move towards Newport and the River Usk. I saw now what he meant about his galley and our consorts. With the wind and the oars, we led the other ships which all had sails. The tide and the wind helped. Travelling back upstream would take a longer time.

"There are twenty ships, Captain, and they are putting out to sea to meet us." The lookout's voice drifted down to us.

"Any standards?"

There was a pause as the lookout peered at the approaching fleet. "Aye, Captain, one which keeps to the rear has a red standard with a beast upon it."

I grinned. "That is Simon de Montfort. He has put to sea."

"Then we make for her. That will be the most valuable prize. Men, arm yourselves. The wind and the tide will take us to our foes," said the captain.

The oars were stacked, and then the men armed themselves with a variety of weapons. I saw that short weapons were favoured, and most of the men had not only a short sword but a hatchet, an axe or a curved gutting dagger. Most wore a leather jerkin and had a leather cap upon their heads. Some wore helmets, but they were few and far between. As I watched the converging ships, I saw the brilliance of the plan conceived by de Clare. The approach of the army down the coast road would be disguised by the fleet of ships, for their attention would be on the nautical threat. When de Montfort was far enough into the channel, he would see Lord Edward and his army. What would he do? He could return to shore or try to battle his way through our ships, and the three galleys which led our fleet were like knights on warhorses. We were the most powerful vessels in this battle. If we survived the initial contact, then we would win. Of course, the opposite was equally true. If we lost then my company and I would die, and we would enjoy a watery grave.

Captain William One Eye was clever. Had we gone into action with oars run out, then we risked having men injured when the oars sheared.

His crew cowered beneath the gunwale, and if we collided, they would not be the ones struck by savage splinters. The captain said, "When you are ready, archers; the enemy ships also have archers."

I nodded. The nearest ship was approaching our larboard side and I turned to it. "Archers, I will try a ranging arrow." If anyone was going to look foolish then it ought to be me. I was aware that I had the wind behind while the enemy archers would be loosing with the wind against. We were travelling faster than they were. I had told my men to loose at one hundred paces, and we were 200 paces from the leading ship. I would waste an arrow.

I pulled back as far as I could and aimed the arrow in the air. I was aware that all eyes, save the captain's, were on me. I aimed at the centre of the ship and released.

I watched it soar. Normally, I would have nocked a second and not watched my flight. This time, I followed it as it rose. It seemed to hang in the air – that was the effect of the wind – and then it plummeted. I saw an archer on the ship drawing back on his bow. I had not aimed at him, but the wind, the speed of their ship and a little luck ensured that he was the first to die in the battle of the channel. The arrow pierced his skull. He and his bow stood on the gunwale briefly and then tumbled into the water. Our crew cheered and the battle began. The enemy archers took cover.

John of Nottingham laughed as he said, "Can we loose now, Captain?"

I nodded as I selected another arrow. "Aye. The wind, it seems, favours us."

We began to drop arrows into the well of the ship. We could not see the effect, but the converging course meant all of our arrows hit something. The other two galleys were having the same effect, and the first three ships of de Montfort's fleet were all under attack. The captain of our ship pushed home his advantage and he closed with the leading ship; it was bigger than ours with a forecastle and an aft castle but, in the centre, our gunwales would be the same height. My men cleared the forecastle of archers, for arrows were no longer returned, and men with shields appeared. We switched to the aft castle as the lookout shouted, "Captain, the last four ships are putting back to Newport! The red standard falls back!"

I heard Captain William One Eye curse, "Then the richest treasure is gone. Let us take this one first, eh, lads?"

We could now see the effect of our arrows as our ship rose and fell. We had hit many men. I saw our hulls approaching each other rapidly and I shouted to my men, "Brace!"

I grabbed a rope – the sailors called them sheets. It was fortunate that I did, for there was a crash and the sound of wood splintering; tiny shards flew into the air. Lewis Left Alone tumbled to the deck.

The captain shouted, "To the steerboard side, Captain Gerald, there is another vessel there."

We could no longer send our arrows into the Montfortian ship as his crew were swarming aboard ours, and we heard the sound of slaughter. It was the hack of savage weapons and the scream of men who were dying. There was a second vessel, which had escaped the attention of the galleys. She was attempting to turn, to head back to Newport. The rest of our fleet laboured towards her.

I nocked an arrow and loosed it. As the rest of my company joined me, we sent arrow after arrow towards the ship, which seemed to take an eternity to turn. As the ship was manoeuvring, its tiller came closest to us. We cleared the quarterdeck and she lost way. One of our ships struck her and the crew quickly surrendered.

The ship our own crew had attacked also surrendered. Our captain had clearly done this before. He left a small crew on board and then set off after the fleeing fleet. It would be a race to catch them before they made the safety of the Usk and Newport.

My men and I now had our eyes in, and we managed to capture one more ship by the accuracy of our arrows, which incapacitated the men steering the enemy ships. I saw now that ships had a vulnerable and fatal weakness. If the steersman was killed then, no matter how many men there were on board, the ship was lost.

We stopped just 400 paces from the shore. To go closer would be to risk attack by archers and crossbows, which sheltered behind walls and shields. We were close enough to the shore to see Lord Edward, the Earl of Gloucester and the rest of our army approaching the bridge over the Usk.

Captain William One Eye nodded and smiled at us. "I thank you and your archers, Captain Gerald. We are all rich men this day, for we have captured two ships and all that they contain. I am an honest man, and this day, you were part of my crew. I take half and the crew shares the other half. I promise you, Gerald War Bow, that you will receive a just share, and should you ever tire of fighting for Lord Edward, there will be a berth for you on my vessel – for I have never seen bows used so well. You put the Welsh to shame!"

"I thank you, Captain."

The lookout's voice drifted down again. "Captain, they are signalling from the shore. They wish to speak with you."

"Oars!"

We headed in to the beach where I saw the Earl of Gloucester and his squire. They had waded their mounts into the shallows to speak with us. "Well done, Captain! What news of de Montfort? Is he taken?"

The captain shook his head. "His ship put back into the river."

"Is it possible to land our archers?"

The captain turned to me. "It will be waist-deep water, can you manage that? For I dare not go closer and risk grounding. The tide is on the turn."

"We can manage that, eh lads?"

Jack of Lincoln was already placing his bow in his bow case. "No offence, Captain One Eye, but I would like solid land under my feet the next time I loose an arrow."

I unstrung my bow and put it in my case as the captain used his oars to edge us as close to the shore as we could manage. I wrapped my cloak around my neck to keep it dry. I also took off my boots. It was a wise decision – Robin of Barnsley did not. I landed in the sea and the shock of cold water almost paralyzed me, but the water came over the top of Robin's boots and that, allied to the shock, knocked him from his feet. John of Nottingham and I were close enough to grab and steady him. Tom grabbed his bow case, which was floating away. We struggled ashore and then watched the archers from the other two galleys have the same difficulties we did. More of them were doused. I dried my feet on my cloak and, while the others sorted out their wet gear, I walked across the sand to the road, where Lord Edward awaited us.

He smiled. "We have no time to waste, for I wish to get to the bridge as soon as we can. It may be that we can end this rebellion here and now. Follow us when you can. I know you are on foot, but we will try to get some horses for you."

"Aye, my lord. It will take some time to dry off. We will follow when we can."

The army moved off, and the three galleys headed back to Chepstow with the six captured ships, now crewed by our men. The other companies of archers each had their own captain and at least one was older than I was, but I served Lord Edward and so they deferred to me.

"We have a three-mile walk to the Usk. Let us step out smartly. If any horses are spied let me know, for I would rather ride than walk. Tom, take the fore!"

We were in enemy territory and so we strung our bows. The baggage train had already passed us, and we had a road that was empty except for the piles of dung left by the animals. That hampered our progress. The road had been built, I guessed, by Henry the First, to connect the castles of Chepstow and Newport. Consequently, it headed directly north and west.

We soon left the low-lying ground, which went from beach to swamp to bog. There were patches of high ground to our right, and hedges and small copses. None of us were used to marching and our progress was slow. The rest of the army was mounted. Sometimes, fate intervenes, and that suggests an order from some higher being. The Earl of Gloucester's men were struggling and so I, reluctantly, ordered a halt. Tom was out of sight, having just crested a rise, and so I hurried after him. I saw him as I reached the high ground; he was sheltering behind a dry-stone wall.

He heard me and did not turn. "Get down, Captain! Horsemen!"

I dropped next to him and he turned. "Sorry, Captain, but there are thirty horsemen ahead and I think they are the enemy, for they trail the baggage train."

I raised my head above the wall and saw, on the slope to the right, the thirty horsemen. They had tried to hide behind trees, but the sharp eyes of my archers spied them. The high point we were on allowed us to see the baggage train, and it was less than half a mile away. The last few miles had seen us catch up with it. I shaded my eyes and looked at the shields. I recognised the livery; quartered red and white with a black diagonal – they belonged to Hugh le Despencer, who had been King Henry's chief justiciar. He had gone over to the rebel side, and I had killed some of his men after Lewes. I saw that they were descending to the road, but they had to negotiate a steep hill. We had time.

"Wait here and I will fetch the men."

I scurried back and said, "To arms! There are horsemen ahead. String your bows and be ready to loose as soon as I give the command."

There were forty of us and we outnumbered the horsemen, but if they were well led and they turned on us rather than the baggage train, then this could end in disaster. I was aware of the weight of leadership upon my shoulders. As soon as we reached the rise, I saw that they were crossing to the road and the leading riders were just thirty paces from it. They were strung out in a long line and were less than 150 paces from us. They were riding good palfreys and could cover that distance quickly.

I nocked a needle bodkin. Tom rose from concealment as I joined him and he also nocked a bodkin. I could not afford to wait for all of our men to reach me, and as soon as there were fifteen of us, I shouted, "Loose!"

My shout and the sound of the bowstrings, allied to the whoosh of arrows, alerted the horsemen. It was too late for four of them, who were plucked from their saddles. The others reacted quickly and pulled up their shields. I saw that three more had been hit by war arrows, and the riders were contemptuously brushing them off.

"Use bodkins! Are you fools?"

I was not shouting at my men for I knew that they would have nocked bodkins. We should have emptied more saddles. As the other archers scrabbled around for bodkins, my men and I sent another flight of bodkins at the enemy, but the horsemen were now charging us. As more archers arrived, they too nocked arrows – but I knew that some of them had also used the wrong arrow. It cost them. My men and I were together and our arrows threw men from their saddles, but the horsemen to my right were using their shields for protection, and fifteen of them struck those archers who had made the mistake of using the wrong arrow. Archers have neither helmet nor mail, and ten archers fell to swords. We cleared the men to our fore and turned to loose at the horsemen. They had, however, carved a path of destruction and escaped.

"Grab the horses! John, have men search the dead."

I ran to the dead and dying archers – the wounds were terrible to behold. Captain Harry, the leader of the Earl of Gloucester's men, had half of his jaw hanging off. The sword had also bitten into his shoulder. He tried to talk but could not. His eyes pleaded with me to end his life. I was about to do so when God showed his mercy and he died. Captain Ralph led the rest of the men. They came from many lords. Evan, Baron Wigmore's archer, was with them.

Captain Ralph shook his head. "A horrible way to die. He could not even ask God for forgiveness!"

Evan closed the dead captain's eyes. "He and his men had not enough bodkins. That is why they died. They must have wasted them in the sea battle."

I stood. "We saved the baggage train. We will bury our men here, it is the least we can do."

We used the hatchets and swords of the dead to bury them. Their arrows we would take, but their bows were buried with them. I mumbled some words over them, but I was no priest and hoped that God would understand.

There were ten horses and Captain Ralph and I rode two, while the rest went to eight of my men. We draped the mail over the saddles and strapped the swords onto our belts. The archers who walked now moved more quickly, for they had seen the folly of moving too slowly. However, we still did not catch up with the army until we reached the bridge over the Usk.

I saw then that we were too late. Simon de Montfort had destroyed the bridge. There would be no decisive battle of Newport. The wily old campaigner had managed to evade battle.

CHAPTER 15

I had led the detachment of archers, and it was my responsibility to report the sad news to Gilbert de Clare. He was with Lord Edward and the other nobles. They had commandeered a house on the east side of the Usk. I was admitted by one of Captain William's men.

They looked at me expectantly. "I have to report, my lord, that we surprised a company of horsemen who were about to attack the baggage train. We engaged them but we lost twelve archers, including Captain Harry."

Lord Edward's eyes narrowed. "Who were they?" To him, it mattered more whence came the horsemen rather than the loss of archers.

"They were men at arms, and they bore the livery of Hugh le Despencer."

Baron Mortimer smacked one fist into the palm of his other hand. "That damned traitor! He was rewarded by your father, my lord, and this is the way he pays him back!"

I turned to the Earl of Gloucester. "I am sorry about your captain and archers, my lord."

He nodded, almost absent-mindedly. "What? Thank you, but the loss of a few archers is better than the loss of the baggage train."

I wondered if my death would have the same effect. Captain Harry had died, and his lordship seemed unconcerned.

Lord Edward said, "We retrace our steps to Gloucester. Once there we will make our plans. Sir Gilbert, you know this land better than I, what can de Montfort do now?"

"He has lost the opportunity to travel by sea. I would say that he will travel through the Black Mountains. He still holds strongholds on the west of the Severn and he will regroup. Hereford still holds out for the rebels."

Lord Edward looked at me. "Captain Gerald, now is the time for you and your men to find out where the rest of the rebels are to be found. Gloucester, how long for de Montfort to reach his strongholds?"

"Nine or ten days."

"Then you have that time, Gerald, to find the enemy. You will need horses."

"We captured some."

"Good, then take others. I will be in Worcester. Bring me word as soon as you can."

I hesitated. Once I would have said, 'Yes, my lord' and scurried off like a good little boy. I had changed. "My lord, if the rebels are in the Midlands or London, even the south coast, then it might take me ten days just to reach there."

Lord Edward rubbed his chin. "You are right. Then let us say if you have not returned in ten days then we will assume the rebel army is not close."

I nodded. "Or that we are dead or captured, which amounts to the same thing!"

He laughed. "You are my rabbit's foot, Gerald, you cannot die! I forbid it!"

We left before dawn and we rode hard. We reached Gloucester by sunset. We had covered almost forty miles in one day. Sir John was eager for news and I dined with him. I knew that Lord Edward trusted him implicitly and so I was candid. He too had news, which helped me. "We have heard that young Simon has raised the siege of Pevensey and is heading west to help his father."

I nodded. "That helps but a little, for I believe that Pevensey is more than 150 miles from here. There are many routes he could take. He could come due west to Bricstow, north-west to Oxford or even due north to Northampton and the Midlands."

Sir John was sympathetic and he was also a clever man. "The middle road is to Oxford. If he has a large army then you should hear of it on that road. My suggestion would be to go to Oxford, for that is loyal to the king." He shrugged. "It is a starting point!"

He was right, and it made sense. We knew the town and it was loyal. More importantly, it was the junction of many roads. Travellers were the best of spies, for they were invisible and always willing to talk.

We took four of the horses we had captured as spares and Peter led them. We reached Oxford two days later, and I used the inn where I had buried my gold. We were greeted like old friends, for we wore Lord Edward's livery and had paid well each time we had stayed there. The landlord was also a mine of information. He added to our knowledge of young Simon de Montfort, telling us that he was in London gathering an army. The fact he was to the east of us was good news. While we could be in London in two days of hard riding, even if he headed for Oxford then it would take at least four days for an army of knights to reach us. I sent Mark the Bowyer back to Sir John with the news.

After he had gone Peter asked, "Do we just wait, Captain, or do we head for London?"

I shook my head. "Heading for London would be the worst thing we could do. Here we are amongst loyal men. London is filled with rebels. In addition, he could head north to the Midlands or south to the coast. He could take ships and land an army close to Bricstow. We wait and we keep our ears open."

I used the time to walk the streets and talk to merchants. They heard much. Sometimes it was rumour and sometimes it was fact. Two days later I had my first solid lead. Simon de Montfort was leading an army to Winchester, which was a stronghold of the king; he was trying to draw Lord Edward away from his father. It was time for us to move. Mark had rejoined us, and so I sent William of Matlac back to tell Sir John of this new direction. "Tell him that we will close with Winchester and trail his army. You are to return here to the inn and I will send for you."

We headed for Winchester, which we knew was a loyal city with a strong wall around it. Once the capital of England, the burghers there would defend the town. We reached it shortly after St. Swithin's Day. The city had fallen. Refugees who had fled told of churches and property being destroyed and Jews being whipped and hanged.

We were less than two miles from the city and I had a dilemma. Did we camp close by and see which way this army went, or did we head back to the centrality of Oxford? We were south of King's Worthy on the crossroads there. We had watered our horses and I was debating whether or not to ride the last mile to Winchester when, from the west, we heard the sound of hooves. Hooves meant armed men, and I quickly strung my bow and shouted, "Stand to!"

The horsemen saw us as we saw them. I recognised the livery: they were the men of Hugh le Despencer, except that this time, they were led by a knight and a squire. There were twenty of them.

I nocked a bodkin and loosed it at the knight. He was quick-witted and his shield came up. His squire was slow, and the bodkin sent by Tom pierced his shoulder. John and Jack sent their arrows into the air while the others used a flat trajectory.

"Peter, ride north! We will follow!"

The combination of plunging arrows and flatter arrows had an effect, and three men at arms were hit. I sent another arrow at the knight and then shouted, "Mount! We have done enough. Head north!"

My last bodkin caught the knight on the helmet. The ringing must have deafened him, but it also made his horse rear. The wounded squire fell from his saddle and I mounted Eleanor. I slung my bow and drew my sword. The men at arms were trying to get to the side of their lord but milling horses and wounded men impeded them. The squire's horse was dragging the wounded youth to and fro, for his boot was caught in the stirrup. I rode at the knight. He must have been disoriented or else inexperienced: he allowed his shield to drop. It was not much, but it gave me a chance. Standing in my stirrups I brought my sword across and swung at his shoulder. His full-face helmet did not help his judgement, and although his sword came towards me, my sword hit him hard before his had a chance. I broke a couple of links, but I also hit him so hard as to knock him from his saddle.

"Captain!"

Sheathing my sword, I wheeled and headed up the road. John of Nottingham was in his saddle with an arrow nocked. It came towards me! It was not aimed at me, but at the man at arms who was leaning forward with his spear to skewer me. The arrow passed within a hand-span of my face, and then I heard it strike the mail of the man at arms. He tumbled from his saddle. His horse kept galloping, and as it passed me, I grabbed the reins. We soon caught up with the others outside the church at King's Worthy. They were waiting with nocked arrows. I reined in.

John of Nottingham shook his head. "One day, Captain, I will not be there to save you!"

I nodded. "I owe you a life, John."

"I am still in your debt, Captain, but I am not anxious to pay it." I saw him cock his head. "The hooves are receding. They are not following us."

I worked out that the horsemen were taking the news of the sea battle and the flight of the Earl of Leicester to the rebels. They were messengers, and the news they delivered was more important than a handful of archers, although they would remember us. This changed everything. The south coast would be of little importance to the son of the Earl of Leicester now.

"We will head back to Oxford. Geoffrey, you will ride to Sir John and tell him our news."

We could not do the journey in a day and so we camped in woods. Any army heading north would take longer than we had.

William of Matlac was back in Oxford and he had news for us when we arrived. "Sir John said that the Earl of Leicester is at Hereford. He has reinforced it. The lords who support him in the west are gathering to his banner. Lord Edward is at Worcester. Sir John said that our master is pleased with our work."

"And now it becomes interesting. His father is in Hereford, and so heading to Bricstow does him no good, for we hold Gloucester. Young de Montfort needs to get to Hereford or the Severn at the very least. He will try to join up with his father. Jack of Lincoln, take Robin of Barnsley and Lewis Left Alone. Find us a camp north of Oxford. I want to be able to watch the roads north, east and west."

They left and we waited. They returned after dark. "We have found somewhere from which we can watch the roads north and east, and the best road west leads from Oxford, for there is the Thames to cross. We can be on the road to Lord Edward quickly if they reach us."

I nodded. "Then let us make the most of our time in this inn, for from now until we return to Lord Edward, we camp in the greenwood." I turned to Lewis. "And I want you to ride to Gloucester. Take the news of what we have discovered. We will be here."

He grinned. "I will ride like the wind!"

"Just ride carefully, eh?"

Jack laughed. "Will Yew Tree made the right decision then, Captain. I know that he would not have enjoyed going without ale for so long!"

For some reason, the thought that our old comrade was enjoying life in Easingwold and drinking beer to his heart's content made us all happy.

Travellers and refugees from Winchester arrived in Oxford two days later. They came the same time as Lewis. All of them brought news of an army heading up the road from Winchester.

I was summoned to the home of the Mayor. He looked nervous. "Captain, we know that you are one of Lord Edward's archers. There is an army coming from Winchester, and if they spy you here, then there will be a battle. We know of the great mischief these godless men caused in Winchester, and we intend to open our gates to them. We will not welcome them, for we are loyal, but we will not fight them."

"And you need us to be gone."

"Just so. We have food for you, and if you need silver…"

I shook my head. "We will take the food, but we are paid by the future King of England. Keep your silver."

I did not blame the burghers. The tales from Winchester had been truly horrible. Those loyal to the king and his son were, by and large, at Worcester. I found myself in total agreement with Lord Edward;

233

we needed a battle just so that we could have peace. The next battle would be the last.

We rode directly north. Jack led us to the camp he had selected, and it was a good one. As we set up the camp, Lewis told me his news. "Lord Edward was in Gloucester, Captain. He is pleased with our work and asks that you send word when this rebel army is within a day's march of Worcester."

That would be easier said than done. The enemy would have scouts out, and I had to assume that they were as good as us.

"From now on when we ride, we each have a strung bow. We are well furnished with bowstrings."

Peter asked, "Captain, when will I need a bow?"

John, who was the one responsible for the training of Peter, nodded. "Soon. I think that by September you can try the hunting bow."

It satisfied Peter. I know how he hated being the one who did not fight.

"We will have to fight enemy scouts and keep ahead of the enemy. It will not be easy."

That evening I changed into my better clothes and headed for Oxford. I took Tom with me, but he would remain outside the city. We took our bows and our swords although I did not think that we would need either. I just wanted to discover, if I could, the direction the enemy would take.

The roads were empty as we approached Oxford. The castle was at the northern end of the city, and that gate would be the best guarded. I saw that there were eight men at arms gathered around a brazier. Although It would weaken their night vision, it still meant we would be seen and would not be able to gain access to the town. The double gate was closed, but there was a small sally port which was open.

There was an old ramshackle house – in all the time I had been coming to Oxford I had never seen anyone living in it. Only two walls remained, and most of the roof had fallen in. We secreted the horses there. "Tom, I shall head around to Westgate. It may not be as well guarded as this one."

"How will you pass the sentries, Captain?"

"I shall simply walk in the shadows. If I make a noise, they may hear, but they are busy talking anyway. It is a chance I will have to take."

I was about to move when there was a shout from the gatehouse. "Ware the gate! Riders coming out."

The gates creaked open, and two lightly-armed horsemen came out, a sergeant at arms along with them. He had a voice like a bull and, even though I guessed that he was trying to speak quietly, we heard him, despite being 200 paces away. Some words we missed, but we gathered the salient points. The two men were to ride to Northampton and order the muster of as many barons and knights as possible.

We had our answer. The rebels were heading north and east. I had no need to enter Oxford. The two riders took the northern road. Our camp was also on the northern road. I toyed with the idea of chasing after the two men and preventing their news getting through, then I realised that we would be better off by simply getting to Northampton and waiting there.

We broke camp before dawn and headed the forty-three miles to Northampton. As we rode, it struck me that I had criss-crossed this part of England so many times I should have known every blade of grass and leaf. As we neared the rebel city I thought that, as they would have to march west if they were to help Simon's father, Upton was a good place to intercept them. I knew that we would be ahead of the enemy army and so, when we reached Upton, we hid out in a wood just 400 paces from the west road. John of Nottingham changed into ordinary clothes and, leaving our bows at the camp, we rode into Northampton. By being in the city when Simon de Montfort the younger arrived, we would not arouse suspicion. We left Jack in charge. The wood was his domain still.

We had coins, which we had taken from the men at arms we had killed near Newport. I intended to use that silver to pay for a good room at an inn close to the castle. It was all part of our disguise. We arrived in the morning, and before we went to the inn, we visited a barber. The town had a surgeon-barber, and I decided to have my beard shaved. I had been seen with the beard by the men at arms and I wanted to change my appearance. I also had the barber trim my unruly locks, and he noticed the scar on my face as he shaved me. It was now a red line that would fade, eventually, to white.

"I can see that you have had trouble already in your life, young sir."

I nodded, affably. "It seems to me that there are few men in this realm who have a trouble-free life, my friend."

"Wise words from one so young. When I began to shave you, I took you for a much older man. Why now that your hair is trimmed and your beard removed, you look unrecognisable."

I laughed and, standing, paid him. It was what I wanted to hear. The visit had cost me as much as a night in an inn, but if it disguised me, then it was worth it. With my courser and best clothes, I now looked like a young gentleman. The silver I used to pay for the room, without an attempt to haggle, confirmed this, and I knew that, in the inn at least, we would not have aroused any suspicion.

We ate in the inn and then walked around the town in the afternoon. I made purchases, which added to the impression that I was a well-off young man with money to waste. It was only in the room we shared that I could be myself.

John of Nottingham smiled as he breathed a sigh of relief. "You know, Captain, you could be a mummer. That was as fine a piece of acting as I have seen at any Easter play!"

"I am aware of the mistakes I made in the inn in Gloucester. That will not happen again. Tonight, we will talk as much as any and keep our ears open."

"A fine trick, if you can manage it."

"We must, for here we are two days from Worcester. Simon de Montfort is less than half a day from the Severn. If the two Simons join their armies then Lord Edward is in trouble. We have endured a great deal to get this close to victory. Let us not throw it away recklessly."

When we dined that evening in the tavern there were no soldiers, just merchants and men from Northampton. That is not to say we did not learn much to our advantage. That young Simon de Montfort and his young knights were coming to the town was no secret, and it was common knowledge that he would join up with his father. As I listened, I knew that Northampton was too far away for young Simon to threaten Lord Edward but, equally, Lord Edward could not attack Northampton without risking Simon de Montfort escaping across the Severn. The crossings were watched, but Lord Edward would need all of his army if he was to defeat the de Montforts. Although I paid close attention to their words, I also spoke so that no suspicion was aroused. John and I agreed with the merchants and burghers.

That night, safe in our room, we discussed what we had heard and the implications. "It seems to me, Captain, that they have spies too, and the Earl of Leicester must be sending messages to his son."

"We know that already, John. How does it help us? Where will they wait before they attack? It has to be somewhere within striking distance of the Severn, and it has to be west of here." I lay back on the bed and stared at the ceiling. "At least this time we can give an accurate account of the men in this army. That will be a help."

"Aye, so long as we are not recognised. You have become famous in the last couple of years. I know that shaved face and trimmed hair help, but…"

"I know John, I know."

The first elements of the army poured into the city from noon onwards. We joined the cheering crowds who greeted them. As they rode through the town I saw that they all bore white crosses upon their tunics. They had worn them at Lewes. Young Simon had a horse with horse armour, and he had a breastplate over his mail as well as poleyn on his legs. His helmet was a magnificent one – Lord Edward's was more functional than the work of art which paraded before us. He received the cheers as a conquering hero, yet, in truth, all he had done thus far was to slaughter Jews and steal from churches.

All afternoon his men rode through the town. There were more than 300 knights followed by their squires and men at arms. What I did not see were archers, nor were there any crossbowmen. To me, that was a weakness.

When the baggage train entered the crowds filtered away, and we went to an inn close to the square in the centre of the town. Here, the mood was one of joy. Northampton supported the rebels. They were part of the people's parliament created by the Earl of Leicester. Younger men shouted that they would get a horse and follow the army, to end the tyranny of King Henry. I knew they were fuelled by drink. There was little chance of Simon de Montfort ridding himself of the King of England. For a start, de Montfort was married to the sister of the King of England. He might wish to kill Lord Edward and then have King Henry abdicate in favour of him, but the king was safe.

The next day, more knights and their retinues poured into the city. It was now getting on for the last week of July, and the army would need to move on soon.

The landlord came to speak with us as we ate a late breakfast. "Gentlemen, how much longer will you be needing your rooms?"

"Why landlord, do the extra men in town mean that you require them for better-paying guests?"

He laughed. "Oh no, sir, you have paid well, and besides, the army moves out tomorrow morning. It is just that we normally change the bedding today, but if you are leaving soon, then…"

"I can put your mind at rest then, innkeeper; we leave for York in the morning. But if the army leaves tomorrow, then we had better leave this night, for I am accustomed to good rooms, and if they get ahead of us, we may have to suffer poor accommodation."

"I am not certain that they will be heading north, sir. The rumour is that they go to fight Lord Edward, and he is to the west of us."

"Nonetheless, we will leave tonight." I gave him a smile. "And then we will not upset your bedding arrangements!"

"Oh no, sir, I meant no harm, and…"

"We were ready to leave. We conclude our business this morning and we shall leave after noon."

We had not discovered the army's next port of call, but it would be to the west, and we could follow them. We made our last purchases: bread, good cheese, two ale skins, oatcakes and some sweetmeats. I had felt guilty about eating and dining so well while my men endured cold comfort in the woods, and the purchases were for them.

We made certain we were not followed and headed up the Great North Road. Once it was convenient, we took the first track which led west and found ourselves in our camp well before dark. Our men, not least Jack, were relieved to see us. They enjoyed the food and ale we had brought.

"We need to be ready to ride first thing in the morning. So, get to sleep early. The day of reckoning is nigh."

The scouts ahead of the army alerted us to its presence the next day. Jack and the others had not wasted their time, and they led us by hidden paths and trails so that we kept ahead of them. We knew where the roads had junctions or forks, and once the scouts had passed them, we hurried on.

We used farms and fields to disguise our movements. We rode further than the army of young Simon, but we kept hidden. It soon became apparent, to me at least, that we were heading for Kenilworth. It was a mighty castle defended upon one side by a lake, and it was close enough to Worcester to strike at Lord Edward and his army. Most importantly, it was the gaol of Richard of Cornwall. When we were just five miles from Kenilworth, and as the afternoon was almost through, I took a chance. "John, I leave you in command. I will ride to Lord Edward. I will take Tom with me. Find a camp to the west of the castle."

"And if it is *not* the Castle of Kenilworth that is the young de Montfort's target?"

"Then I am wrong – but I do not think I will be! They will not reach it until late, and there is nowhere twixt here and Kenilworth that they could use. They will be weary and, I hope, will stay there tomorrow to rest their horses." I had noticed that there was little grazing. If the young Montfort intended to attack Lord Edward then he would need fresh horses. "If they move then send word to me at Worcester unless I have already returned."

Once Tom and I were ahead of the scouts we used the road and made good time. We reached Worcester after dark. I went directly to Lord Edward's quarters. He, Henry Almain, de Clare and Mortimer were seated around a table and were drinking wine. Lord Edward looked up expectantly.

"Well?"

"They are at Kenilworth. They will be camping even as we speak. They have knights and men at arms."

He stood and, placing his hands on my shoulders, said, "You are the best of men!" He turned to the others. "I want our destination kept secret, so tell the men that we ride north tomorrow. I want only knights and men at arms."

De Clare said, "And what of the Earl of Leicester?"

"We have two armies we need to fight. One, to the west of us, waits for our attack. The other, to the east, knows nothing of our intelligence. We risk leaving the river unguarded, but I will have Sir John de Warenne command the rest of the army, and I will speak with him before we leave." He turned again to me. "And your men?"

"They watch the enemy."

"Good, then get some rest. You and Tom shall lead us to Kenilworth, and you will ride to glory with us!"

We had all day to rest. It was in the late afternoon when the trumpets sounded and men mounted their horses. None were mailed, but squires had sumpters with war gear upon them. Any spies watching would have been confused as to our purpose.

I rode with Lord Edward, Baron Mortimer and the Earl of Gloucester. If the people of Worcester wondered why an archer rode with such noble lords, they were not alone, for I saw some strange looks from the men we left in camp. Once we reached Droitwich we turned northeast and took the Kenilworth Road. Night came late in early August.

I sent Tom ahead when we neared Kenilworth, and he returned to lead us to a valley not far from the castle. With him rode John of Nottingham.

"My lord, the enemy host is camped outside Kenilworth. They have few sentries!"

"Then now is the time to don our armour!"

It seemed a noisy affair as men put on mail and, in some cases, plate. Some horses wore mail too. John of Nottingham assured me that we were too far from Kenilworth for them to hear.

Lord Edward was ready first, and he rode up to me. "As a reward for your sterling work, the three of you may join this charge. I have told my men that we do not bother with ransom. When this war is over, we shall simply take the castles and the lands from their heirs. They have rebelled, and that will be the price they pay!" When he became king, he would be ruthless. That day showed me that he had changed since first I met him.

That ride through the Kenilworth camp was not war, it was slaughter. I had never entered a battle from the back of a horse and yet, that night, it was the easiest fight I had ever had. I had no shield and needed none, for the men who rose from their tents simply grabbed any weapon they had to face us. The first knight I slew saw just my sword as it swept towards his head. His hand did not even rise to block the blow. The sword seemed to have a life of its own as it rose and fell, slicing open skulls, tearing open faces and hacking through necks.

The knights who rode behind Lord Edward had even more success, for they knew what they were doing. Eleanor, too, was in her element; she snapped and bit at all that she saw. I had a strong right arm, but it rose and fell so many times that I felt as though I had loosed a hundred arrows.

By the time we were halfway through the camp, the knights had broken. Many had run towards the castle while others threw themselves into the lake or the river. Lord Edward ordered us to turn, and we galloped through the camp. My archers had followed us and, with their bows, they picked off fleeing knights.

Dawn came early in August, and it broke over a grisly sight. The camp was filled with the felled flowers of young knights. Many fled inside the castle, and we captured ten knights and their horses. Of Simon Montfort the Younger there was no sign, but it mattered not. The army he had promised his father had been shattered. We had not slain all of them, I only counted the bodies of sixty knights, but his men at arms were totally destroyed.

Lord Edward led us back towards Worcester, along with the captured knights, in chains. We were at my archers' camp and feeding our horses when he said to me, "Gerald, I want two of your archers to watch the camp at Kenilworth. We have not destroyed this army, but it is hurt. Let us use what's left. They know where de Montfort will be meeting his father. When your men know the direction, then send to me."

I nodded and waved over Tom and Jack. I gave them their instructions. "Is this not over, Captain?"

I shook my head. "We have had a victory, but so long as Simon de Montfort lives it will never be over. We must trust to Lord Edward and to God! As soon as the survivors regroup and move, then let me know."

Once we were all ready, we headed back towards Worcester. I could see now that Lord Edward was planning ahead. He was keeping this part of his army moving so that he could react to whatever the enemy did next.

We stopped at Alcester where we fed our horses and ourselves. Some slept, but I could not, for I was haunted by the images of butchered bodies. Lord Edward found me grooming Eleanor.

"You are troubled, Gerald?"

I nodded. "I am an archer and I do not see the arrows as they bite into flesh. Last night I killed men and watched the life leave their eyes. I butchered men and boys who could not defend themselves."

"Yet you killed fewer than had you used a bow."

I nodded. "I know, there is no sense to it, but..."

"I have placed much on your shoulders and you are still young, but we must show steel and then we shall have England back under the control of my family, and that is all that matters!"

We rested during the day, for we had endured a hard ride. Messengers arrived from the west with the news that Simon de Montfort had crossed the river. I was close by Lord Edward, and I thought he would have been angry, but he was not. He appeared calm and reflective. It was almost as though he had expected the news. It was de Clare who reacted angrily.

"Were the fools not watching? We were fighting our enemies, and all that they had to do was to watch!"

The messenger was a young knight, one of John de Warenne's men. "My lord, that is unfair. We had all the crossing points watched!"

"Then how did he evade you?"

"It was the day after St Peter in the Chains, and the river was unusually low. He and his army waded across close to Kempsey. It was not a crossing point, my lord. None was watching it."

Lord Edward held his hand up; he looked like a priest giving his blessing. "Peace, it is done now. He is across the Severn and his son is at Kenilworth. We are between them. They have men they use as I used Gerald War Bow and his men; they will head for each other. When we know where young Simon leads his men then we will know where we fight this battle. De Clare, go to Worcester and fetch the rest of my army."

"Where to, my lord?"

He smiled. "In truth, I do not know." He looked at the young knight. "You say he crossed close to Kempsey?"

"Aye, my lord."

"Then, de Clare, you head south and east along the road to Oxford. Parallel his line of march and stop him moving due east. If he can combine with his son then that will give him the chance to hold until he is reinforced by more men from the Midlands. I will do the same with his son. I will not wait for you word, Gerald."

"My lord, you divide your army!"

I saw him nod. "I am learning, my lord, that with great power comes great responsibility. Now ride. We will also begin to move. We will head south and west."

De Clare and his horsemen left us. I hoped that Lord Edward knew what he was doing. The only archers with him were my men, but he had Captain William's men at arms, along with those of Baron Mortimer. I did not know how many men de Montfort had, but he had had almost a fortnight to gather men and prepare for this battle.

It was getting on for the middle of the afternoon when Jack of Lincoln rode in. He threw himself from his horse. "My lord, the young lord lives, and he is leading men from Kenilworth. They are taking the road to Stratford. They are heading in this direction. Tom follows them, and he will ride to us if they change their route."

Lord Edward quickly grabbed a nearby map. I was close enough, with Jack, to see what he did. He put one finger from his right hand on one part of the map and a finger from his left hand on another and moved them towards each other. He beamed at us. "Evesham! They are heading to Evesham! Baron Mortimer, we ride. Send a rider to de Clare and tell him: Evesham!"

CHAPTER 16

Lord Edward turned to me. "Take your men and ride to Evesham. I need to know the lie of the land before the battle."

"Aye, lord."

It was only seven miles to Evesham and we made it before dusk. We had seen no other riders on the road, and that was not a surprise. If an enemy had been in the vicinity, they would have had to pass Worcester, which lay between Wales and the rest of our army.

A small farmhouse lay just off the Twyford road; we smelled the smoke and heard the cow lowing to be milked. We dismounted and tethered our horses there. The farmer came to speak with us. He looked fearful and barely opened the door.

"Friend," I said, "there will be a battle here. I pray to God that my lord, Lord Edward, is victorious, but I cannot promise. If you have somewhere you could shelter it would be better for you and your family."

He opened the door wide and spread his arms. We could see his wife and children. "But sir, my farm!"

I smiled. "Will not be touched. You have my word, and I am Captain Gerald War Bow, Lord Edward's archer." He looked reluctant still. "I was at Lewes, and I know that even the finest of soldiers can lose his head in battle. When men have the battle lust in their eyes then it can blind them. You would not wish to put your family in harm's way, would you?"

He shook his head in a resigned manner. Farmers knew exactly what soldiers were like after a battle. "No, sir. My brother has a farm at Lenchwick. I will go there."

Despite the urgency, I saw that he still took his milk cow, and his wife and children carried boxes of their valuables. He had not totally believed my oath, and I did not blame him. If I was dishonest, I could have sounded equally sincere.

"Peter, put the horses in the barn. Tomorrow you will be kept busy fetching us arrows."

"Aye, Captain."

"John, come with me. The rest of you, prepare food. Tomorrow, we will fight."

A village and bridge across the Avon lay to the south of the farm, with a hill above them. John and I climbed to the top of it. August sunsets could last a long time but the shadows cast could be confusing. I saw the abbey to the east of the village church and I saw, in the village, armed men moving around. There were no banners, which meant they were not knights – but the scouts of de Montfort's army were there, for light reflected from helmets and mail. Lord Edward had been right.

John and I lay down and I looked back behind the hill. As at Lewes, there was dead ground the other side. When we had walked from the farm, we had not seen the village. The enemy were in Evesham and, looking up the hill, they would not see Lord Edward and his men as they approached down the Alcester road. I looked back to Evesham. Simon de Montfort was planning to head up the road to meet his son, probably at Alcester. It was a clever plan, but Lord Edward had, I hoped, thwarted it; he had half of his army between the father and son.

I could see that the bridge was a narrow one. If de Montfort fought here and we secured the dead ground, he would have an uphill struggle, and his line of retreat would be difficult. The late afternoon sun showed me that the ground was flat, but there was a slope from the river up to the hill. It was almost the reverse of the situation at Lewes. There, King Henry had been trapped against a river and the Earl of Leicester had the advantage of height and dead ground.

John pointed. "Captain, look!" There were horsemen heading up the road which led from the village.

"Fetch the men and my bow. We cannot let them see this dead ground. We must take out these archers."

"Aye, Captain, but they are Welsh archers. This will not be easy!"

"John, we have trained our company. We are better."

He disappeared, leaving me alone. I saw that there were twelve horsemen. Even as I looked, I saw more men arriving in the village, across the narrow bridge. If they headed up the road as well then we might struggle to contain them.

Lord Edward, Mortimer and de Clare would not reach the hill until dawn. We had to keep the enemy at bay until then. It was obvious that de Montfort had forced a march. If we had not raided at Kenilworth then they would already be combined. Perhaps Lord Edward had been unerringly correct in all his decisions; he was behaving and acting like a king. We had needed the slaughter to avoid a repeat of the disaster at Lewes.

My men scurried up the hill and John gave me my bow.

"We use war arrows. Tomorrow we will need every bodkin we can muster, and more. There are twelve horsemen and they are archers, but they are riding. It will take them time to nock an arrow. We wait at the bottom of the hill so that when they pass by, we can pluck them from their saddles."

I led them down the slope. We could hear them talking as they moved up the road on their horses. It was obvious that they did not expect to see anyone, for they sounded relaxed. They were, as John had said, Welsh. David the Welshman knew their words and he whispered, "They are saying that they hope they find a farm with a comfortable farmer's wife!"

Had we not arrived then the poor farmer and his family would have lost more than a milk cow. I nocked an arrow as the horses' hooves drew closer. There were nine of us, and we stood in a line with two paces between each of us. The sun was setting in the west, which meant that it was in our eyes – but that also meant that we were in shadow. As they passed us, we would release. They were riding in pairs and that meant there would be just six targets for our nine arrows. The other six would dismount and nock their own arrows. With their horses as a barrier, they would have the advantage. Even as the first horses rode up the road, I was planning what to do when that happened.

These were scouts. I expected them to be as good as us but they were not, for they did not have their version of Tom riding ahead. Even so, they were archers, with an archer's sense of danger. Before the last horseman was level with our last man, Jack of Lincoln, they had spied us. A Welsh voice shouted the alarm.

"Release!"

I was at the fore of my men and I sent my arrow at the left-hand man in the column. David the Welshman took the one next to him. Both were knocked from their saddles, and their horses, frightened by the smell of blood and their falling riders, galloped up the road. The two leaders were down. Five more men were hit by my archers, for they were so close that we could not miss – and then a Welsh voice shouted an order.

Dropping my bow, I unsheathed my sword. "John, with me!"

The milling horses of the fallen archers, and the fact that the five survivors had dismounted, meant there were no targets for us at the front. I did not want news of our presence to reach Evesham: the Welsh archers had to be taken.

The horses hid us. I could hear the Welsh jabbering but their words meant nothing to me. Three arrows soared over their horses. They were releasing blind, and the arrows would be silhouetted against the last rays of the setting sun; my men would see them. Two archers were just drawing when John and I appeared next to them. They were quick and turned their bows towards us. We were archers and knew the danger we faced. With swinging swords we charged them, and our blades broke their bows in two as they tried to use them to strike us. My sword took the right hand of one archer and I back swung my blade to hack into his chest. John's blow had not only broken the bow, it had sliced across the archer's throat. Our charge made the fallen men's horses move up the road towards the other horses and, as they did so, six arrows flew and the last three Welshmen died.

One horse began to move back down the road. "Lewis, get that horse! The rest of you gather the other horses. We need to move these bodies from the road else when dawn comes, they will be seen."

I regretted having had to kill fellow archers but knew that it was necessary. When they did not return, de Montfort might assume that they had found a farm and the road north was clear.

When we had taken the horses to the farm we returned to the hill. "We bury them."

Jack of Lincoln shook his head. "What for, Captain? They would have killed us without a second thought and left our bodies to rot where they lay."

"We bury them because, when we die, I would hope that another would lay us in the ground and cover us with soil, and besides, this will be the ground where we fight on the morrow, and I would not have malevolent spirits in the air!"

"The captain is right. William and Mark, fetch tools and we will bury them by the road. Robin, fashion two of the bows into a cross. We will mark their grave."

It was a couple of hours later when we finished. It was a dark night and hard to see, but we stood around the graves and bowed our heads. It was a case of there, but for the grace of God, go I. After they were buried, we walked up the dark road back to the farmhouse. The first action of the battle of Evesham had taken place. We ate and divided up the arrows and bowstrings we had taken. Leaving John in command, I rode back to Lord Edward. He was still camped at Alcester.

He was not abed, but was speaking with Baron Mortimer and Henry Almain.

The baron held up a piece of parchment. "My wife has sent me a letter, Captain. She commends our efforts thus far and asks for the head of the Earl of Leicester as a trophy! Think of the warrior she would have made if she had been a man! She asks after you, Captain, for you have made an impression on her."

I saw that Lord Edward was slightly annoyed with the baron. "Enough of that, what have you to tell me, Captain?"

"The army of your foe is moving into the village of Evesham. We dispersed their scouts. It seems to me that they are heading on this road to ride to meet with the Earl of Leicester's son."

He nodded and stood. "That confirms the news your archer brought. Young de Montfort is now heading east towards Alcester. Mortimer, wake the camp! We ride now. I would be in place at dawn! Send the captain's archer to him." When he had gone Lord Edward said, "I ignored your advice the last time we fought de Montfort. Give me your assessment of the battlefield."

"There is a hill, my lord, and it masks the line of advance from the north. You could hide your whole army there and those in Evesham would see nought. The road and the ground slope up from the river. It would suit horses, my lord, and the hill would allow archers to loose over the heads of the horsemen."

He smiled. "And this time I have no king to tell me to ignore archers. We did so the last time, at a heavy cost."

His cousin nodded. "Aye, a year of captivity and the mocking from our inferiors! I will not endure such an event again!"

Lord Edward nodded. "And the bridge?"

"It is narrow, lord. If many men try to cross it then it will become jammed."

Outside, I could hear the noise as men were woken. It would take some time to arm and saddle, but Lord Edward would reach the field before dawn.

Baron Mortimer returned with Tom. Lord Edward said, "And have you chosen your men, Baron?"

"Aye, Lord Edward, they are all keen to have the honour of slaying the great rebel."

"By your leave, my lord, Tom and I will return to my camp and observe the enemy movements. We are camped at a farm less than a mile from the hill. The farmer and his family moved out when I requested it."

He smiled. "You and I have grown up in the last year, Gerald. I now know what I must do when I am king and you know how to fight a war. Together we can do great things! The battle this day is just the beginning!"

He turned to a chest and took out some red crosses. "This day, we all wear a red cross. It is the cross of the crusader and will mark us from the white crosses of the rebels. Have them sewn onto your tunics."

Tom and I left a camp that was a maelstrom of activity. Every man of Lord Edward's army was mounted. The men on foot were with Gilbert de Clare, and I worried that they might not reach the battlefield in time.

Captain William and Ralph saw me and waved us over to them. "Once more we will fight together, Captain. I am of the belief that we lost Lewes because we did not do so then. Today we will ensure that we win!"

"I will see you on the field at Evesham."

I was weary when I dismounted at the farm. Peter rose from his bed to see to Eleanor and Bess. John was by the fire and he had some ham frying. He saw my look and shrugged. "The ham would have gone off and we will leave some pennies for the farmer. The bread we use would be stale by the time he returns."

The smell of cooking ham drove all guilt from my mind and we ate the fried meat and bread. When I had washed it down with ale I said, "Today, there will be a battle. Rouse the men, and we will stand on the hill and watch the dawn. I would know if de Montfort has come."

"Aye, Captain. It has been a long year, but now we can make the world right again!"

The food refreshed me. I handed out the red crosses to my men as they came into the kitchen to eat. "Lord Edward wishes us to have these red crosses on our tunics. The enemy wears white."

Jack nodded. "And if they wear them over their hearts it will be a good target!"

We had needles and thread. It would not need to be pretty work, just so that it could be seen on the battlefield. That done, we took our bows and spare bows as well as all of our arrows. We were like pack animals as we climbed the hill. While Peter organised the arrows and bows, we stood on the crest. I now had my full company back together and felt satisfied. It was still dark and I could see the lights in the village. Men were there, moving around. The neighing of horses and the jingling of mail told me that it was an army. Dawn was not yet here and John of Nottingham said, "I know that we have no priest but I would make my peace with God before we fight this day. Ronan and Dick, son of Robin, fell at Lewes. I am not sure if they confessed."

"You are right." I laid down my bow and, facing the east, for there was a thin line marking the dawn there, knelt with the rest of my men. We prayed and we confessed. I made the sign of the cross and then asked God to forgive my sins past and the sins I would commit on the battlefield.

Each man said his own prayers and then stood when he was done. John of Nottingham was the last to rise. He smiled. "I am the oldest archer now, Captain. I have much to confess!"

We picked up our bows and stood on the top of the hill. I knew that we would be seen. That did not matter, for de Montfort would expect scouts. He would dismiss us as irrelevant, for he was a knight and regarded other knights as the superior weapon. We needed the height to be able to see into the village. From the noise, it became obvious that there was an army below us both in the village and before it. As the first rays of sun lit the village, I could see the army as it prepared. They had fewer horsemen than Lord Edward, and I could see that they had many who were neither men at arms nor archers. It was unlikely that they were the Londoners from Lewes; I guessed they were Welshmen. There seemed little order to their movement, but then they did not know how close they were to Lord Edward. They thought he was still in Worcester.

The hill was less than a mile from where their forward units were forming up. I saw de Montfort's distinctive banner: red with a white gryphon upon it. We were indeed seen. Other knights rode to him and I saw them pointing at us. Behind me I heard Peter shout, "Captain, it is Lord Edward. He and the army have arrived."

There had been a slight fear that de Montfort might send men to shift us from our lookout, but the arrival of Lord Edward meant that would not happen. David the Welshman pointed to the west. "Captain, in the distance I see the banners of the Earl of Gloucester; the rest of the army has arrived!"

We now had both elements of our army together. Young de Montfort was still on the road to Alcester. Lord Edward had a chance. He, Baron Mortimer and Henry Almain dismounted close to Peter and walked up the hill to join us.

When he reached us, he scanned the rebels as they arrayed. "You were right, Gerald War Bow, this is a good site for a battle. Cousin, have our men come around the hill from the east, we will form our battle lines before the hill. Captain, you will command the archers."

"Yes lord."

"Baron, you and your battle will be to the east of us. Send a rider to de Clare. I want his men to fill the line between the hill and the river."

The two men disappeared. Lord Edward leaned in to me. "I will tell you my plan, for you deserve to know. De Montfort now needs me dead – and dead in battle. He still holds my father captive and I believe that, with me dead, he will have my father abdicate in his favour. I put myself in the centre to draw him to me. Then, de Clare will attack the enemy left while the baron will go for the head of the gryphon. You and your archers must kill as many knights as you can. Use bodkins."

"You do not wish ransom, my lord?"

"No, for I will cut out the bad hearts of my nobility. I can always make new knights who will be loyal to me!" He clapped me on my back. "God speed, Gerald War Bow, and I shall see you after the battle."

When he had gone, I said, "You heard him, bodkin arrows!"

While Peter fetched more bodkin arrows, I saw the enemy forming up. Already Lord Edward's men at arms and knights were filtering around the hill as archers joined us and John placed them in position. The last to arrive was Gilbert de Clare's battle.

I saw that de Montfort was not using a broad line of attack as at Lewes but a narrow point. His knights, gathered around his banner, would lead the attack. There were more than 200 of them. Behind them was the main part of his army, and it was a long, narrow column, led by mailed men. They were on foot. He was going to use his men like a human battering ram.

The enemy formed up on our right. John of Nottingham walked amongst the archers under my command to ensure that they all had bodkin arrows ready. He looked each archer in the eye as he walked along the line.

"Now remember, Gerald War Bow is our captain and this day he is yours. You listen to his orders. I have mighty hams, and I will use them to fetch a clout to any who disobey or are tardy in the execution of his commands."

I had planned on giving a speech but now there was no need, for John's words had the desired effect.

"String your bows! Select your arrows!"

I chose eight bodkins and jammed them in the soil. I had known archers to defecate and then dip the arrowheads in the dung, for that would make a poisoned wound which would be fatal. It was unnecessary. Today, we had the advantage of height and our bodkins would fall like rain. Their helmets might save some, but a bodkin in the shoulder or arm would disable a horseman. Some of their horses had mail, but even they would die when the bodkins fell. We would only stop once our knights engaged. Then we would change to war arrows and send them at the men on foot, who wore no mail.

The two armies were lined up. I saw priests moving amongst de Montfort's men: Lord Edward had been shriven and our men were prepared. A horn sounded from the Montfortian side and the huge metal snake came towards us. I saw that, along the flanks of the charging horsemen, there were dismounted men at arms and knights. The Earl of Leicester did not have as many horses at his disposal as he might have liked. His knights would be equally matched with those of Lord Edward – Baron Mortimer and the Earl of Gloucester had twice as many knights as de Montfort.

"Draw!"

The range was extreme, but Lord Edward's counter charge meant that we would only have a short time to use our bodkins. After the initial contact, we would have to release at those who were further back. Simon de Montfort seemed eager for battle and urged his mighty steed up the hill.

"Release!"

I had a hundred archers at my command and the arrows slammed into the rebels. The elite of the enemy were at the fore, and all had mailed horses and wore plate. A handful were hit and none fell, for our bodkins could not penetrate plate.

"Release!"

The second flight had more success as they hit knights and men at arms wearing mail. Ten, at least, were plucked from their saddles. The next five flights caused increasing casualties and then I shouted, "War arrows!"

The charge by the rebels had driven them deep into our lines. Gilbert de Clare led his men into the enemy's left flank. Our war arrows had an instant effect, falling amongst those who wore no mail. Most did not have a helmet and few had a shield. Every arrow found flesh. After five flights and with the pressure of the Earl of Gloucester's knights, the men on foot broke and fled. The rebel knights and men at arms fought on, but the backbone of the men on foot were gone. Their archers had barely a chance to draw their bows.

It was then I saw Baron Mortimer and his handpicked men. They charged into the right flank of the men around Simon de Montfort. The rebel lances had shattered in the first contact, so now the rebel knights defended themselves with their swords. I saw Roger Mortimer's lance hit Simon de Montfort below the helmet, driving into his skull.

The rebel leader fell to the ground.

This was the point where, normally, knights would surrender, but not at Evesham. The knights around de Montfort were butchered. I saw Hugh le Despencer knocked from his saddle by Roger Mortimer. When he fell to the ground Baron Mortimer dismounted to hack into his body.

Sir John rode up the hill. "Lord Edward commands the archers to join the general pursuit. No prisoners!" Sir John wore no helmet and had a simple mail coif on his head. I saw the sad expression on his face.

I nodded. "You heard the command!"

Dropping our bows and arrow bags, we hurtled down the hill. By the time I reached the last stand of Simon de Montfort, Roger Mortimer was hacking his head from his body. His wife would have her trophy.

My men stayed close to me. We had swords and daggers ready. When you hunt, the most dangerous of beasts is the wounded one. The bridge would be like a stopper in a bottle, and when they knew they were to be slaughtered, then they would fight even harder. We ran through knots of rebels, surrounded by knights and men at arms. The enemy were being butchered.

Some of the other archers were faster than we were, and they were not staying together. Suddenly, I saw them begin to fall as they ran into a wall of steel. The men at arms who were fighting them knew their business and the archers were cut to pieces. I recognised the livery of the men who stood together, it was de Ferrers' men at arms.

I saw Henry Sharp Sword as he ran through the captain of John de Warenne's archers. His shield blocked the archer's sword, and he drove his own sword under the rib cage to emerge at the neck. I recognised some of the men as having been in the woods when we had captured them, but I only had eyes for Henry Sharp Sword. He had a mail hauberk and a coif upon his head.

As soon as he spied me, he lurched towards me. "Now I shall have the price placed upon your head and I will take your head back to my lord!"

I think I might have died swiftly, had he not been so keen to get at me. I ignored his words and concentrated upon his sword and shield. He had forgotten that he was moving uphill, and the slope was slick with blood. His right foot slipped as he swung at me. I did not even need to block his strike with my dagger for it bit into the turf. I swung at his head. He was quick and his shield flicked up, but not quite quickly enough: I hit the side of his head. It was a glancing blow but I could see that I had dazed him. In addition, I had angered him.

I was aware of my men fighting his company. We outnumbered his men, though they were better armed. But I had my own battle to fight. Henry Sharp Sword moved towards me again, but this time he balanced his feet. I leaned away from his blow. So far, my dagger had been unused. I was slightly above him and he shuffled his feet around so that we both had one leg higher up the hill than the other; it weakened the benefit that height afforded me. I still had a slight advantage, for it was my right leg which was uphill and I would be swinging down at him. He swung at my leg, which was unprotected. I jumped in the air and, as I landed, my feet trapped his sword beneath them. It was my turn for fast hands, and my dagger darted out. I missed the eye I was aiming at, but drove the dagger through his cheek. As I ripped it out I sliced the bottom of his nose off.

He was now so angry that he forgot all he knew. He wanted to kill me at all costs. With blood pouring down his face he ran at me, swashing his sword. I danced backwards out of the way. It was a dangerous move as there were men fighting all around me. The last thing I needed was to trip on a body – then he would have me.

"Come back, you cowardly archer!"

I had been taught many years earlier that words could do me no harm. I was now looking for a blow that would end this quickly. He was bloody, but none of his wounds would slow him up, and he was still a most dangerous opponent. I preyed on his fear of my dagger and I lunged at his eye; it was a feint. He swept his sword up, but I was already swinging my sword at his head again. He did not bring up his shield in time, and this time my sword sliced through some of the mail links on his coif. I saw him stagger at the blow. I feinted again with the dagger, and this time he did not bother to block the blow. Instead, he swept his sword at my left arm. Fate intervened for my feet let me down and, as I stepped away, I slipped on the blood that covered the greensward. They let me down but also saved me, as the sword swept over my body.

I was exposed on the ground and I was helpless. With a cry of joy, he raised his sword. Any blow across my body or head would end my life – but my strong right arm saved me. I raised the sword to block the blow and then, as the swords rang together, rammed my dagger through his kneecap and twisted. As I ripped it out he collapsed, screaming, for I had torn tendons and ripped cartilage. Leaping to my feet I raised my sword and drove it down into his throat.

He was dead.

I looked around, panting. Lewis Left Alone lay dead with a mass of cuts and wounds. His killer lay next to him, also dead. The rest of my men were still standing, although Robin of Barnsley had a leg which was bleeding and Tom was attending to it. I saw that John of Nottingham had a bloody coxcomb, but other than that we had survived.

"Do we continue the chase, Captain?"

I looked at David the Welshman and shook my head. "I do not know about you, but I have had enough slaughter for one day. Besides, the men on horses are the ones who can catch them."

I saw that, now that the bridge was blocked with the dead and the dying, many men were heading up the Alcester Road. Our knights and men at arms would catch them. The only one of our leaders who I could see was Roger Mortimer, despoiling the body of Hugh le Despencer. I could not conceive how a man could hate someone who was already dead. Surely he had done all that he could to him?

I went back to the body of Henry Sharp Sword. He had a good sword and I took it. I pulled his mail from his body, it would fetch a good price. His coif was ruined. He had a full purse and there was gold in it. The rest of my men did the same with the men they had killed. We picked up Lewis' body. We would bury him. Then we headed back up the hill. We had bodkin arrows to recover and the treasure from the knights we had killed to take. They were easy to identify. They were the bodies stuck with arrows.

"Tom and I will take Lewis back to where we buried the Welsh archers. They are all archers together. We will bury him at sunset."

When we passed the corpse of Simon de Montfort, it was hard to recognise him. His head was gone as were his arms, legs, feet, hands and genitals. If it was not for his livery, I would not have known who it was. The body of another of his sons, Henry, was also cut about.

As we neared the hill Peter ran down to greet us. He had obeyed his orders and guarded our arrows and bow staves. He looked at Lewis. "Poor Lewis. He had a sad life, Captain."

Tom shook his head. "The first part of his life was sad but I know, for I spoke with him, the time with this company was his best. He is a lesson to us all, Peter – live each day as though it is your last. Who knows? It may be."

Dusk had come upon us before Lord Edward, Henry Almain and the Earl of Gloucester returned. They were leading their horses for they were weary. All had tunics which were covered in blood. Behind them came their knights and men at arms. Every horseman was walking.

I heard a shout from the road below us and saw Roger de Leybourne leading a man wearing Montfortian armour. I prayed that the man would be allowed to live, for he was the first prisoner I had seen. To my amazement I recognised him. It was Lord Edward's father; it was King Henry!

The reunion was touching but the king, I could see, was a broken man. He was no longer the arrogant aristocrat who dismissed commoners as irrelevant. He had endured a year of captivity and had almost died when our men took him for an enemy. He was king in name only. From that moment Lord Edward was really the king. He had been the king in waiting, and now he just waited for his father to make the throne his. The king's life had been saved by Roger de Leybourne. For his services, Lord Edward knighted him on the battlefield and, at the same time, conferred a knighthood on Captain William who was now Sir William of Evesham.

Prince Edward came over to me and said, "Do not fear, Gerald War Bow, you shall be rewarded too. It will not be a knighthood, but you shall not lose for your loyalty and for following my banner."

"And young Simon, my lord?"

"Fled. I fear that Kenilworth will still be a thorn in our side, for those who escaped us entered that castle and there are now 1,700 rebels within." He smiled. "At least we know where they all are!"

And so the bloody battle of Evesham was over. Many men called it the murder of Evesham, for there had been no honour. Knights had been butchered. Lord Edward had his vengeance for the defeat at Lewes, and his grip upon the land was a firm one.

EPILOGUE

The day after the battle I was summoned to the side of the king and the other lords. "Captain Gerald War Bow, you have done the cause of England and King Henry great service. In recognition of that fact, you are hereby made a gentleman and given the manor of Yarpole, which lies in the land ruled by Roger Mortimer, Baron of Wigmore. Baron Mortimer is also given the castle of Ludlow, for he has shown himself to be a stout defender of our border.

I was stunned. I was not a knight but I had land and an income. I knew not what to say.

Lord Edward smiled. "I can see that this has come as a shock. Take your men and ride to Yarpole, for I believe that Baron Mortimer has a task he would charge you to undertake." Lord Edward continued to confer honours and to knight young men who had served him at the battle.

The baron was pleased, for he now had Ludlow Castle. He took me to his tent and handed me a sack. "This is a present for my wife. Give it to her with this letter. I will follow as soon as Kenilworth falls or we apprehend young Simon de Montfort!"

"Of course, my lord."

"Yarpole is small, but it will give you a good income and I will be a generous lord, for you have served our cause well."

My men, of course, were delighted. I was now a gentleman and that raised their status, too. We left immediately. We had spare horses and treasure to sell. Ludlow would be the place to become richer, for King Llewellyn was now at war with King Henry. He had allied himself with the loser in the civil war and now owned five English castles in Wales. There would be war and the mail we sold would be worth more. We stayed overnight in Ludlow and sold our treasures at the market. We shared the proceeds. Even our youngest, Peter, was rich!

We rode through Yarpole. I had the deeds with me, but they were unnecessary as the hall was unoccupied. I discovered that the gentleman who last owned the manor had died at Evesham. He was a rebel and had chosen the wrong side.

"John of Nottingham, I leave you and my men here. I will deliver the letter and present to Lady Maud and return." I put a purse of coins in his hand. "See what the ale in the village is like, eh?"

"Do you not want to look around first, Captain?"

I shook my head. "I will have time enough for that. I wish to deliver this present and then my work is done. We will have war again soon, and this time it will be with the Welsh. Let us enjoy this brief time of peace, shall we?"

I was taken directly to Lady Maud.

"I come bearing a gift and a letter, Lady Maud."

She grabbed the letter and broke the seal. Her daughters came down when she squealed.

"What is it, mother?"

"You have the best of fathers! We now have Ludlow Castle and he has sent us treasure!"

She took the sack from me and, reaching in, pulled out the head of Simon de Montfort. I found it sickening, but her daughters seemed as excited as she was.

They were so engrossed and excited that they did not notice me leave. I yearned for the company of my men. They were rough and they were common, but they were honest and they had a code. I had been amongst royalty and nobility and saw that they did *not* have a code; chivalry was an illusion.

I was still Lord Edward's archer but I knew not for how long. I mounted Eleanor and rode to my new manor and my men. I found myself smiling. Once out of the castle the air smelled sweeter and life seemed better.

I began to whistle. It was a new start!

GLOSSARY

Badequelle – Bakewell (Derbyshire)

Battle – a medieval formation

Bricstow – Bristol

Chedle – Cheadle (Staffordshire)

Chevauchée – A raid by mounted horsemen

Haverberg – Market Harborough

Leueton – Luton

Murage – A medieval toll for the building or repair of town walls.

Namentwihc – Nantwich Cheshire

Sennight – a week (seven nights)

Slo – Slough

HISTORICAL NOTES

The Battle of Lewes should have been a royal victory, but Lord Edward wished to punish the men of London and it was his departure which left the king and his brother vulnerable. The incarceration in Wallingford and the meeting at Westminster all occurred as I wrote them. The rescue of Lord Edward, improbable though it might seem, did occur. The words I used as he is rescued are, allegedly, the actual words used on the day. The character of Gilbert, Earl of Gloucester almost needs a whole book. He changed sides at the drop of a hat, but if he had not defected to the royalist side, then the rescue could not have happened. Within the space of just over a year, Lord Edward went from prisoner without hope to a prince who would be king, for his enemy was dead.

There were many spies. The spy who told Lord Edward of the Kenilworth camp was a female spy who dressed as a man: her name was Margoth.

Mortimer did send Montfort's head to his wife, Maud de Braose. She sounds like a powerful woman. I have changed the rescuers of Lord Edward because this is a story and I am a writer, after all! My story is the story of Gerald the archer. The kings and lords are incidental. It is the archers of England and Wales that I celebrate in this series of books.

Books used in the research:

The Normans, David Nicolle

The Knight in History, Frances Gies

The Norman Achievement, Richard F Cassady

Knights, Constance Brittain Bouchard

Feudal England: Historical Studies on the Eleventh and Twelfth Centuries, JH Round

Peveril Castle, English Heritage

Norman Knight AD 950–1204, Christopher Gravett

English Medieval Knight 1200–1300, Christopher Gravett

English Medieval Knight 1300–1400, Christopher Gravett

The Scottish and Welsh Wars 1250–1400, Christopher Rothero

Lewes and Evesham 1264–65, Richard Brooks

A Great and Terrible King – Edward I – Mark Morris

.